LoserDeals

PETER VIERTEL

DONALD I. FINE, INC.

New York

Library of Congress Catalogue Card Number: 94-68103
ISBN: 1-55611-434-6

Manufactured in the United States of America

10   9   8   7   6   5   4   3   2   1

Designed by Irving Perkins Associates

To Camilla and Fred

friends and neighbors

Part I

Under Hollywood rules one player is dealt eleven cards to his opponent's ten. After the first hand has been played, the loser always deals.

—THE GIN RUMMY MANUAL

My first wife's shrink, during one of their early sessions, suggested she write down the contents of her dreams as soon as she woke up, especially the erotic ones. He advised her to keep these compositions in a safe place, "so that they would not fall into enemy hands," by which he was apparently referring to mine. It was a needless warning. By that time our marriage had passed the point of no return, and I wasn't particularly interested in her dreams, or even her nightmares. I was concerned more about her fantasies, her daydreams, like the one about her coming home to find me lying dead in the living room of our apartment, which she had admitted was a recurring one. Anyway, nothing much came of this therapy as Dr. Ravitch was called back to duty by the Medical Corps of the U.S. Army for the duration of the war in Korea. That meant Phyliss would have to start her treatments all over again, which she decided not to do. Instead she hired a private detective, and that unpleasant alternative resulted in our divorce, probably the same conclusion her sessions with the shrink would have achieved at even greater expense to her father, who admitted at a later date that he had financed both of these ventures.

Phyliss was the only child of a Beverly Hills dentist who had disapproved of our marriage from the start. It wasn't that he disliked me, he told me once I was single again—he merely thought that for his daughter to tie herself down to a mostly-out-of-work, although promising young actor, was a mistake she would one day come to regret. It was not a viewpoint I could dispute with any conviction, and as our brief union had not been blessed by an offspring, we parted company quite amicably. My ex-father-in-law even extracted two of my horizontally impacted wisdom teeth free of charge, a parting gift that I knew to be a generous one, his fees being among the highest in that expensive town.

All this happened more than thirty-five years ago, and I haven't really thought very much about my first wife recently, but then a few weeks ago I became involved in an escapade that brought back some of these old memories—not so much of Phyliss, her doctor and her dad, but rather the mechanics that were responsible for the end of my first marriage, i.e., the hiring of a private eye to follow a straying spouse. I was also reminded of Dr. Ravitch and his instructions to my then wife, and although this is not a record of my erotic dreams, it is nevertheless an account of an experience that has some of the aspects of a nightmare, which is why I have decided to commit it all to paper as a kind of therapy, a summing-up that seems appropriate now that the game may be almost over.

1

IT ALL BEGAN ON A RAINY SUNDAY MORNING in March, one of those days
on the shore of the Mediterranean when you find yourself wishing
you were almost anywhere else. The inclement weather had come
along at the end of a sunny winter, and now there seemed to be no
limit to the amount of water falling out of the gray sky. The southern coast of the Iberian peninsula, where ten years ago I decided to
retire, is a pleasant enough place when the sun is out, but when it
fails to appear the rows of high-rise buildings and advertising posters take on the look of one big modern slum. You can no longer see
the nearby mountains that have not as yet been invaded by the
many real-estate developers who have been raping this coast for
two decades, which adds to the depressing scene.

I was seated in the bed-sitting room of the apartment I had
rented on the Paseo Maritimo of this seaside town, and was reading
the Sunday papers. After I had finished the magazine section and
had fed Fergy, my auburn-haired cat, I walked across the hall and
let myself into the office of my son-in-law, Enrique Tomson. Kiko,
which is his nickname, is the local representative of a Madrid firm
that sells security hardware, burglar alarms, electric gates and all

the other electronic equipment that is in demand now that Franco has left the scene and petty thievery is somewhat more widespread than when the Generalissimo was in power. There was always a good deal of it, but with the advent of drugs and democracy it has become a national pastime that is almost as popular as soccer.

As Kiko is an enterprising young man, he has opened a detective agency as an adjunct to his security hardware business. Potential customers are advised of its location here in San Pedro by a neon sign that reads: DETECTIVES TOMSON. It flashes on and off twenty-four hours a day, and if nothing else, helps amateur sea captains to determine their whereabouts on a stormy night. Kiko was the head grip on the set in Almería of the spaghetti western where I performed my swan song, and it was there that he met my daughter Susan who was visiting me during her summer vacation from college. A week before the end of principal photography she announced that she was planning to marry her young Anglo-Iberian suitor, for Kiko, it turned out, had been brought up in London where his parents had taken refuge during the Spanish Civil War.

I was not under the illusion that my only daughter would marry into the Spanish aristocracy, but an Andalusian film technician was considerably less than I had hoped for. Like the extractor of my wisdom teeth long ago, I foresaw a limited future for the young couple, and suggested to Susan she return to Santa Barbara and discuss her plans with her mother, my second wife, who had divorced me to marry a building contractor. Susan accepted my offer to return home, which included a proposal that she finish college before getting married. To my dismay Kiko accompanied her, and eighteen months later they both returned as man and wife. Kiko had enrolled in a course offered by a security equipment manufacturer in Oakland, and so now they were both prepared for what they foresaw as a rosy future. My second wife had given them her blessing, I learned soon after their arrival. So that was that. More of my family problems later.

My reason for moving over into Kiko's office on that rainy

morning was a simple one. I had borrowed a tape from a golfing friend, and as I don't own a VCR, intended to use the machine Kiko had installed in his office in order to demonstrate the advantages of the gadgets he sells to his customers. Having left the door of my flat ajar, I made a small adjustment in the Venetian blinds, and inserted the tape into the black mouth of the Grundig that stands facing Kiko's desk. The title on the cardboard cover was a provocative one. *Mastering the Fundamentals,* Arnold Palmer had chosen to call his little gem, and by viewing it perhaps twice I was hoping to cure my slice, and thus be able to shed the name of the banana-ball king, which is how I have become known in the small circle of my high-handicap golfing pals.

For most of my life I have been a better-than-average tennis player, and only lately have taken up the game that for geriatrics is supposed to provide an all-consuming interest, as well as taking the place of sex, grandchildren and the more violent sports that become too much of a health risk with the passing years. Golf is also meant to fill the long empty afternoons that confront men and women who have given up their professions, and keep them from morose contemplation of "the last great fairway leading to the sky." That this frustrating game can cause deep depressions in one's psyche was a danger no one had warned me about prior to my abandoning my racquet and sneakers.

I touched the start button, and Arnold appeared dressed smartly in matching slacks and sport shirt, standing on the sunlit grass of a practice range, seven iron in hand. He had just launched himself into his opening lecture when the sound of high-heeled footsteps became audible from the hallway, and a few seconds later there was a knock on the door. I said: *"Pase,"* my eyes still on Palmer, thinking it was probably Maria, our cleaning lady, stopping by on her day off to retrieve one of her belongings that she had, as usual, left behind. Then I realized that a woman in a yellow slicker and a tweed hat had come into the room.

She was of medium height, neither young nor old, but what

impressed me immediately about her evenly tanned face were her eyes, which, although not oriental, were almond-shaped and deep brown, leading me to assume that her place of origin was somewhere in the Middle East, a notion that was dispelled as soon as she opened her brightly rouged lips. "Am I in the wrong place?" she asked, with what I recognized to be a carefully camouflaged South London accent.

"That depends on what you're looking for," I said, and got up to cut off Palmer in midsentence.

The oval eyes narrowed. Their owner was apparently not accustomed to impudent replies from anyone she considered to be of an inferior station. "You are not Señor Tomson, I take it," she said.

"No, I'm not," I replied. "He doesn't come in on Sundays."

"I didn't think you were," the woman said, frowning. "I expected to find a much younger man."

I am not overly sensitive about my age, but I was irritated by her remark. I said: "Then I suggest you come back tomorrow morning at ten. This office is closed on Sundays and holidays."

"No offense intended," she replied. "I merely thought that a private detective—with all the crime we have on the coast now . . ."

Anxious to get back to Arnold Palmer as soon as possible, I said: "Tomson is in his late thirties, he'll be happy to talk to you Monday morning."

"Tomorrow will be difficult for me. Perhaps I could discuss my problems with you now, and you could pass on the information to your partner."

"I'm not his partner, I'm just minding the store."

"Ah, I see. You're a friend."

"Sort of," I said. "He's my son-in-law."

She made no move to depart. Instead she unzipped her slicker and revealed a pair of sturdy shoulders and a prominent bust under a white silk blouse. Rain or shine the climate on this coast is inclined to be damp, and I could see by the tiny drops of perspiration on her upper lip that the climb up the stairs had raised her body temperature. "It would help a lot if you could spare me a moment or two," she said. "I've come all this way, and as you're a member of Señor Tomson's family . . ." She was staring intently at me. She paused for a brief moment. "I have the strange feeling we've met somewhere before," she continued. "I'm almost certain of it."

"I don't believe we have," I replied evenly.

"Are you sure?"

"Maybe in another life . . ."

She gave me a sour look. She was not a person who enjoyed being made fun of, I decided, even in a good-natured manner. "Well, it really doesn't matter," she said. "But I do have a good memory for faces." She slipped off her right glove. "I'm Pamela Collins," she stated icily, offering me her hand. It was, I noted, equally cool to the touch. The conversation had taken a turn that was familiar to me. People have often assured me of a previous encounter, insisted even, until usually in the past I have confessed that I was for some years a minor Hollywood actor, a "featured player," the friend of the leading man who gets speared by the Apaches at the end of the third reel, or the cowardly pilot in a "service drama" who crashes during a training exercise, or, as had been the case in my last role under contract to one of the majors, the unsuccessful suitor of the female lead in what used to be called "a screwball comedy."

But on that rainy Sunday morning I was in no mood to admit, as I had often done before, that my interrogator might have seen me on the late night television in an old movie, which usually prolonged a boring conversation. Besides, I have never enjoyed discussing my early years in "the industry" with "civilians," as we used to call them, for inevitably doing so caused me to recall the less than happy circumstances in which I came to grief in Hollywood, an incident I was given to ponder often enough without any outside assistance. So instead of continuing my denials of a previous encounter, I said: "Maybe you've run into my *doppelgänger,* or it could be that I don't have a particularly unique face. Anyway, what's the message you want me to pass on to Señor Tomson?"

"I didn't catch your name," Pamela Collins said.

"Masters," I told her. "Robert Masters. Robert will do."

"It's a rather delicate matter," she said slowly. She took off her tweed hat, and held it out at arm's length to shake it, sending out a shower of raindrops in my direction where I stood seated on the front edge of Kiko's desk. Pamela Collins had, I noticed, a full head of dark brown hair that she had pinned up in a mound under her hat to keep it dry. "Do you play golf?" she asked, her eyes having caught sight of the cardboard cover of the borrowed tape.

"Yes, a little."

"And Señor Tomson . . . does he play golf, too?"

"No, he's into karate. The martial arts."

"Does he speak English?"

"Oh, yes," I said. "He was trained in the United States." Fergy had sauntered through the partially open door, and was shame-lessly rubbing herself against my visitor's shapely legs.

"I hope you like cats," I said, snapping my fingers to catch Fergy's attention.

"I like all animals," Pamela Collins replied, leaning forward to scratch Fergy's neck. "I prefer them to humans." With her eyes on the cat, and lowering her voice, she began to state the purpose of her visit. "You see, I have a friend," she continued, "a close friend who is more than a little concerned about her husband's conduct." She paused significantly. "She suspects he's being unfaithful to her."

"So she wants him followed."

"You're very intuitive," she said, sarcastically.

"I also have a hunch that your close friend doesn't exist," I replied.

She left Fergie to her own devices and turned her attention

back to me. The minor constellation of freckles on her chest rose slightly as she took a deep breath. "All right, there is no friend," she replied. "It's my own husband I'm concerned about. He's an ardent golfer, which provides him with an excuse to stay away from home most days."

"The very best reason I can think of to play."

"You're not married, I take it."

"No, but I was a couple of times."

"Bully for you," she said. "But you still play?"

"It keeps me busy now that I've retired. I've always been a tennis player, but now that I'm a senior citizen I've taken up golf."

"How fascinating," she said, coolly, and studied her scarlet fingernails. Then she added: "It's where my husband goes after he leaves his club that worries me."

"Are you contemplating divorce? Because if you have him followed that's how it will end. Why don't you ask him if he has a mistress and save yourself time and money?"

"I have asked him," she said, "and all I get as an answer are lies. Lies and denials. I want to confront him with the truth." She took a handkerchief out of the sleeve of her slicker and raised it to the corners of her eyes that had become moist with tears.

"The truth usually doesn't help matters."

"I know that. I'm not a child."

I shrugged and returned to Kiko's chair behind the desk. In the right-hand drawer I found a stack of lined yellow paper and a ballpoint pen. "All right," I said in my most businesslike manner, "then I suggest you give me your address and directions how to get to your villa. Also the name of your husband's golf club, the make of car he drives, and a description of his person. I'll pass the information on to my son-in-law, and leave the matter in his hands. He'll need a telephone number at which you can be reached."

"I don't want you to call me," she said. "I'll call you," familiar words out of my professional past.

"Fair enough."

She rose and came around the desk to stand beside me. The scent she wore was anything but unpleasant. In a faint voice she began to supply the answers to my previous questions. She seemed suddenly unnerved, as if she had finally realized that she was taking a serious step in a betrayal she had only contemplated previously. For the first time since her intrusion on my peaceful Sunday morning I found myself feeling sorry for her.

"What's your husband's full name?" I inquired once I had finished my notations.

"Cecil Collins," she replied. "He has a title, but I suppose that's not important."

"It's not important to *me*."

Her eyes narrowed. "Have you ever been told that you were less than charming?"

"Not by anyone that mattered to me." I got to my feet, and we stood facing each other. She was trying to control her temper. I half expected her to reach out for the yellow piece of paper on Kiko's blotter and tear it to pieces. She stared at me for a few more seconds, perhaps remembering one of my rare close-ups that had provided her with the impression of *déjà vu*. "I still feel we've met somewhere—possibly many years ago. Before I met Collins."

"I wish we had," I said with my most winning smile.

"I assure you that it would not have made the slightest difference," came the answer, and turning back to grab her oiled-leather handbag, she started off toward the door.

"Your hat!" I called after her, and after retrieving it, handed it to her.

"What's the telephone number here?" she asked.

I stepped over to the desk for one of Kiko's business cards, and she snatched it out of my hand. "I'll call next time so I can speak directly to Cuko, or whatever it is you call him," she said.

"Kiko," I corrected her, but she was already halfway out of the door, and slamming it shut behind her, almost decapitated Fergy, who had made a rush for the warmer climate of my apartment across the hall. The cat's shrill cry rang in my ears, but when I attempted to console her, she escaped to her favorite hiding place under the bed.

2

"YOU MEAN TO SAY YOU'VE NEVER HEARD of Sir Cecil Collins?" Kiko asked. It was Monday morning and there had been no improvement in the weather. This had not deterred my son-in-law from taking his early morning jog, and he was seated now in his black leather chair, freshly showered, his black beard recently trimmed, all of which gave him the appearance of one of the current ministers of the Spanish socialist government.

"No, I haven't," I told him. "I don't read *Hola,* or any of the other magazines that report on the doings of the jet set."

"He's one of the British superrich," Kiko informed me. "I don't know how he made his money, but he's got plenty of it. He divides his time between Monte Carlo and Marbella. He's a baron."

"Tailing him is still a nasty job," I said.

"If I don't do it, somebody else will."

"Kurt Waldheim's words."

Kiko made a face and shrugged. In the dozen years we have known each other our relationship has changed considerably, as has Kiko's appearance. Although he has maintained his athletic figure, he has lost most of the hair on the top of his head, probably the reason for his beard.

He now smokes a pipe instead of cigarettes, carries a snub-nosed revolver for which he has a license, and has acquired the demeanor of a Latin Sherlock Holmes, tight-lipped and anything but talkative except when it comes to discussing the virtues of Real Madrid, the football club of which he is a fervent partisan. Where once he treated me with filial respect, he now has an attitude toward me of gentle tolerance, no doubt due to the decline of my personal fortune. If I had consulted him before making my various investments in the local real-estate market, he often reminds me, I wouldn't be in the precarious financial situation in which I find myself at present. Not that Kiko is rich, but his cash flow is somewhat steadier than mine. That is the reason I occupy the rented apartment adjoining his office instead of the villa I built for myself in the hills above San Pedro, which I had been forced to lease to a retired Belgian couple at the beginning of the present recession.

He relit his pipe and said: "The normal fee for this kind of job is thirty thousand pesetas a day, plus expenses."

"Three hundred dollars a day," I said, for my own benefit. "Not a great fortune. Let's say, for argument's sake, that you discover Sir Cecil has a paramour after three or four days of snooping. You make a thousand dollars, but then you'll probably have to go to court with her ladyship, at a reduced fee. You'll also have to pay overtime to one of your little helpers."

"Who says it'll only take three or four days?" Kiko asked. "Chances are the job will last at least two weeks. We'll have to furnish proof, and that usually takes time."

"You mean photograph his lordship *in flagrante?*"

"Could be."

"Are you that desperate for business?"

"We're in the middle of a recession," Kiko said. "In case you've forgotten!"

"Well, then take the damn job."

"I will. We're not being asked to commit murder, you know. Anyway, Lady Pamela's request is nothing unusual. A detective agency is often asked to do that kind of work."

"Okay. Say no more. The woman will probably call tomorrow. Then you can advise her of the fee involved and assign a member of your staff." Kiko's staff consisted of two unsavory characters, Alberto, a former Spanish legionnaire with a shaved head, and Pepe, a reformed truant from Algeciras in his late fifties.

"You could take it on," Kiko said. "It just involves hanging around a golf course, and you're better suited for that than anyone."

"I'm not interested in that kind of work. And I don't think I have to remind you that I'm not a licensed detective. I don't even have a Spanish work permit."

"There's no risk, for God's sake. What could happen?"

"Collins could make a *denuncia.*"

"On what grounds?"

"Invasion of privacy. Molesting him."

"I assume you're not going to get caught."

"Forget it," I said. "I'm not your man."

Kiko scowled. He had a stubborn streak I had run up against before. "Money makes the world go round," he said, as I started for the door.

I said: "I seem to remember you used to say it was love," and went back to my own quarters. Fergy was asleep on my bed and the telephone was ringing. It was Susan, calling from the real-estate office where she worked as a secretary.

"How are you, Daddy?" she asked in an ominously friendly voice, the one she always used whenever she was about to make a difficult request.

"I'm fine," I said. "What can I do for you?"

"Would you like to take me to lunch?"

"When?" I asked.

"Today. I need to talk to you. Could you meet me at La California at one-thirty? My car's on the blink."

"It's not much of a day."

"So what else is new?"

"Okay," I said. "Don't be late."

"I never am anymore," she replied with a girlish giggle. "I'm a businesswoman now."

3

I CAN ONLY GUESS that the poetic name of my native state has always conjured up a land of milk and honey, even to the people living on this equally sunny coast. Why else had the owners of the small *tasca* on the eastern edge of Marbella chosen to call their establishment La California? The one long room with its white-tiled floor was certainly unlike any restaurant you might find on the West Coast. There is a long counter adjacent to the bar where a variety of seafood is on display so that you can choose what you want to order as you enter. A raised television set stands in the far corner that is always going at full blast, drowning out the uproar of raucous Latin voices once the premises are fully occupied. But the place has a strange charm of its own.

Despite the heavy traffic in the center of town, I had arrived on time, and was able to find an empty table next to the row of glass windows that give out onto the street. I ordered a *caña*, a tall glass of the local draught beer that along with the fresh seafood is the main attraction of this *tasca*. Then I began to play the game I have become addicted to these last years. How many of the people standing at the bar were at least forty years younger than I was? I reckoned. Or thirty years? Or twenty? I was no doubt the oldest customer in the room, with the possible exception of the crippled lottery salesman who was standing in his usual spot near the door.

At ten minutes to two I caught sight of my daughter on the sidewalk outside. A few minutes later I watched her squeeze past the crowd of locals at the bar, and then she sat down opposite me with an apologetic smile. She was wearing jeans, a tightly fitting red sweater and a baseball cap that only partially protected her abundant blond hair. At times she looked alarmingly like her mother, except for her nose, which prominent feature I had passed on to her. She said: "I'm sorry I'm late, Daddy . . . but it wasn't my fault."

It was never her fault, I couldn't help thinking, no matter what had happened to her. Someone else was always to blame for her misadventures, and the list of these was long. Automobile accidents, broken bones, failed exams, missed airplane connections, even running out of gas on the way to an important appointment. I, of course, was a paragon. "Never mind," I said. "I got here in time to find us a table."

"Just as I was leaving the office the boss decided to dictate a letter," she said, smoothing back her moist hair with her two hands.

A plump Spanish woman in black came over to where we were seated, and asked if the far end of our table was unoccupied. I nodded to her, and she was joined an instant later by her equally plump friend. Susan made a face.

"Don't you own an umbrella?" I asked her.

"I was in such a hurry I left it at the office. I didn't want to keep you waiting."

I waved to Encarna, the waitress that had been there as long as I could remember, and she came over to take our order. The two Spanish women across from us had lighted cigarettes. I ordered a plate of cooked shrimps, two portions of San Pedro, the fish Encarna recommended as being freshly caught that morning, a tomato salad with onions, and another *caña* for Susan.

"*¿Hay chanquetes?*" she asked the waitress.

Encarna nodded. *Chanquetes* are the tiny fish that are a delicacy of the region, served fried. But because of their popularity and modern fishing methods they are becoming extinct. "They're illegal," I said.

"I know, Daddy," Susan said, adopting a tone of filial tolerance. "But I didn't catch them."

Encarna left us after promising our neighbors to return in a moment. The place was beginning to fill up. There were no more tables, and the people at the bar were glancing enviously at the seated customers.

Susan, who had only recently given up smoking, glared furiously at the two portly women seated only a few feet from us, who were puffing away at their Ducados while placing their order with Encarna.

"Spanish cigarettes, yuk!" Susan said, and added, "It's been a while, I never seem to get to see you alone. Actually I've wanted to talk to you for quite some time." There was something slightly ominous about her tone of voice, but the shrimp had arrived, and she paused to help herself to half a dozen of them. "*La caña,*" she reminded the waitress.

"*Por favor,*" I reminded her.

"*Yes,* Daddy . . ."

"What's wrong?" I asked. "Anything unusual?"

"Well," she said, "it's a long story. Kiko and I haven't been getting along all that great recently. I suppose I'm partly to blame. We've been married for twelve years, and ever since the kids arrived . . ."

"That's normal in every marriage."

"I know . . . and I also remember that you warned me, so there's no use going into the past, is there? We got along pretty well in the beginning, but now I feel I can't hack it anymore. Culture clash, isn't that what it's called? He can't change, and I don't want to."

I have never enjoyed listening to the marital woes of others, probably because I've had enough of my own. My daughter's problems should have been an exception. "You're not contemplating divorce?" I asked, echoing the words I had spoken to Lady Collins only twenty-four hours earlier.

"No," Susan said, vaguely. "I just want to get away for a while, and I thought maybe spending Easter with Mummy might be a good idea."

"In Santa Barbara?"

"Yes. Why not?"

"What about Tommy and Carmen?"

"I'd take them with me. Mummy has never seen Carmen, and she says she's anxious to . . ."

"Has she offered to pay your way?"

"No, of course not. But she might chip in if asked."

The tomato salad and the *chanquetes* had arrived. Susan beamed at the cluster of tiny fried fish, like a pad of worms on the white plate. "Want some, Daddy?" she asked.

"No, thanks."

"Nobody'll know," she said, with a little laugh.

"I'll wait for my order." I was making a mental calculation as to the cost of the trip. Two thousand dollars was, I reckoned, a conservative estimate. "How long do you think you'll be gone?" I asked. "If you go."

"Three weeks. A month."

"And that'll help solve your problems?"

"No, but it'll give me time to meditate," she said, adding, "I won't have to borrow more than two thou from you."

"That's good news."

"I'm sorry, Daddy."

"Not half as sorry as I am."

She shrugged. "I haven't asked you for money for quite a long time . . . not since you helped me buy a car."

"Can't you put off your trip until summer? I'm not exactly flush right now."

"There's somebody else," she said.

"Holy smoke!" It was an expletive that dated me, but it was all I could think of at that moment. "Does Kiko know?"

"Of course not."

"Well, don't tell him, please."

Encarna had placed a plate of grilled fish in the center of our crowded table. I wasn't in the least bit hungry. "The San Pedro is for both of us," I said.

"You've hardly eaten anything."

"I seldom do at lunch."

She glanced over at me quizzically. "I guess I inherited a lot of things from you. It isn't as if you've never had problems like these. Right?"

"I never had to ask my dad for money to get out of town," I told her. I took a deep breath. It seemed uncomfortably warm inside the *tasca*. "I'll try to figure out something," I said glumly.

"Thank you, Daddy," Susan replied. "I'm sorry," she added. "But it isn't all my fault."

"Yes, I know. It takes two to tango."

"No, I mean it."

"Eat your illegal baby fish," I told her, "and let's get the hell out of here." There was now a game show on the small TV screen in the far corner, and even driving around in the rain seemed preferable to remaining at our table.

4

I HAD LENT SUSAN MY UMBRELLA, since she was temporarily without wheels, so that *I* was obliged to take shelter in a public telephone booth once we had left La California. I watched her run across the main thoroughfare as the traffic lights changed, and noticed that she stepped into a puddle, splashing an elderly gentleman who was on his way to the covered bus stop, cane in hand. That wasn't her fault either, I couldn't help thinking. But she apologized. I could see that she had taken the trouble to speak a few words to her victim. Then she turned, blew me a kiss and waved before the blue bus arrived to cut short our farewell.

By that time it was a quarter past three, yet the rest of the afternoon promised to be long. I made a run for a nearby phone booth, slid a twenty-five-peseta coin into the appropriate slot, and punched out Evelyn's number. Visiting the one person who might listen sympathetically to my family problems seemed like a good idea. We have been lovers for quite a few years, although her empathy was not a patent certainty. Evelyn has no children of her own, and I had noticed in the past that she becomes rather detached whenever I mention Susan and her vagaries. After the fourth ring

Evelyn's pleasant voice, carefully taped in English and Spanish, advised me that I should leave my name and telephone number after the beep. That left me with the rest of the afternoon as empty as before.

I waited a minute or two for the rain to subside, then hurried to where I had parked my car, a Ford Fiesta I had purchased some years ago. It started almost at once, for which I was grateful. I would drive up to my house, I decided, as I had not checked how it was surviving the storm in more than a fortnight. When things went wrong my tenants, the overweight Belgian couple, had always been prompt in reporting all minor disasters by calling me at my flat, so I assumed the drains had not as yet been clogged by leaves and mud, and the electricity had not been cut off as a result of the storm. Nevertheless I thought I would drive past the place to have a quick look.

Long ago, when I had first arrived on the coast, I had hoped to find a small house by the sea, but the high price of seafront real estate had made me settle for an old *finca* in the hills above Marbella. It had turned out to be a prudent choice, as I soon learned the damp climate of the region made the upkeep of a residence by the sea extremely costly. Immediately after the war, motivated by the same impractical desire, I had built a small house on the beach at Trancas twelve miles north of Malibu. Then when my career in the motion picture industry had come to an abrupt halt, due to the fatal indiscretion that I will go into later, I had sold the place for many times my initial investment. It was a windfall that decided me to abandon any thought of returning permanently to the West Coast. Of course the value of land and houses in that region has risen astronomically since, and the last time the small shack changed hands the price paid had been reported to me to have exceeded a million dollars. Still, I have had no regrets.

The *poniente,* the harsh west wind from the Atlantic, was blowing hard when I arrived at my converted *cortijo.* I noticed that the green shutters on the upstairs windows were closed, as was the front door. I stopped my car and got out. Pepe, my aging gardener, was picking up the fallen leaves on the front lawn. He saw me and gestured for me to join him. I went slowly up the flagstone steps, hesitant to intrude on the privacy of my tenants. But I soon learned I need not have worried. *"La gente se han ido,"* Pepe informed me, the people had gone. To judge by the gray stubble on his chin, he hadn't shaved for a couple of days and looked almost as unkempt as the lawn. I asked him when the people had left, and he told me that a week earlier they had packed their belongings into their station wagon and driven off, never to return. They were, I realized, two months in arrears for the rent.

I went back to my car to collect the key ring for the house that I kept in the glove compartment. Then I climbed back up the stone steps and went inside. The place was a mess. Two rotting tomatoes and an open can of tuna was all that the frigidaire contained. The bed in the upstairs bedroom had not been made. Pepe informed me that Maria, my maid, had not appeared since the Belgians' departure, she hadn't been paid her last month's wages. Nor had Pepe received any money for two months. I assured him I would bring him a check the next day, and he got on his motorbike and rode off.

I locked all the doors and went outside to sit for a moment on the wicker chair that stands on the covered terrace. On the way up to the *finca* I had listened to an interview with the English doctor who does a guest spot every two weeks on the local British radio station. Monday was the day of the week that most heart attacks occur, he had told his listeners. Stress was usually to blame, caused by the return of office workers to their duties after a weekend of relaxation. Well, it was Monday all right, Monday in spades. Only a heart attack was the least of my worries.

The sky over the Rock of Gibraltar showed a patch of blue, promising an improvement in the weather, although the sea was still a dark gray. It was the view that had decided me to buy the ruin of an old farmhouse. The long curve of the bay and the mountains hovering over the sea reminded me of southern California. They say that as you grow old you begin to long for the landscape of your childhood. But it had been more the strong dollar that had made rebuilding the place a tempting proposition—even a sound investment. So in spite of my son-in-law's advice I had bought twenty-five acres of the adjoining land without investigating the zoning laws. It was agricultural land, I soon discovered, with the result that I was land-poor when the recession came along. I planted lemon trees because of the scarcity of water. But lemons were soon a glut on the market. I would be able to drown my sorrows in lemon juice, so it seemed.

The patch of blue on the horizon disappeared. I roused myself out of the dilapidated armchair and returned to my car. With any luck, I reckoned, Evelyn would be back in her cottage, and avoiding the potholes, drove slowly down the narrow road. It was worth a try. Anything was better than returning to my flat and facing Kiko, who would undoubtedly be waiting for me in his office.

5

THE SMELL OF A WOOD FIRE greeted me as I arrived at Evelyn's front door. El Refugio is the name of the *pueblo* where she lives. Contrary to its appearance, the village is not an old one. Thirty years ago it was planned and built by a well-to-do young Spaniard from the north who created an Andalusian town center, complete with cobblestone streets and picturesque houses that he went about selling to his friends at modest prices, hoping to create a haven for artists and bohemians. Right from the start it had turned out to be a modestly successful venture, and although the young promoter died of alcoholism before its final completion, El Refugio had not lost any of its original charm, had retained an atmosphere of picturesque bohemianism without the usual pretensions of artiness. There was a small church and a restaurant called La Parilla, the latter frequented by the locals on a more regular basis than the chapel, which was used occasionally for weddings and Masses for the departed.

I never regretted having turned down the chance to buy the small house that had been offered to me some years ago by an American writer's widow, for El Refugio was noisy at night, which didn't seem to bother Evelyn, who was a sound sleeper, having lived most of her life in cities. Then, too, once we had become a couple, nearly seven years ago, I had gained the status of outpatient, and was thus able to enjoy the ambiance of the place without being subjected to all of the disadvantages of communal living, such as the barking of dogs and the constant dropping-in of neighbors.

I tapped on the front door with the brass knocker and went inside. Evelyn was seated in her favorite rocker with Hercules, her golden Labrador, at her slippered feet. But she was not alone, I discovered. Kathy Vernon, her friend and confidante, was seated on the small green couch that stands with its back to the front door. The two women were having tea. Kathy was puffing on one of her evil-smelling Spanish cigarettes as I crossed the room.

"Ah, Roberto," Evelyn said. "What a pleasant surprise!" Her blonde hair looked as if it had been freshly curled, her face made up as it always was late in the afternoon, no matter what her plans for the evening might be. She is one of those English women who feels she is not completely dressed until her hair and face are what she calls presentable, an idiosyncrasy I admire.

Kathy rose, and tossed her lighted cigarette into the fire. "I was just leaving," she said, her usual polite lie whenever I happened to interrupt one of their get-togethers.

"Don't rush off just because of me," I said, which was not the truth, either.

Kathy is Scottish, a weather-beaten forty-five, recently divorced from her American husband, who agreed to a generous settlement after only three years of marriage, not a bad coup considering the couple had been childless. Evelyn, who is ten years older than her friend, occasionally comments on Kathy's good fortune, sounding vaguely envious. These statements never fail to irritate me, as they suggest a degree of dissatisfaction with her own lot. "It's not too late for you to do the same," I tell her whenever she mentions Kathy's nest egg. "You look ten years younger than she does, so act now while you can." These remarks she never fails to shrug off, although I know she is pleased with my compliment, which is based on fact, as Evelyn has a younger appearance, probably due to her having avoided cigarettes and booze all of her life.

She smiled now and said: "Get yourself a cup and join the party. You know where everything is in this house."

"I need something stronger than tea today," I told her. I went into the kitchen, got myself a glass and filled it with ice from her fridge, then returned to the living room, where I knew there was an open bottle of whiskey and a bottle of Lanjaron water with which I topped off my drink. The two women sat watching me.

"Hard liquor in the afternoon?" Evelyn said. "That's not like you."

"I've had a bad day."

"Oh, really? Tell us about it."

"I'd rather not," I said.

Kathy rose and picked up her package of cigarettes. "I really must be off," she said. "It was nice seeing you again, Robert. Even briefly."

"Make it longer next time," I replied, with equal hypocrisy.

"I'll call you later, Ev," she said, and was gone.

Hercules raised his head to watch her go. His mistress emptied the ashtray into the fireplace. "She always buzzes off as if we were about to fuck," I said.

"She's just being polite."

Evelyn never comments on my occasional profanity, although I know she doesn't like it. In all of the years we have been together I have never heard her use strong language. She is conventional in that way, true to her middle-class upbringing, even though she lives an unconventional existence. She had come to the Costa del Sol on a holiday with her husband in the sixties, and then after his death at the early age of forty-eight, she had returned, mainly because the climate and the informality of life suited her. Spain was cheap in those days, and her husband's insurance policy had provided her with enough money to live comfortably. But she had become bored with doing nothing and had gone to work for a French porcelain manufacturer who felt he needed a presentable "public relations person" who spoke English as well as Spanish. The small salary the job paid turned out to be a blessing, as inflation and the falling pound had made it difficult for her "to keep head and shoulders above water," as she put it. She had no thought of marrying again, one of the basic reasons our relationship suited her, as it did me.

"What happened to spoil your day?" she asked once I had taken over Kathy's place on the green couch.

"My Belgian tenants have buggered off. The house is a mess, and besides not paying the last two months' rent, they neglected to give Maria her wages, so she decided to take a holiday."

"Is that all that's troubling you?" Evelyn asked with an ironic grin.

"Wait. There's more." I sipped my drink and told her about my lunch with Susan.

"I'm glad I never had any children," Evelyn said. "Oh, I regret it occasionally, but not for long." She poured herself a fresh cup of tea. "Are you going to give her the money?" she asked.

"I haven't got it to give."

"Well, maybe Kiko will help out. He *is* her husband, after all."

"That's another story," I said. I then related in detail my morning encounter with Lady Collins and my morning interview with my son-in-law.

"Good Lord!" Evelyn said. "All this while I was visiting my aunt in Soto Grande."

"Was that fun?" I asked to change the subject.

"Not really. That part of the world is too quiet. I was glad to get home." She paused. "So what are you going to do? Take on the job of private eye?"

"No way, José. I'm not that demented."

"But you must have played the part of a private detective in one of your early movies, so it shouldn't be all that difficult."

"You've got me confused with Humphrey Bogart. Anyway, I've

retired from that profession, remember?" I got up to replenish my drink. "Incidentally, have you ever heard of Sir Cecil Collins?" I asked her.

"Indeed I have," she replied. "I've seen his photograph in *Country Life* dozens of times. He has an attractive wife."

"They're rich, I take it. Did he make his own pile?"

"I haven't a clue. But he's nobody's fool, I'm certain of that. I shouldn't like to get on the wrong side of his lordship."

I said: "Call Kiko and tell him that."

She shook her head. "Poor Roberto," she said. She held out her hands. "Come take a nap, and forget your troubles," she added with her most alluring smile. "I'll join you in a while."

"Not today, Josephine. I'm beat."

"We'll see about that," she said. "But first you'd best lock the front door. People have a way of stopping by on rainy afternoons. It's part of the charm of El Refugio."

"That's the one thing you don't have to tell me to do, lock the door," I told her.

She looked puzzled, but not for long. Then she got up from her chair and crossed the room to lock the door herself. "I'll try to overlook that last remark of yours," she said. "I don't know why you always have to refer everything to your past."

6

LONG AGO SCREENWRITERS used to insert the word FLASHBACK in their scripts to denote a time change, an interruption in the continuity of their stories that was usually preceded by a lap dissolve. But in the scripts and movies of today this device has been abandoned, today's audiences having been conditioned to a more radical method of storytelling. The film editor cuts to the distant past without warning, knowing that the minds of viewers are more alert than the popcorn addicts of my youth. However, as I am a neophyte at this trade, I shall fall back on this outmoded convention, and a flashback is what follows, motivated by Evelyn's suggestion that I lock the front door, which took me back more than three decades to a sunnier climate and easier times.

In the early nineteen fifties I was, like everyone else who had been in uniform, grateful to be alive. I was also under the illusion that I had done my small share to make the world a better place—this despite the fact that some of my former comrades in arms, like Dr. Ravitch, had been called back into service and sent off to Korea. A bachelor once again, I had been signed recently to a term contract by one of the major film studios, and was being well paid for my services, so that I was even able to purchase the small beach house in Trancas, as I have mentioned earlier. Freed of all of my obligations, I was convinced that I had nothing better to do than enjoy myself.

My closest friend was a young film editor who like myself had served in the Navy. His name was Harry Lessing, and as he had been excused from work on this particular Saturday in October, we decided to drive to the desert for the weekend. We set off in two cars on a Friday night, having concluded that it would be better for each of us to have his own wheels. We met at a motel Harry knew about in Palm Springs and went to a Chinese restaurant for a relaxed dinner. The next morning we drove to Charlie Farrell's Racquet Club, the most popular establishment in the resort, that was, however, too expensive for our modest means.

Harry had been a local tournament player before the war, which was the reason we had been invited to play some men's doubles by a successful screenwriter who was staying at the exclusive club. But when we arrived the man had already gotten himself involved in another game, and so we made for two deck chairs in the shade of the terrace and sat waiting for our turn to play. Because of the heat only a few courts were occupied, and after a while a woman I had met a couple of times at the house of friends in Brentwood came over to us and asked if we would like to play a set of mixed doubles. She was the wife of a prominent agent, and although neither Harry nor I were enthusiastic mixed-doubles players, we felt it would be discourteous to refuse.

Our fourth arrived a few minutes later, and the agent's wife made the introductions. They weren't really necessary, we had both recognized the girl. Her name was Sue Wilson. She was a talented young actress who had appeared in a couple of movies and who was also known to be the mistress of one of the executives in charge of the studio where I was under contract. It was common gossip that the man was in the process of divorcing his wife in order to marry his new find, so that it came as no surprise that she was spending the weekend alone in Palm Springs. We spun our racquets to determine our partners, and Harry wound up with the agent's wife.

Instead of the usual tennis dress, my partner was wearing a sky-blue sunsuit that showed off her figure as well as her evenly tanned skin. She was a brunette, a rarity among the starlets of the day, and she wore her dark hair like a Grecian helmet to frame her pert face, somewhat in the style of Clara Bow or Louise Brooks, seductresses of another era. She had a winning smile and was graceful in her movements, although it was obvious that she had only recently taken up tennis. Harry's partner was more serious about her game, and there followed a long set with interminable rallies and a great deal of hilarity.

As we changed sides for the last time Sue asked me in a low voice what plans I had for the evening, and more in the nature of a joke than anything else, I said that I was "available." "So am I," she replied, "later on." She explained that she was having dinner with some boring people from the studio but suggested we could meet for a drink at ten-thirty. "That makes me a cheap date," she added with a giggle. We decided to meet in the parking lot of the Dunes, a gambling establishment, and she asked me to be patient and wait for her in case she was detained.

It is obvious that words spoken so many years ago cannot be remembered verbatim, so I must be permitted a degree of author's license, but I do recall that as Harry and I followed the two women off the court, he said: "I hope you know what you're doing, pal," apparently having overheard a part of my previous conversation with my tennis partner.

I thought I did, needless to say. I was twenty-four years old, recently divorced and not as broke as I had been when I was discharged from the service. In the Navy they tell you "never take your finger off your number," by which is meant that it is better for an officer to remain inconspicuous, keep his serial number covered at all times and wait for routine promotion. But I had left all of that behind me and I didn't think my "cheap date" would amount to much more than an evening of flirtation, an amusing way to spend Saturday night. Sue Wilson, although a few years younger than I, was obviously no fool, so I felt safe.

We went to a small nightclub on the outskirts of the town, had a couple of drinks, danced and chatted aimiably for a couple of hours. Then I drove her back to the parking lot to collect her car. Before getting out of mine, she suggested I follow her back to the bungalow where she was staying and come in for a nightcap. I remember that I hesitated for a moment. It was already fairly late. "You're not chicken, are you?" she asked me. "A little," I said. "This is a company town. I know, I was brought up here. And I've got news for you . . . I'm not Clark Gable." She laughed. "I'm glad you're not," she said. "I hear he has a teeny-weeny whatsit." In any event, she added with a grin, she would use her influence to have the studio pick up my option.

The bungalow she had rented for the winter was in one of the new developments. A large picture window looked out on a swimming pool and the desert beyond a low white wall. She made stingers for both of us and turned out the lights. We sat on a white leather couch enjoying the moonlight. By that time she had already told me quite a bit about her past. After graduating from the chorus she had done a brief stint as a nightclub singer, had been the girlfriend of a minor gangster before being discovered by a talent scout. My life had been more sheltered, I confessed. My father had owned a bookshop in Santa Monica, and I had grown up in the safe environment of that small town.

"So you read a lot of naughty books when you were a kid . . . *Fanny Hill* and all the rest," she said with a giggle.

"Just *Fanny Hill* and *Lady Chatterley's Lover.*"

"And how did you get into this business?" she asked.

"By accident." I told her how one day Lewis Milestone had walked into our store in order to buy a copy of *War and Peace,* and while my father was getting the Tolstoy novel for that famous director, Milestone had wandered into the back room where I was un-

wrapping a shipment of new books. He looked at me with his piercing eyes, studied my face and then asked me if I had ever thought
of becoming an actor. I told him I hadn't, and he grinned. "That's
where the money is," he said, "in front of the camera." My father
had joined us. He told Milestone that he wanted me to go to college and get an education before the draft caught up with me. Then
I could make up my mind what to do. "Well, if he wants to finance
his college career, have him come and see me. I need a kid with his
looks for a bit part in a movie I'm about to make." He scribbled his
name and telephone number on a scrap of paper and I called him
the next day.

"I know," Sue said. *"All Quiet on the Western Front."*

"No, that was before my time," I said. *"Lucky Partners* was the
name of the movie. It was a flop."

"But it got you out of the bookstore," Sue said, "and away from
dad."

"Not really. I didn't leave home until I joined the Navy."

She said: "What a good boy. Well, it's high time you lived a
little, Bobby." She moved closer. We kissed, not all that passion-
ately at first, and then I followed her into her bedroom. Sue had
barely mentioned her liaison with her powerful beau, except to say
that like any woman involved with a married man, "a girl gets tired
of waiting," and I had refrained from asking her for more details. I
had other things on my mind.

At dawn I drove back to the motel where Harry and I were
staying. The sun had just risen over the summits of the surrounding
mountains, and the smell of the desert filled my car. Sue and I had
made no plans to meet again, although we had exchanged telephone numbers. But the following week she came to visit me at my
shack, which is how she referred to my small house on the beach. I
was not in love with her, but after the dentist's daughter, Sue's
lighthearted ways were a relief. Undeniably there was also a strong
physical attraction. I was on layoff, as it was called then, and I had

plenty of time to play tennis and walk along the edge of the sea and think of Sue.

Then one Sunday morning she called and asked me to visit her at *her* house for a change. Eddie, her protector, was in New York, she told me, attending a series of meetings with bankers and exhibitors, and as she had given the help the day off to go to the races at Santa Anita, "the coast was clear." I suggested that it would be safer if she came to Trancas that afternoon, but she said she couldn't face the long drive back to town through the weekend traffic. Besides it would be better if she stayed home in case there was a call from New York. She had invited her best girlfriend and her beau for tennis, which would decrease the risk, she assured me.

The house was high in the hills above Sunset Boulevard, and after following a narrow, winding road that had not been left unscarred by the recent rains, I found my way there. She must have been on the lookout for my arrival, for as I stopped my car, the black iron gates at the bottom of a steep drive opened, and I drove up to the entrance of the house. I noticed that there was a tennis court that looked as if it had been recently added to the property; for the house itself was anything but new. It had the look of belonging to another era, which turned out to be the case as Sue informed me soon after we had started on our guided tour. It was a "love nest" built by one of the famous leading men of the silent era for his fourth wife, a somewhat daring undertaking in the days when the great stars preferred to live on Hollywood Boulevard.

"Is it yours?" I asked, impressed by the lavish decorations of the living room we were passing through.

"Well, sort of," she replied. "Eddie bought it for me. It's in the name of some sort of company I'm supposed to own someday. Anyway, I live here now."

I followed her into the adjoining master bedroom. Beyond it there was a covered terrace above a small swimming pool, with flagstone steps leading to the tennis court. The telephone rang, and putting her hands to her lips, she picked up a nearby extension. It was her girlfriend calling to tell her that she wouldn't be able to make it for tennis. So tennis turned out to be a mere formality. We swam in the heated pool, I recall, Sue having shed her tennis clothes, and I, with greater propriety, in my shorts. We kissed, treading water. Sue said: "Enough of this. Let's adjourn to the bedroom."

With my head buried deep in the perfumed pillows of her king-sized bed I thought I had heard the sound of footsteps. She was whispering: "Wait for me, wait for me," as I pulled away from her embrace. "Why are you so damn nervous?" she asked, annoyed that I had interrupted our lovemaking. "I heard something," I said, and she said: "Nonsense," and winding her arm around my neck, tightened her hold on me. At that precise moment the door of the bedroom opened to reveal a slim gray-haired woman in slacks and a black cardigan. She was carrying a leather briefcase that slipped from her grasp, accentuating the look of surprise on her pinched face.

"My God!" the woman exclaimed.

Two words. That was all. Then she bent down, her right hand searching for the handle of the briefcase, her eyes fastened on us in horror. Once she had recovered her belongings she turned and ran off.

I can remember every detail of that moment, have never forgotten it. Sue leapt out of bed and crossed to the windows on the far side of the room. She pushed the curtains aside and stood looking down at the garden. My heart was pounding inside my chest. I heard the front door slam shut, and a few minutes later the noise of a car starting. "Who the hell was that?" I asked.

"Eddie's secretary," Sue replied in a jittery voice. "She has a key to the house."

I went into the bathroom, got a towel to wrap around me, and followed Sue out onto the terrace overlooking the pool. She had dropped into one of the wicker armchairs and was lighting a cigarette. "We forgot to lock the goddamn bedroom door," Sue said. "How fucking stupid can you be?"

"It wouldn't have made much difference," I told her.

"Yeah. I suppose not." She closed her eyes and sat back in the chair. Then she opened them again. "Well, that does it," she said. She shook her head slowly.

"Will she talk?"

"What do you think? Miss Davis is Eddie's loyal slave. And she hates my guts . . . always has." Strangely enough, she seemed angry rather than frightened.

"Why do you think she came here?" I asked.

"I don't know. Probably to collect some papers Eddie told her to get out of the library. He must have called her from New York. Or maybe his wife sent her to check on me."

I sat there not knowing what to say. Then foolishly I reminded her that I had told her it would be better to meet at the beach. "I'm sorry I got you into this," I added.

"Yeah . . . sure. You forced yourself on me." She laughed an unhappy laugh. "Well, we might as well have a drink and return to the hay," she said. "Better to be hung for a sheep than a lamb, or something like that."

"The only thing you can do is lie and deny everything. Tell him the woman invented the whole story."

"That won't work," Sue said. "Eddie's no dumbhead." She rose very slowly from her armchair. "I guess it's back to the chorus for li'l ole Sue," she said. "Well, even that's not the end!"

But things turned out differently. She didn't go back to the chorus and she didn't lie. Instead she confessed all. And Eddie, whatever his name was or still is (I remember it all right, but it isn't important), forgave her. Which was not surprising, or at least it doesn't surprise me now. He was in his late forties, a stocky man with a potbelly and thinning hair who chain-smoked cigars. He obviously realized that losing Sue would be extremely painful, and admitting to having been cuckolded would make him look ridiculous, a figure of fun to be snickered at all over town.

That he was madly in love with her was understandable. Everything about her was pleasing and seductive, her skin, her body, her wholesome smell. "What was she like, your Nemesis?" Evelyn and everyone else I had been with afterward had often asked me. But who in his right mind is willing to describe the quality of long-ago kisses, as well as the rest? Better to pretend a loss of memory of the distant past than to provoke unreasonable jealousy in the present.

Eddie forgave his mistress, but he didn't forgive me, the lowly contract player who had dared to trespass on his property. I was also the one person who knew that although he was tough in business, he was weak as far as Sue Wilson was concerned . . . pussywhipped was the current expression. That was probably what made him decide to condemn me to an everlasting anonymity in the industry, a vengeance easily available to him because of the power he wielded in the business. Later I learned that one of his conditions for reinstating Sue in his affections was for her to give up her career, to which she agreed. They were married less than a year later, after Eddie had paid off his wife.

The story never became public gossip although a good many people knew about it at the time. My agent and friend Paul Levin was one of them. "The best thing for you to do," he advised me in the privacy of his office, "is leave town for a while." He was not brave enough to represent me, he admitted with a nervous laugh. "I'm only a small shark swimming among the big ones," he added. "So go to Europe for a couple of years." Runaway productions, as making movies abroad was called in those days, was my best chance to make a living, and maybe even save my so-called career. I took his advice there and then, called a travel agent and made a reservation on the *Ile de France.* The next day I was able to rent my shack on the beach to a property developer, and packed up my belongings. Going by boat seemed like a good idea because I could take my car along. And I was in no hurry to get there.

The evening before setting out to drive across the continent in my Chevrolet convertible Paul Levin gave me a farewell party in his small apartment south of Wilshire Boulevard. It was not the best-attended social event of the season, although a few of my friends showed up. While the drinks were being served, the butler who had been hired for the occasion informed me that "a lady" was asking for me on the telephone. I took the call in Levin's bedroom. It was Sue. She was calling, she said, to say goodbye. "You won't believe this," she added in a low voice, "but I wish I were going with you."

"What? You and Eddie?"

"Don't be bitter, Bobby."

"I'm not," I told her. "Just sad."

She said: "I'm going to miss you."

"No, you won't," I replied. "You'll be too busy shopping for your trousseau." I was bitter, I guess. Bitter *and* sad.

7

IT SOON DAWNED ON ME that my remark about locking the front door
had been a mistake. When Evelyn finally appeared in the bedroom
she was still fully dressed. She had added, I noticed, a red-and-
white-checkered apron to her attire. "So you're not joining me?" I
asked with pretended surprise.

"I thought I'd let you wallow in your unsavory past for a while,"
she replied. "In the meantime I've prepared my best spaghetti
sauce. You're welcome to stay for dinner."

"That's very kind of you."

"You told me that you were tired, anyway."

"I was. I feel better now."

"Well, rest for a little while longer. I'll let you know when
everything is ready."

There was a definite coolness in her voice, and I regretted
once again having told her about the errors of my youth. I had
never tried to delve into her previous relationships. She was a
widow, after all, and had remained discreet about her own life.
Women are less inclined to confessions about their love life than

men—I had learned that early on. Sue Wilson had been the exception to the rule.

"Do you want me to make the salad dressing?" I inquired, in an attempt to get back into her good graces.

"I think I can manage," she said, another indication that all was not well. She had always deferred to my making the salad dressing, had pretended, probably, that mine was superior to hers. "The girl who got you into trouble . . . did you like making love to her more than you like making love to me?"

"Of course not. Anyway, that was nearly half a century ago."

"But you still remember her."

"Sure. It was a turning point in my life."

"Have you ever thought of going back to California?"

"What for?" I asked her. "To celebrate my sixty-fifth birthday in the Motion Picture Relief Home?"

"You might be able to find work there. That would solve your financial problems, wouldn't it?"

"I can't even afford to buy Susan a ticket back to the States, for God's sake. Nor do I want to leave you."

"It was just an idea, darling," she said, in a friendlier voice.

"But not a good one," I replied. "Are you coming to bed?"

"No, I don't think so."

"I'll make it worth your while."

"Big talk," she said. "Rest for another half an hour, then get dressed and join me for dinner. I'm going to take Hercules for a walk. It's stopped raining and he hasn't been out all day." She closed the door. I got up and put on my clothes, thinking I would join her for the dog's outing, but when I stepped into the living room I discovered that she had already departed. My watch told me that it was only six-thirty, too early for dinner. I threw a fresh log on the fire and turned on the television, hoping to catch the evening news. Not that what was happening in the world mattered all that much to me at that moment. My own problems were uppermost in my mind.

The screen cleared and revealed a group of cavalrymen galloping through a canyon. A western! A late afternoon show for the Spanish kiddies and their mothers, holed up in their high-rise tenements on a rainy winter evening. The picture was in black and white, dating it to the late forties or the early fifties. Alarmed at the prospect of stumbling upon the image of our next to last president, Ronnie, I was about to change channels when the scene shifted abruptly. We were now in a crude cabin, the three inhabitants of which, dressed in boots and frontiersmen's garb, seemed to be feverishly preparing themselves for an attack by hostile Indians. One of the two men, crouching at a slit in the logs of the cabin, rifle in hand, was none other than myself, aged about nineteen!

I stepped back, and sat down on the arm of Evelyn's chair. The news could wait. The distant cries of the Indians could be heard on the sound track. The young woman was struggling with a chest of drawers, attempting to move it toward the front door of the besieged shack. I watched myself cross the scene to help her. My hair, I noticed, was long, almost shoulder length. And I was thin. There was no sign of a paunch above my gunbelt. Our eyes met, mine and the terrified leading lady's. There was a shot of the leading man, John Payne. He registered no jealousy. I was the young woman's brother, I remembered, also that I was not long for this world, a casualty before the cavalry could arrive. Now the Indians were milling about on their ponies. Wild cries, then the attack. Back to the cabin, and John Payne firing his Winchester. More gunfire on the sound track. Then, finally, a close-up of myself, aiming and firing. No wrinkles in the young face. To my surprise I noticed that my upper lip was graced with a wispy mustache. Then a well-aimed Apache bullet made me crumple to the floor. My last moment was cut short by a soap commercial, featuring a pretty German girl rubbing suds on her smooth cheeks. I shared my death scene with her.

Evelyn was now knocking on the door. She handed me Hercules's leash. "Hold the dog for a minute," she said. "I've got to get the wine out of the car. I forgot that I was fresh out."

I said: "Well, hurry up," but she merely looked puzzled and went off.

She came back minutes later carrying a shopping bag. "Why did you want me to hurry?" she asked. Then she glanced over at the television set. "One of your old movies?" she asked.

"An early effort. Nothing memorable."

She put her shopping down on the coffee table and turned to face the TV. But the Apaches were already in full retreat, and the log cabin was on fire.

"You've missed the fun," I said. "I've already gone off to the happy hunting grounds."

"Oh, damn!" she said. "How did you look?"

"Young . . . too young. So it's just as well you didn't arrive in time . . . you've always preferred older men."

She said: "I did until now," and smiled, and I knew I had been forgiven.

8

It BEGAN TO RAIN AGAIN while we were having dinner, and by the time I started home the main road was flooded. But love and spaghetti had improved my mood. Apart from everything else, Evelyn's common sense always had a positive effect on me. She had suggested I get a small mortgage from a Gibraltar bank in order to refurbish the house, which would make it possible for me to rent the place during the Easter holidays, an easier proposition given the importance of the *Semana Santa* in this country. As far as Susan was concerned, she advised me to tell her that she should postpone her plans for the summer until she had heard from her mother, who might well be willing to come up with the fare to California. At the very worst this would prove to be a delaying tactic and would relieve my immediate financial problems. Wise counsel.

It was a quarter to eleven by the time I arrived back in San Pedro. I parked my car on a side road, pulled the radio out of its slot on the dashboard, and went upstairs. In recent years a removable car radio has become a necessity on this coast. This prevents the local drug addicts from breaking into a vehicle as they are only interested in selling the stolen radio to replenish their supplies of cocaine or marijuana.

There was a slit of light showing at the bottom of Kiko's door, and I could hear the sound of voices coming from inside. I inserted the key to my apartment in the lock without turning on the hall light, but Kiko must have heard my footsteps, because he appeared behind me a second later. "I was waiting for you," he said. "Come in for a minute." He seemed tense. A football game was in progress on the screen of his TV set. "Yesterday's fiasco," he explained. "They played like pigs, Real."

"I'm tired," I said. "What's on your mind?"

"Susan wants to leave me," he said, relighting his pipe. "A temporary separation, she calls it."

I did my best to look surprised. "When did all this happen?" I asked him.

"She called me from her office this afternoon. She said she'd been wanting to tell me for some time. It's pretty shitty of her, don't you agree? . . . to give me that kind of news on the telephone."

Obviously I was not the only one who had had a bad day. "She was probably afraid to face you," I said. "Some women are like that."

"You had lunch with her, didn't you?"

"Yes . . . but she only mentioned that she'd like to visit her mother during the Easter holidays."

"You're sure that's all she told you?"

"She also asked me to help finance her trip."

He grunted and went over to the TV set to turn down the sound. "I asked her if she'd been screwing around, and she half-admitted there was somebody else. She wouldn't say who it was but I guessed it was her boss and she didn't deny it. I know the guy. He's got a wife and four kids."

"I don't know anything about that," I said. "So what are you going to do?" I couldn't imagine why Susan had decided to tell him the truth, after agreeing with me that it would be a mistake to do so. "Maybe you'd better go home and talk things over," I said, halfheartedly.

He nodded and returned to his chair. "Is that what you would have done in my place?" he asked sarcastically. "Talk things over? What the hell is there to talk about? So when Lady Collins called, I decided to stay here and wait until she turned up." He opened the top drawer of his desk and produced a wad of five-thousand-peseta bills. "She made a deposit of a hundred thousand, and I was in no mood to turn her down."

"Well, money makes the world go round."

He stared at me for a long time. "I guess I had that coming to me," he said. "Anyway, you've got to help me."

I said: "Look, Kiko . . . I've already told you that I can't help you. It's just not possible. I'm sorry as all hell that you and Susan are having a bad time. But you remember I warned you years ago that you were too young to get married."

He put the palms of his hands together. "One day," he pleaded. "Maybe two. No more. I've been talking to an old friend of mine who's out of work, and he'll take over from you. It's no big deal. All you have to do is hang around Collins's golf club. I wouldn't ask you if we weren't all in the deep shit. I'd do the job myself, but everybody knows me. And a private eye on a golf course would look pretty silly, you've got to admit."

"What makes you think one day will be enough?"

"Because after that my friend will help out."

"Then wait until your friend is free."

"That's not on," Kiko said. "Next week Collins will be in London. His wife wants the job done before he leaves here. Please, Roberto . . ."

"Okay, then, *one day,*" I said, "but that's all. And if the weather doesn't improve, your man takes over whenever he can."

Kiko said: "This guy's English. He's out there rain or shine."

"We'll see," I said. "What about Susan?"

"Susan," Kiko repeated with a crooked smile. "I think I'll let her dig her own grave. The chance of her *señorito* leaving his wife is about as likely as my winning the lottery this week, even if I had bought a ticket." He put his right hand on top of the stack of bills in front of him. "You want to draw twenty-five thousand for your expenses now or later?" he asked.

"I don't expect to get paid for doing a favor," I said, regretting that I'd allowed myself to be talked into helping him out for even one day.

"What about your gasoline and the greens fees?" Kiko asked. "Those are legitimate expenses. So keep track of them."

I said: "Forget it. Favors always cost you money. You know that. Or maybe you don't."

9

THE HOUSE REMINDED ME of Beverly Hills, the old Spanish mansions that line the flats, the no longer fashionable area between Sunset and Santa Monica boulevards. The smooth lawn with a flagstone walk leading up to the front entrance, the red tiled roof and the green wooden shutters, all in good repair, gave the place a look of opulence you find only in the most exclusive urbanizations on this coast. The main difference was that the Collins villa stood only a hundred yards from the Mediterranean. There was a private road that ran along the beach, which was where I had parked my car. The *poniente* was still blowing at gale force, the breakers churning up brown sand.

A uniformed guard in brown corduroy trousers and jacket, with a small caliber rifle slung across one shoulder, was walking along the road in my direction, holding onto his hat to keep it from being carried off by the wind. I opened the newspaper I had bought early in the morning and spread it out over the steering wheel, pretending I was a winter tourist killing time on a miserable day. The *guarda* glanced over at me as he passed and mumbled a greeting that I answered with a wave of my left hand. I felt ill at ease although I knew I had a legal right to be parked there, the access roads to the sea having been declared public property by the socialist government. The guard continued on past the stone pillars of the Collinses' gate and was soon out of sight.

It was Wednesday morning, and as it had continued raining all of Tuesday it seemed that there was only a small chance that Sir Cecil would be venturing out for a round of golf in the blustering gale. I had taken up my post half an hour earlier, and as the minute hand on my watch ticked away I couldn't help speculating on the twists and turns of fate that had contributed to my present condition: a so-called senior citizen in a foreign land, short of funds and plagued by family responsibilities, making him desperate enough to take on this kind of nasty job for "expenses."

A good many other thoughts were plaguing my brain that morning, such as concern for my daughter's future, the financial problems facing me due to the abrupt departure of my Belgian tenants, so that I was almost caught off guard when the green Bentley I had been waiting for came into view. It was Sir Cecil all right. The silver hair and the handsome face of the driver fitted the description his wife had given me. I pressed the ignition key, and thinking it was wiser to keep a safe distance, started up the narrow, winding road of the urbanization.

But I need not have worried that Collins would notice he was being followed. Ignoring the thirty kilometer signs posted along the road, he sped off, scattering fallen leaves and cutting a wet trail through the puddles left by the rain. Fortunately he was obliged to stop at the junction of the main highway leading into town, and for an instant I found myself less than ten feet away from his rear bumper. Sir Cecil glanced briefly to his left, then veered recklessly into the path of the oncoming traffic. A workman in an ancient truck gave him a blast of his air horn, and once the truck had passed, I ventured out into the right lane of the divided *carretera*.

A traffic light at the entrance of the town put an end to the brief chase. The Bentley passed through the intersection while the light was yellow, and I was forced to stop when it turned red. It had started to drizzle, and given the state of my worn tires, I knew it was better to reduce my speed. However, in order to keep my promise to Kiko, I decided to proceed on to the golf club where Lady Pamela had informed me that her husband was a member. Given the inclement weather, it seemed more than likely that his lordship was on his way to a rendezvous with his mistress, and secretly relieved that my unpleasant mission had failed, I drove on.

The light rain abated as the clubhouse came into view, and as I passed through the entrance gate of the parking lot I caught sight of the green Bentley standing with its radiator against the wire fence that runs along the border of the first fairway. So much for my intuition. Now two choices of how to proceed presented themselves: I could wait in my car until Collins had finished nine or maybe even eighteen holes, or I could pay the greens fee and follow him for the first nine holes. The latter course of action appealed to me more than the first. I hadn't played for a week.

Tomás, the chronically ill-tempered starter was on duty, and he looked up with surprise after I had dropped two five-thousand-peseta bills on his desk. Nine thousand was the fee for any outsider not accompanying a member, four hundred for the rental of a pull-cart. As a grandiose gesture I told him to keep the change. Tomás managed a crooked smile, and once he had supplied me with the handle of the cart, I said: *"Hasta luego,"* and left him to his paperwork. I got my shoes out of my golf bag, slipped them on, attached the handle onto the pull-cart and dropped my bag of clubs in place.

Then once I had taken up my stance between the yellow markers, I was visited by that brief moment of euphoria known to hackers the world over. For a few seconds I even forgot that Collins was out there ahead of me, and after a couple of practice swings, I lashed out at my virtually new Titleist 5 and sent it rising into the humid air. The ball veered crazily to the right and struck the trunk of a eucalyptus a hundred and fifty yards from where I was standing, ricocheted to the left and came to rest in the middle of the fairway. I returned my driver to its place in my golf bag and moved forward.

Off the tee of the sixth hole I hit another drive that spiraled off into a copse of trees at the bottom of a deep gully. I was tempted to tee up another ball but decided to walk down the hill and look briefly for my first missile. When I reached the gully a small stream made me turn off into the wooded area a hundred yards or so from the green. Suddenly I heard what sounded like someone thrashing around in the undergrowth, and an instant later I saw a tall man swinging an iron at the thick grass that had grown in abundance under trees that had hidden him from view.

It was Collins. He was dressed in sky-blue trousers and a white jacket. There could be no doubt about his identity. Even allowing for my late arrival, no other player could have teed off between us. Then, too, his wife's description of him fitted perfectly: the silver hair and the handsome face that she had said resembled that of Cary Grant. He glanced over at me, looking slightly annoyed.

I apologized. "I didn't see you," I said. "I'm sorry." On a three-par hole it is impolite and possibly dangerous to drive off before the preceding player has cleared the green.

"That's quite all right," he replied. "Your ball is over there, on the other side of that small tree. I heard it land. You go on through."

"I'm in no hurry," I said.

"Neither am I."

I was tempted to offer my assistance in his search and then suggest we play on together, but there was something about his stern manner that made me decide not to. I stepped over to the eucalyptus he had indicated and identified my Titleist 5. "What kind of ball were you playing?" I asked to prolong the conversation.

"A Maxfli 4," Collins replied, and continued his chopping at the underbrush. He stopped momentarily. "Go ahead," he commanded.

Under what I felt was his critical gaze, I kept my head in what might have been a vise, swung and sent my ball flying off in the direction of the green, an effort that would have made Arnold Palmer proud of me.

"Good shot," Sir Cecil said.

I caught the handle of my pull-cart and moved off, the seven iron still in my right hand. I had gone about fifty yards and was on my way to the green where my ball had landed, when I turned back. More than anything else, I was curious to see how much longer a multimillionaire like Sir Cecil would go on searching for a three-dollar ball. Another figure was visible among the trees, a slight young man dressed in ragged jeans and a yellow shirt. He was holding his cap in both hands, and I realized that it was filled with golf balls. A *bolero,* I thought to myself, as these urchins who hunt for lost balls on the local golf courses are called. It is against the rules for players to buy cheap balls from these young men, as many of them are known to be drug addicts and thieves. Signs are posted in most clubs to this effect.

Collins and the *bolero* stood facing each other. Then suddenly the boy dropped his cap and pulled what looked like a knife from the rear pocket of his jeans. Collins stepped back, tripped over a branch and fell to the ground. He got up right away and was brushing off the seat of his trousers.

What the hell . . . abandoning my pull-cart but with my seven iron still in my right hand, I ran down the slope. I don't know if I was motivated by the part of the detective I had agreed to play or was merely responding to some basic instinct that demanded I go to the rescue of a fellow golfer my own age, or whatever, but in less than a few seconds I arrived on the scene. Forgetting that while on shore-patrol duty in the U.S. Navy I had been instructed never to strike an assailant but to punch him in the stomach with my nightstick, I down my seven iron, intending to knock the knife out of the *bolero*'s hand.

He stepped aside, and I missed. Then with a dexterity that proved to me in retrospect that it was not the first time he had used his weapon, he thrust it at me. I felt a slight pain in the upper part of my right arm, saw a gash in the sleeve of my windbreaker. The youth turned and fled, scooping up his cap as he went. The dozen or so golf balls he had offered for sale lay at my feet. I glanced over at Collins. He seemed amazed rather than frightened. "Bloody hell," he said. That was all.

I peeled off my jacket. There was a long gash in my upper arm. My torn sport shirt was marked with a trail of blood. I said: "Shit, I think he got to me." There was very little pain and I could raise my arm without undue difficulty. My muscles seemed to be functioning normally.

Sir Cecil was surprisingly calm. "I could have dealt with the little bastard, you know," he said. "As a rule I am of the opinion that it is always better to part with one's money instead of risking injury."

I managed a grim laugh. "I guess I overreacted," I said sheepishly.

"Well, I appreciate your coming to my rescue," Collins said in a friendlier tone of voice than before. He stepped over to me, and together we inspected my wound. "I think we had better return to the clubhouse," he observed. It had started to rain. "Not a particularly nice day to play anyway," he added, while helping me to slide my arm back into my torn jacket. Shock was beginning to set in.

"I'm all right," I said.

"I think you'll find," Sir Cecil replied with a wan smile, "that your wound will interfere with your swing."

10

BY THE TIME WE HAD COVERED half the distance to the clubhouse I began to feel slightly dizzy. Sir Cecil insisted on pulling my cart as well as carrying his own bag. Then as the first tee came into view I caught sight of a young woman walking toward us through the downpour. She was dressed in a beige raincoat and was leading a small terrier on a leash.

"Shirley," Collins said. That was all. It was enough.

She was pretty, I was not too much in shock to notice, not a ravishing beauty but a normally pretty young woman in her late twenties. She wore a floppy hat that concealed her hair. Collins made what I sensed were the slightly embarrassed introductions, omitting the woman's last name.

"We've had a very unpleasant adventure," he said. "This gentleman has been injured."

The remainder of what occurred is jumbled in my mind. Tomás insisted we call the Guardia Civil, but Collins was adamant about our not standing around and waiting for the police to arrive. I agreed with him. They would never find my assailant. Furthermore, our description of the man was anything but accurate. Neither one of us could remember his face, or be able to identify him accurately by his clothes.

"I'll drive myself home," I said, "and call my doctor."

But when I tried to lift my golf bag off the cart I found that I was unable to do so unassisted. "Shirley will drive your car back to town," Collins said. "She'll leave it at the Don Pepe and take a taxi back to her car here. That is if you don't mind the dog riding in your automobile."

I thanked him and insisted that I was all right. Collins shook his head. "I'll take you to my place," he told me. "I think you'll find my doctor will respond more readily to my call than yours. And I do feel responsible, you know."

"Well, you needn't," I said, sounding British. Tomás was watching us with a tense expression on his face. He had already called the Guardia Civil, he said, and he felt certain they would be arriving in less than half an hour. Collins paid no attention to the man. "We're not going to wait around for them to arrive," he told me. "Come along to my car."

"I'll get blood on your upholstery."

"Blood spilled in a worthy cause."

There was no arguing with him. Johnny, the terrier, refused at first to get into my Ford Fiesta and had to be lifted in. "Dogs are snobs," Sir Cecil said. "Worse than humans."

I got into the Bentley and we started off. My arm had started to ache. I did my best to keep my right side away from the beige leather seat. "It's not a serious wound," I told Sir Cecil again. He didn't reply at once. Then he glanced over at me. "When we get to the house," he said, "I'd rather you didn't mention meeting Shirley."

"I understand . . ."

"No, you don't. Not really." There was a long pause. It was obvious that he didn't want to say any more on that subject. I looked over at him. At close quarters he had the not unpleasant aura of a polar bear: not dangerous per se but possessed of a dormant fierceness that was undeniable. It caused me to be vaguely uncomfortable. "You know, to be quite honest," he said, ending the silence, "I was thinking of having a go at that fellow myself. But you came charging down the hill before I could make up my mind about the right move."

"Mine certainly wasn't."

He grinned. "There was no element of surprise," he said. "That's absolutely certain. You started your backswing while you were still ten yards away." He picked up the telephone receiver from its cradle between the two upholstered seats and dialed a number. "Hello . . . this is Sir Cecil Collins," he said, speaking into the small handset. "Will you ask Dr. Wiesner to come as quickly as possible to my house? It's an emergency. Thank you." He returned the instrument to its cradle and glanced at his wristwatch. "Wiesner's an excellent GP. He's an Englishman, been practicing out here for some time."

"I don't think I'll need more than a little mercurochrome," I said.

He raised his shoulders. "As my Irish ancestors would say: It's a mistake to keep a dog and bark."

I managed a polite laugh. "Are you Irish?" I asked.

"Way back," he said. "My family has lived in England for many years, as indeed have I."

We were approaching the villa at high speed. Collins turned up the steep drive and stopped near the front door. "You all right?" he asked solicitously.

"I'm fine," I told him. "I'm sure I could have managed to get home by myself."

"I believe you," he replied. "But I prefer to have you taken care of by my own doctor."

He rang the doorbell, then pounded the door with the brass knocker. A maid let us in, a small Spanish woman dressed in a black uniform with a starched white apron. "*¿La señora?*" Collins said in heavily accented Spanish. The maid nodded. We were both moving rather gingerly across the beige marble floor of the entrance hall, neither one of us having thought to take off our golf shoes. There was the sound of high-heeled footsteps, and Pamela Collins came slowly down the carpeted stairway facing us. She was dressed in navy blue slacks and a white blouse. "Your spikes, darling," she said to her husband long before she looked over at me. "They scratch the marble."

"I know," Sir Cecil replied irritably. "But there's been an accident."

A look of recognition crossed Lady Pamela's face when finally she glanced in my direction. I introduced myself and we shook hands.

"We were attacked on the golf course," Collins told his wife. "Mr. Masters came to my rescue." Then, turning toward me, he added: "Let's go into the library. The doctor should be here shortly."

"He called a few minutes ago," Pamela Collins said. "He's on his way."

The maid pushed open a large wooden sliding door and I followed my host and hostess into a huge room lined with bookshelves. There was a stone fireplace in which a log fire was burning. "I'll just get out of these wet clothes," Collins said. "I'll bring you a jumper and a pair of dry trousers," he told me.

"Don't go to a lot of trouble," I said.

"No trouble at all," he replied, and left the room.

I undid my shoelaces with my left hand, and the maid scooped up my golf shoes as soon as I had shed them. I managed to straighten up with some difficulty and stood facing Lady Pamela in my soiled, soaking socks. She said nothing for a moment, crossed to a silver box on a low carved table, selected a cigarette and lit it.

"I know now why I was under the impression that we'd met," she said in a low voice. "You're a movie actor." There was a note of disdain in her voice.

"I was once," I said.

"You were in a film they showed yesterday on the Spanish television," she continued. "You're no more a detective than the man in the moon."

"I didn't pretend to be one."

"God, what a farce!" she exclaimed guardedly. "How did you meet my husband?"

"I was following him on the golf course, per your instructions."

"And I suppose you told him everything."

"I'm not that big a fool," I said.

Collins had reentered the room, dressed in a sky-blue dressing gown and carrying a sweatshirt and a pair of gym pants. "Why hasn't Mr. Masters been offered a drink, darling?" he asked. "I'm sure he needs one, and so do I."

"I was just about to do so," Lady Collins said acidly.

"Go into the guest loo and put these on," Sir Cecil said, handing me his clothes. He shook his head. "It seems I have to do everything in this house. You'd think that with a staff of four, plus a wife, there'd be a tray with ice, glasses and a variety of bottles, wouldn't you?" He pulled on a bell cord next to the fireplace and glared at his mate.

Pamela Collins eyed him coolly. "You know, darling," she said, "sometimes your charm escapes me." I realized that it was one of her favorite sayings.

11

THE DOCTOR LOOKED LIKE HE'D BEEN SENT OVER by Central Casting. He had a pale, rather thin face, crowned by thinning hair worn straight back that was gray at the temples. He wore a shirt and a tie that matched his tweed jacket, gray flannels and brown shoes. He explained almost at once that his parents had been German and that they had escaped Berlin in the nick of time and settled in London, where he had been raised and had gone to school. All this while he pressed the upper part of my right arm to make my wound bleed, then applied a disinfectant that he warned me would sting, which it did, although the pain from his pressing my arm was considerably greater.

Listening to him with my eyes closed, I decided that he sounded as English as the Duke of Devonshire, or at least how I have always imagined His Grace might sound. "I will give you an antitetanus shot just to be on the safe side," he said after blowing on my arm to cool it. "I'll just bandage the cut and you'll be as right as rain by the end of the week," he added.

"Probably hit the ball a lot straighter," Collins observed, "now that your right arm is damaged." The three of us had moved into the gymnasium in the back of the house at Lady Pamela's suggestion, so that there would be no danger of getting blood stains on the Persian carpets in the study.

"You were fortunate, young man," Dr. Wiesner said with a smile. "I trust you will report the incident to the police."

"Fat lot of good that will do," Collins said.

The bleeper in the vest pocket of Wiesner's tweed jacket was making a shrill noise. While he went off to call his office, Pamela Collins came into the gym.

"I'll take Mr. Masters home," she said. "That way you won't have to get dressed, darling."

"I don't intend to stay in my dressing gown the rest of the day," Collins said. "I'll drive him."

"You'd do better to jump into a hot tub," his wife told him. "If you catch a cold you'll only pass it on to me." It was the kind of wifely remark I sensed Sir Cecil did not appreciate but he did not reply.

Less than ten minutes later I found myself seated next to Pamela Collins in her red Mercedes convertible.

"I thought we'd better have a little chat," she said. "First of all, where are we going? To San Pedro?"

"Not that far. My car is at the Hotel Don Pepe."

"How did it get there?" she asked suspiciously.

"We dropped it off on the way home. Your husband thought it better I didn't drive, but I insisted I go half the way. Of course I didn't tell him I knew where he lived."

She said: "That was just as well. But why didn't you stop at the clinic. You passed right in front of it?"

"He wouldn't hear of it. He called Dr. Wiesner from his car."

"That sounds like Cecil," she said. "He always has to have his own way."

"He was being kind."

"He always is with strangers. Was he alone at the golf club?"

"He started out alone. I caught up with him at the sixth hole. I seem to remember he told you all that."

"I never believe what he says. What made you decide to play? You could have waited for him in the parking lot."

"I was supposed to follow him, wasn't I? It's lucky I did, as it turns out."

"I suppose it is," she said. "You're certain there was no one else with him?"

"Of course," I said. I was well on my way to becoming a double agent. I would have to call Collins in order to make our stories gel, but I didn't have his number.

"If I find out that you've been lying to me," Pamela Collins said, her hands tightening on the varnished wooden steering wheel, "you'll live to regret it."

"Why should I lie to you?"

"Oh, I don't know," she replied. "It might turn out to be to your advantage to change sides. My husband is the one with the money."

"Listen," I said, and I meant it, "I promised my son-in-law to take on this job for one day. That's *all*. He'll be taking over from now on."

We drove on in strained silence until she turned into the parking lot of the old hotel. "Where did you leave your car?" she asked.

"I don't remember. But I'll find it."

She stopped the Mercedes behind a delivery van and turned off the engine. "I'll wait until you do," she said.

"You don't need to bother."

She looked over at me. There were tears in her eyes. "You think I'm just another stupid jealous woman, don't you!" she said. "Silly enough to spy on her husband. Well, it's not that simple. We've been together for over twenty years. I helped him get where he is today. Right from the very beginning I was his partner as well as his wife. You think I'm going to let him dump me now? Just because he likes to roll around in bed with his secretary?"

"You should see a lawyer."

"Yes . . . or a priest!"

I got out of the car. There wasn't anything I could say, nor did she give me time to answer, for as soon as I had closed the door of the Mercedes she drove off with a squeal of tires. I crossed to the entrance of the hotel, and the uniformed doorman nodded to me without tipping his hat. I suppose I wasn't looking my best in my borrowed clothes and so he hadn't recognized me. The pay telephone was downstairs next to the toilets, and although I didn't have my reading glasses with me I managed to find the Collinses' number in the local telephone directory. A maid answered. Then after a long wait Sir Cecil came on the line. "Just thought we might as well get our stories straight," I told him. "About my car."

"Ah, yes," he said. "It's very kind of you to call."

I gave him my version of the story.

"That makes sense," he said. "By the way, Dr. Wiesner rang after you left. He'd like you to drop by his surgery tomorrow afternoon so that he can have another look at your wound. Change the bandage."

"Can you give me the address?"

"I'll go with you."

"I can find it on my own," I told him.

"Nonsense. We can meet at the golf club around six. If it's a fine day I'll play early and then wait for you in the bar."

"I can probably change the bandage myself."

"Don't be ridiculous. And if I come along you won't be kept waiting. Anyway, I want to return your things. The police will want to see them as evidence. They'll probably come around in a day or two."

I said: "All right. I'll meet you in the bar at six. I have your trousers and your sweatshirt. I'll return them as soon as they've been laundered."

"You needn't bother," he replied. "I have plenty of people to do that here."

He was used to having his own way. There was no doubt about that.

12

"YOU'RE A HERO," Evelyn said with that special laugh she reserved for my small disasters. We were dining that evening in her favorite Italian restaurant that was ersatz Italian but was the best inexpensive place in town.

"An idiot, you mean."

"No, not at all. Although I must say I can't imagine what prompted you."

"I don't know. Guilt, maybe."

"Guilt?" She looked puzzled.

"Yes, guilt. Because I shouldn't have been there. So I overreacted."

"But what else could you have done?" she said, cutting into her tomato and mozzarella salad.

"Walk back and shout. I might have scared him off. He was only a kid, my assailant."

"Next time."

"There won't be a next time. I've turned in my badge."

"Did you tell Lady Collins that?"

"Not in those words."

"Well, my woman's intuition tells me you'll change your mind. You enjoy saving souls . . . especially fair damsels in distress. Like me, for instance."

"What'd I save you from?"

"A lonely old age . . . and the wrong man, or men."

An elderly gypsy had come into the restaurant carrying a guitar. He stopped near our table and started to play *"Una Historia De Un Amor,"* Evelyn's favorite. She applauded enthusiastically and I gave the man a hundred pesetas.

"You know," Evelyn said, thoughtfully chewing her salad, "Sir Cecil should really come up with a reward for your unselfish valor. Make you a chairman of one of his many companies. Something like that."

"You can suggest it to him."

"I might write him an anonymous letter," she said, "and remind him you probably saved his life, for whatever that's worth."

"Forget it. Let's pretend it never happened. Okay?" Our spaghetti had arrived. I realized that eating my portion with one hand might prove to be difficult.

"He's taking you to the doctor tomorrow," Evelyn reminded me. "Perhaps I'd better come along, too."

"That won't be necessary."

"And if I insist? After all, I'll be the one who has to look after you the next few days."

I said: "Eat your goddam pasta before it gets cold."

"You'll be sorry you were unkind to me when they amputate your arm," Evelyn said. She was in a good mood. "You think some of your other ladies cared as much about you?"

"Please," I said. "Can't we skip the past tonight? I'm beat to the wide."

"The past is always there. If you hadn't told me about all your ladies, I wouldn't bring them up. It always sounded to me as if you had a pretty good time in Paris, in your blue period."

"Black and blue," I corrected her. "And what about *your* past?"

"There wasn't much to it."

"Then maybe now's the time for you to catch up?"

"I might, you know. My problem is that I'm a creature of habit. Always have been."

"Then stick with what you've got."

"You, too," she said. We ordered dessert. The strawberries were in season, the first crop. After I had paid the check I drove her home.

Sleep was a long time in coming that night. I couldn't lie on my right side because of my arm. I woke up at three and then again at five-thirty. The sound of the rain had stopped. When I opened the shutters I noticed that the sky was full of stars. The first fishing boats were returning to port. It was too early to make breakfast, so I reread yesterday's papers, the editorial page I had only glanced at. But I couldn't concentrate. Evelyn was right, the past was always there. Especially at five o'clock in the morning after somebody had tried to knife you. So you make a résumé of your life for the benefit of the darkness . . .

The *Ile de France* had weighed anchor. I was standing facing aft, looking out beyond the swirling wake at the receding wharf and the Manhattan skyline. The ship's whistle blew a hoarse blast. I noticed that a young woman in a trench coat was standing beside me. "You off on a vacation?" I asked her.

"No," she replied. "I'm running away from home." She had very brown eyes and brown hair that was hidden in part by a navy blue beret.

"So am I," I said, which was the truth in a way. So we became friends. It was anything but a shipboard romance. Naomi was traveling with her parents. They were in first class and I was in tourist. Her father was a movie director who was leaving the country in order to avoid having to testify before the House Un-American Activities Committee. He was a small, fragile-looking man with graying hair and a friendly manner. I couldn't believe he was a dangerous subversive.

I never got around to telling Naomi the reason for my going to Europe, and so she assumed I was leaving for the same reason as her father. Why else would a young actor desert Hollywood? Then once we were all living on the Left Bank in a small, inexpensive hotel Naomi's father had recommended, we began going out together. She was six years younger than I was, but seemed quite worldly for her age, had advanced views about the relationship between men and women, as well as politics. A day before we became lovers I told her the truth about my flight from Hollywood. She thought it was funny at first, my traveling under false colors, realized that it was really her jumping to the wrong conclusion that was responsible for my charade.

Her father was signed by a French production company to make a movie about the Marseilles mafia. There were quite a few scenes in the script in which French actors were supposed to portray Americans, and although I had no work permit, I got a job as dialogue director. The company went to Marseilles on location, and Naomi stayed behind in Paris with her mother. So we drifted apart. Naomi told me later, when we met again in St. Tropez at the end of the summer, that it was my lack of any kind of political conviction that had made it impossible for her to take me seriously as a lover.

We spent the week together, and remained friends. Her father kept me on as his assistant, and I went with him to Spain for his next film. It amused him to have as his right-hand man someone who had had a love affair with the mistress of one of the Hollywood bosses and was an exile for *non*-political reasons. He gave me a small part in his movie. As a result I was offered a job by an Italian company making a western in Almería. My salary was low but it kept me going.

I rented a small apartment in Madrid and made it my headquarters. As a city it was just the right size in those days, like Los Angeles before the war. The climate was better than in Paris, and the people were friendlier. Nobody resented the fact that you were an American; instead they seemed pleased that you had chosen to live there and were making an effort to learn their language. Meals were served at strange hours in all of the restaurants, but you got better service by appearing early, one-thirty for lunch and eight-thirty for dinner.

Naomi announced her arrival during the winter. She had broken up with her French boyfriend, and to avoid having scenes and useless discussions had decided on a brief Spanish vacation. I was delighted to see her again. At her request we went to the Prado to view the Goyas, the *pintura negra* that occupied a badly lit section on the ground floor. I took her to a flamenco show that she seemed to enjoy less. "How does anyone get to work in the morning after staying up all night?" she wanted to know. "They manage," I told her. "Anyway, most of the customers of this place don't have to worry about showing up at an office."

She couldn't understand why I preferred Madrid to Paris. "Doesn't living in a fascist country bother you at all?" she asked. I admitted that the Wehrmacht-style helmets of the fire brigade brought back unpleasant memories of the war, but insisted that the Spanish people were anything but fascistic. "Yes, and it's easier to get servants," she said, "and the trains run on time." "They don't, as a matter of fact," I told her, "so there goes another one of your pet theories." "You'll never change," she replied. She left for Paris a few days later, where the students' revolt had started that spring and there was a place for her on the barricades, which I had the suspicion she had been looking forward to all her life.

Paul Levin sent me a Christmas card, along with a brief letter on expensive stationery that he had dictated and had not had time to sign. He had joined a big talent agency as a senior partner, so it was apparent that his star was rising. He wrote that Eddie, my nemesis, had retired from business because of ill health, and that no one else in town could remember my early misdemeanor, and even if they did they were totally uninterested. "Why don't you come home?" he added in a postscript. "Business is good and I'm sure I can get you quite a few jobs."

But I had no desire to move back to California. I had bought the old farmhouse in San Pedro which was being rebuilt by a local contractor who had promised that it would be ready for occupancy in the summer. But it wasn't, of course, due to the usual delays that seem to be standard procedure in the construction business the world over. So in order to escape the heat of Madrid I decided to drive north to San Sebastián, where all of my young Spanish friends were vacationing in the month of August.

In those days the entire government moved to that pleasant city, the Generalissimo and all of his ministers, as well as anyone who could afford to go, the aristocracy and their hangers-on, the flamenco dancers and singers, the beggars and carnation sellers and a part of the diplomatic corps. For one month the old Basque town took on the aura of a nineteenth-century spa, with white-helmeted policemen regulating the heavy traffic like symphony conductors, and uniformed nurses parading the infants of the rich along the broad tree-lined avenues. There was a week of bullfights and every other kind of festivity that filled the local bars to over-flowing in the late afternoon. At night, after a late dinner, most of my friends drove to Biarritz for the legalized gambling in the casinos on the French side of the border, and it was there that I met Susan's mother.

Her name was Amanda, she was from Santa Barbara, and she *was* a damsel in distress, I suppose. She was married to a French-man somewhat older than she was. Raymond, that was his name, had a title, was handsome and charming, but he had never held down a job (which wouldn't have mattered, Amanda explained, since his family was well-heeled, except that he was an obsessive gambler). All this I learned the first night we met at the casino in Biarritz, where I had gone with my Madrid companions. While they lost the pesetas they had converted into francs at a bad rate,

Amanda and I chatted at the bar, then moved over to the *brasserie* across the square for a beer and a sausage.

So it all started innocently enough. It was a relief to be able to converse with someone in my own language, a pleasant change she confessed to as well. Then at two in the morning I walked her back to the hotel where she was staying and returned to the casino, and it was this brief absence that provoked numerous jokes from my friends on the drive home. We met again the next night, and the night after that. Amanda's confidences continued. Raymond was a heavy drinker, she told me, and when he lost at the tables he took his rage and frustration out on her. My Spanish friends began to refer to Amanda as my *novia*, fiancée, and amused themselves by warning me that the viscount, or baron or whatever he was, was reputed to be the best shot in France, so that I had better be careful.

I thought of Sue Wilson, and our weekend in Palm Springs those many years ago, and reassured myself that I was older and wiser. I was staying at the Hotel de Londres on La Concha, the lovely half-moon bay that is one of the famous beauty spots of San Sebastián. One morning a few days later, the manager of the hotel intercepted me in the lobby, and after much apologizing, advised me that there had been a booking error and that I would have to move to the Hotel Maria Cristina, where he had already made a reservation for me. He had persuaded the management of this more elegant hotel to give me a special price so that I would not be penalized for having to change my residence. I agreed to move but then discovered that when the tide was out there was an unpleasant smell of sewers that pervaded the whole place. Rather than stay on, I decided to return to Madrid and then head south to my new villa even if work on the house had not been completed.

But my young Spanish friends vetoed this plan. The polo games were about to start in Biarritz, and they persuaded me to move on with them across the border for what was known as the Spanish season. The weather was always better on the French side in September, they assured me, which turned out to be true. Amanda was still there, and was pleased to see me, so she said three or four times during our first evening out on French soil. I was certainly pleased to see her, too. The young women on the other side of the border, the ones I was introduced to, had rather different standards of behavior, and I was getting tired of my monastic existence. Dancing and flirting had been fun for a while, but as a steady summer diet it was becoming tiresome.

Amanda wasn't having a very good summer, she told me; Raymond had been losing heavily at the tables, which did little to improve the few meals they shared, late hung-over breakfasts, and early dinner before the casino reopened in the evening after the afternoon session. As they were well known as a couple, none of the men they knew paid much attention to her, so she became my guide, and while her husband was sleeping off his all-night gambling binges we played a little tennis or, when the sun was out, went to the beach.

Having been raised in southern California, she was adept at bodysurfing, one of the favorite pastimes of my early youth. After which, lying in the sun to rest from our exertion, with loving couples on all sides of us, the obvious thoughts entered my mind, as they probably did hers, although neither one of us said anything. However, Amanda did confide in me that the physical side of her relationship with her husband had ceased to exist. The nervous strain of his long sessions at the tables, combined with his intake of whiskey, appeared to have done away with his libido. Their sex life was a thing of the past, so she said.

Then Raymond was suddenly called to the bedside of an aunt who lay dying in her château somewhere in the Dordogne, and his departure put an end to all of our restraint. This time there was no Harry Lessing around to issue a warning, and I probably wouldn't have paid any more attention to him had he been there than I did in Palm Springs. Desire doesn't listen to reason, even the second time around. I know that this is not the place to expound on the complex motivations of lust, but in order not to appear too much like a fool, I would like to say that certain conditions can make most of us throw caution to the wind. My weakness, if that is what it should be called, has always been the combination of sun and sea, a hangover, no doubt, from my early youth, much of which was spent on the beach in Santa Monica. Kisses tainted by the ocean's salt, as well as a tanned skin, mine or my neighbor's, have repeatedly had an aphrodisiacal effect on me, a phenomenon that I don't think is uncommon, or how else can you explain the popularity of seaside resorts?

The aunt in the Dordogne began to recover, and Raymond's absence continued for a week. By the time he returned, his financial condition unimproved by a hoped-for inheritance, my affair with his wife was common gossip around the swimming pool of the Hôtel du Palais. Raymond reacted in a fairly normal manner. After inflicting a black eye on his wife, he packed up all her clothes and deposited her suitcases outside the door of my hotel room. There was little Amanda and I could do after that. To stay on in Biarritz seemed impossible for both of us. She thought briefly of returning to Paris, but that alternative, she reasoned, would undoubtedly expose her to more of her husband's violent behavior. So I suggested to her that we both pile our belongings in my car and drive to the south of Spain. That would give us time to figure out our next move, as well as providing a cooling off period for Raymond. We did not discuss the future in more specific terms.

It was not an altogether enjoyable trip. Neither one of us was completely relaxed, although the scenery provided us with a few enjoyable moments. One incident still stands out in my mind. On the second day of our journey we came on a traffic accident that had occurred minutes before we passed the usual sight of shattered glass and bent steel. This prompted us to recall similar misfortunes in our lives. Amanda told me that late one night, on her way home to her flat in Paris, she had once hit a pedestrian. She described the circumstances of the accident in what seemed to me to be a callous manner. The man she had run over had been a *clochard,* she told me, an old beggar, and the autopsy revealed that he was drunk. So she was cleared by the police, although she admitted to me that she had been driving too fast.

It wasn't a moment of great importance. We didn't quarrel, nor did I express my misgivings about her behavior. It was, however, a small signal, like the red warning light on the dashboard of a car that comes on suddenly. I realized that I was involved with someone whose reactions were totally different than mine. I remember that all of a sudden I found myself missing Naomi, a feeling that increased as we drove on. Despite Naomi's dogmatic political views, I had never been even slightly disturbed by the way she spoke to waiters or barmen. Amanda, I was discovering, was less considerate, almost rude at times to strangers, imperious.

We arrived on the coast after a hot, tiring journey, and moved into my partly finished *cortijo,* a not entirely happy couple, both of us conscious that we had been brought together by accident. Amanda helped me furnish the house. She was good at that and she enjoyed it. We got along better for a while. In the late fall she became pregnant. Raymond won an uncontested divorce in Paris. In those days you married the girl if you didn't want to be a shit, even if you were an actor. We drove to Gibraltar for the formalities.

But before winter set in we discovered that we really were incompatible. Our marriage dragged on for three years. The final parting was bitter. She returned to Santa Barbara and her parents with our small daughter, Susan. Fortunately she soon met a wealthy businessman who married her, so I was relieved in part of the financial burden, although I had to contribute to my daughter's education. Then fifteen years later Susan came to visit me on the set of the movie I was making in Almería, and there, as I have mentioned before, she met Kiko. Fate. Or *la puta vida,* as they say in these parts.

13

BUT IT WASN'T PART II of *My Amorous Past* that made it difficult for me to fall asleep that night. It was my arm. I have always slept on my right side, and that was impossible for the time being. At four in the morning I finally took one of Dr. Wiesner's magic pills, and the result was that I came to my senses at about noon. After I had shaved and dressed and fed Fergy I ventured cautiously out of my flat. The door to Kiko's office was open, and he was seated at his desk, reading the newspaper. He said: *"En hora buena,"* congratulations. "You've made a new friend, and an important one."

"Who told you that?"

"Evelyn. When you didn't surface this morning I called your lady, and she filled me in with the details of your adventure."

"Did she tell you that I resigned?" I asked him.

"You can't resign. You're vital to the operation. A friend of both parties. You're in a perfect spot."

"Forget it," I said. "I did you a favor, and that's the *end* of it for me."

"*¡Abuelo!*" he said pleadingly. "*¡Por favor!* You're just pissed off because some druggy stuck a knife in you."

Grandpa is not my favorite way of being addressed, even by my grandchildren. I said: "Listen to me, Kiko . . . take my advice, give the woman back her money and wish her luck."

"It's not that simple."

"It's simple as far as I'm concerned," I told him. "I'm out the nine thousand I paid for the greens fee, plus a thousand for the starter. It's all on the house, pal."

"You seem to forget that you're broke."

"You don't say? And what else is new?"

His eyes narrowed. "What else is new . . . well, the bank is about to foreclose on my business."

"What is there for them to take?"

"All my hardware. The two flats."

"Well, I can't help you," I said. I knew that he was bluffing. "Assign your man to tail Collins, and string his wife along. That should provide you with eating money."

"And what are you going to do?"

"Go up to my house and get the place squared away. Then look for another tenant. Have you heard from Susan?"

He shook his bald head. "She didn't come home last night." he said. "I had to make dinner for the kids and take them to school this morning."

I didn't feel sorry for him. "Maybe you should hire somebody to follow *her*," I told him.

"Many thank-yous for the advice, don Roberto."

"*De nada.*"

I went back to my flat, dumped some more sand in Fergy's box and washed my breakfast dishes. Then I looked up Dr. Wiesner's number in the telephone book, thinking I would call his nurse and ask for an earlier appointment. That way I could avoid meeting up with Collins again. But Wiesner's nurse told me the doctor wouldn't be in until six-thirty.

Kiko's door was closed, I noticed, as I left my quarters. There was a lot of traffic because of the good weather, and it was one o'clock when I arrived at my house. Pepe was seated with his back against the verandah wall, eating his lunch. He held out a half-open can of anchovies and a piece of bread. *"¿Quiere comer?"* he asked, as he always did whenever I interrupted his midday meal.

"No, gracias," I said. Maria, the *doncella*, had been there earlier, Pepe informed me, but as she had to collect her daughter from school, she hadn't been able to wait for my arrival. I went inside. The place looked a little better. The fridge had been cleaned out and disconnected, and the bed upstairs in my room had been stripped. The blankets were hanging over the rail of the balcony to be aired. I folded them up and left them on the mattress in case the weather might change. Then I went downstairs, locked the front door and pulled the wicker armchair back under the roof of the front porch. I said: *"Hasta mañana,"* and Pepe waved.

I knew Evelyn would have gone out to lunch somewhere, so I drove to a *chiringuito* on the waterfront, ordered a grilled sole and a beer and sat in the sun on the terrace of the small restaurant. There were quite a few customers because of the weather. All of them were at least twenty years younger than I was. A few tourists were bathing in the cold sea, jumping around like a bunch of albino seals. I noticed that someone had left a copy of the *Herald Tribune* on an adjoining table, along with two empty coffee cups, and I stepped over to borrow it. The paper was a day old but that didn't matter. I hadn't seen it. In my opinion two dollars is too much to shell out for nothing but bad news.

I glanced at the headlines, then leafed through the inside pages on my way to the sports section, stopping briefly to look at the obituary columns. That is another bad habit I have acquired, along with my apathy toward the political events of the day, as the world seems to be going from bad to worse. Not that I am motivated by morbid curiosity. I merely like to check the ages of the deceased, taking comfort in those well over eighty who have died a peaceful death. A familiar name caught my eye: LESSING, HENRY A. The brief paragraph attached to it confirmed that it was indeed my former friend Harry who had passed away.

The paragraph described him as a successful television producer of comedy serials, and gave his age as sixty-eight. It mentioned that he had gotten his start as a film editor, but had left the motion picture industry early on, and had gone into television, and had won two Emmys. The cause of death was given as cancer.

Sixty-eight, I thought to myself, that was right around the corner. Poor Harry. I hadn't heard from him in more than forty years, but my memory of him was as accurate as if we had lunched a week ago. The article failed to mention the Silver Star he had been awarded for valor when the cruiser he was serving on as a deck officer had been sunk in the Coral Sea. Nor did it say whether he had left any next of kin. Not that it would do any good to write his widow a letter of condolence, she wouldn't know who the hell I was. I felt sad, sorry to have lost touch with a man who had been a good friend. Well, neither one of us had ever bothered to write.

My lunch arrived. I had a coffee and a brandy after I had eaten, and took a long walk along the edge of the sea. It was a quarter to four when I drove into the parking lot of the golf club. There were a lot of cars and at least half a dozen players waiting on the first tee. I walked past the practice putting green and went into the bar. Shirley, Collins's girlfriend, was sitting at one of the tables with her back to the television. She waved for me to join her.

"Would you care for a cup of tea?" she asked.

"I'd prefer coffee," I told her. Hatless and without her raincoat she looked different. She was wearing a pair of gray slacks and a light green sweater that hung loosely around her girlish figure. Her blond hair was cut short, with a fringe that concealed her forehead. Men are supposed to fall for the same type, I thought, but that certainly wasn't true of Collins.

"Cecil should be along in a few minutes," she said. "He and a friend teed off at two-thirty."

"I'm in no hurry," I said.

"How's your arm?" she asked. "It's really a shame you couldn't play today. The weather is so lovely."

"There'll be other days," I said. "Wouldn't you rather sit outside?"

"No, I'm not too fond of the sun," she said. "But if you'd rather . . ."

"Right here is fine," I said. We sat in silence for a while. The waiter came to take my order.

"Would you like a piece of chocolate cake?" she asked. "It's very good here."

"No thanks." She seemed to be nervous, ill at ease. I noticed that she was wearing a diamond ring on her left hand. She turned it face down with her thumb, as if to hide the large stone.

"You know Cecil and I are embarrassed to have gotten you involved in our problems," she began. "But it was unavoidable after what happened yesterday."

I said: "Not to worry. It couldn't be helped. I'm sorry you were inconvenienced."

"He'll tell you himself," she said. "By the way, the police insist on seeing you both tomorrow morning."

"That was to be expected."

"I'm sure you have lots of other things to do," she said. "But there you are."

"I'm not too busy," I told her.

She smiled, and folded her hands. They showed very little sign of wear and tear. "You know Cecil was most impressed with the way you acted yesterday. He was even thinking of some sort of present, like getting you a membership here, at his club . . ."

I wanted to laugh, but I kept a straight face. Evelyn must have practiced mental telepathy, although a membership in an exclusive golf club was far short of the chairmanship of an offshore corporation. "I couldn't afford the annual dues," I said. "Anyway, a present is unnecessary."

"Well, he'd like to do something."

"Maybe he can cure my slice."

She laughed. "I'm sure he'll manage to do that," she replied.

The waiter brought my coffee, and Collins came into the bar. A tall blond man with curly hair was with him. Collins led the way to our table. "Ah, my unfortunate friend," he said. "How are you feeling today?"

"Better. A lot better."

He introduced his companion as Bill Leahy, his lawyer, who had arrived from London early that morning. "He's already taken fifty quid off me," he added. "He's shameless."

"You'll win it back," Leahy said. "You were off your game today."

"Bollocks," Collins said. He appeared to be in a good mood. "Lawyers always cost you money, don't you agree? Well, have we got time for a shandy?"

"It's ten after six," Shirley warned him.

"Never mind. Wiesner will wait for us." He grinned. "I have him on a retainer. Just like Bill, here."

"And me," Shirley said.

Collins chuckled but he didn't seem pleased. He said: "We'll overlook that one."

They ordered their drinks, and Leahy took a score card out of his back pocket. Very meticulously he began adding up their strokes. Collins made small talk, but I noticed that he was watching Leahy's calculations at the same time. Shirley was a Scot, he told me, which was why she stayed out of the sun. She was also anxious to avoid getting wrinkles, he added, touching the young woman's hand where it lay on the table. "What was my score?" he asked the lawyer. "Have you added it all up?"

"Eighty-six. Not bad."

"Bad enough," Collins said. He took his wallet out of his back pocket and paid Leahy in sterling. I noticed that he was carrying a considerable amount of pounds and pesetas. "Well, drink up, lads," he said, "and let's be on our way."

The four of us walked past the putting green and the pro shop, with Collins and Shirley leading. They stopped near the entrance gate. "Where are you parked?" he asked the young woman.

"Out on the street. Just over there," she said, pointing to a small blue car standing on the side road.

Collins kissed her cheeks and patted her lightly on the behind. We all stood watching as she crossed to her car. Then she turned to wave. There was the sound of an engine at high revs, and a white BMW coupé came very fast down the narrow road. We all shouted at once, and Shirley jumped back behind the bumper of her car. The BMW missed her by inches. I caught a glimpse of Pamela Collins at the wheel.

Collins said: "Bloody hell," and ran across the street. He put his arm around Shirley's shoulders. She was trembling. Leahy and I joined them.

"That was bloody close," the lawyer said.

Shirley's face was even paler than before. Collins released her. "You all right, darling?" he asked.

"Yes, I think I am," she said in a shaky voice. "No, I'm fine," she added.

"Do you want me to drive you home?"

"No, no . . . you go on," Shirley said. "Dr. Wiesner will be waiting." She unlocked the door of her car and got in behind the wheel. She had trouble starting the engine, but finally it caught and she drove off.

The three of us walked into the parking lot without speaking. We stopped behind the Bentley. Collins took a deep breath and turned to face me. "Leave your car here, Roberto," he said quite calmly. "I'll be coming back this way later to look in on Shirley. She's had a nasty fright."

Leahy got into the back of the Bentley. I took my place beside Collins. Nobody said anything for a long time. Then Leahy spoke up from the back seat. "Have you ever thought of getting a divorce, Cecil?" he asked.

"I haven't, as a matter of fact," Collins replied. "Not until right now."

"I think you'd better consider it," Leahy said. "Before things get much worse." There was a long uncomfortable pause, and I wished I were somewhere else.

"It might not be a bad idea at that," Collins said. We had reached the main highway. The traffic was as heavy as usual. I was thinking of Lady Pamela. She had obviously decided to take over my duties and had followed her husband to the golf club. Collins glanced over at me. "Have you ever been married?" he asked. He was surprisingly calm.

"Yes. A couple of times."

"You're divorced now?"

I nodded. "Yes, I'm a two-time loser."

"Must have been an expensive business."

"Not too bad," I said. "The ladies were as anxious to be free as I was."

"That's the advantage of not being wealthy," Collins said. "Your partners are not as keen to hang on if there are no spoils."

Leahy said: "I don't think you need worry about money, Cecil."

"Spoken like a true solicitor," Collins replied, and smiled grimly. "But I think we should go on with this discussion in private, Bill, don't you? No use boring our friend here with my family problems." He paused. "By the way, we're supposed to make an appearance tomorrow morning at headquarters of the Guardia Civil. At ten o'clock, Robert. It's been a bad couple of days," he continued. "Two attempted murders in a row. That must be a record for the Costa del Sol. More like your part of the world."

It was an astonishing performance. He appeared to be no more upset than if he'd just seen his pet dog avoid getting run over. I glanced back at Leahy. He raised his eyes in the direction of the heavens, then looked quickly over to Collins to make sure he hadn't been watching in the rearview mirror.

14

I T WAS STILL LIGHT WHEN I ARRIVED back in Estepona. The sun was a
bright red ball on the horizon, bathing the Med in gold. Far out at
sea a skirmish line of fishing boats were lighting their lanterns. I
locked the doors of my car and crossed the sidewalk to the small
bar at the foot of my building. Fergy would be impatiently waiting
for my return but she would have to wait a little longer, I decided,
while I had a beer.

Arturo, the owner of the place, brought me a *caña* and a plate
of *boquerones en vinagre,* a variety of sardine they pickle in vinegar
and olive oil, then sprinkle with chopped garlic. There was a side
order of white bread that I dipped in the sauce. I was feeling somewhat more relaxed. The doctor had redressed my wound, satisfied
that there was no sign of infection. There was still a little pain
whenever I moved too quickly, but it was bearable. Collins and his
lawyer had driven me back to the golf club and then had departed
in the Bentley. There had been no further discussion about the
incident outside the parking lot.

I finished my beer and the *tapas* and went upstairs. The front-
door lock seemed not to respond to my key. I turned it clockwise

and discovered that the door was unlocked. Had I forgotten to lock it? I stepped inside, and there was Pamela Collins seated in an armchair facing the sunset outside the open window. Fergy was on her lap and looked over at me as if I had caught her in an infidelity. I said: "Holy God, you frightened me," but the woman didn't move. Fergy jumped down onto the floor and stretched. "How did you get in here?" I asked her.

She rose slowly and turned to face me. The mascara around her eyes was smudged, as if she had been crying. She was wearing a khaki shift with a broad leather belt that showed off her slim waist. "Kiko opened the door for me," she said in a low voice. "I wanted to talk to you, and your son-in-law didn't seem to like the idea of my waiting in his office."

"Would you like a drink?" I asked her, warily.

She shook her head. "I had a couple of vodka-tonics before I left home," she said.

"A couple?"

"I'm not drunk!"

"Well, I'm going to have a beer," I said, and went into the kitchen to get a bottle of Cruz Campo out of the fridge. The sun, I noticed on my way back, had dropped into the sea, and the room was in semidarkness. I turned on the lamp next to my bed. "What made you decide to come here?" I asked Pamela Collins.

"I didn't feel like going home," she said. "Not after what happened."

"That was probably a wise move."

"I was sitting in my car waiting for Cecil when you drove up. I knew he was meeting the little tart, and I wanted to confront them both. Then when I saw them together I lost control of myself. But I only wanted to scare her . . ."

"That's not what it looked like."

"Oh, come on," she said, her voice rising, "you don't really think I was trying to kill her. I'm not that stupid."

"If we hadn't shouted, and she hadn't stepped back . . ."

"I still wouldn't have hit her. I've been a licensed driver for twenty years. I even used to race sports cars." She stopped abruptly. "Can I use your bathroom?"

"Sure," I said, indicating the door.

She reappeared a few minutes later. She had fixed up her eyes and repainted her mouth. "Have you got a jumper or something?" she asked. "It's cold in here."

I wondered how long she was planning to stay. I stepped over to my chest of drawers, found a pullover and tossed it to her. She draped it around her shoulders. "What did Cecil say after I drove off?"

"Not much. He was upset, of course, but he did his best not to show it."

"And Bill Leahy? His toady?"

"He was as startled as I was. He just stood there for a while. Then once we were in your husband's car, after Shirley had driven off, he asked your husband if he had ever thought of getting a divorce."

"That's typical of him. All he's interested in is collecting a big fee." She began to pace up and down the room. "And the little whore?" she asked. "What was her comment?"

"I don't remember, but she was pretty shook up. Understandably."

"Isn't that a shame?" Pamela Collins said with heavy sarcasm. "Well, I'm not finished with her. You don't know the whole story. She was his secretary, his office wife. And she was ever so polite whenever I called. 'Yes, of course, Lady Pamela. I'll put you through.' And all the time she was probably having it off with him on his couch. But she's not going to get her way. I'll see her eight feet under the ground first, I assure you."

"I don't think you should say things like that. Not even as a joke."

"I'm not joking. They tell me that for five thousand pounds you can get rid of almost anyone. Just ask Kiko."

Was she demented? I wondered. I said: "I doubt that's the best way to patch up your marriage."

"And what do *you* suggest?" she asked, turning to face the window. She had a good figure, I noticed, not for the first time. She reached into the pocket of her dress, took out a crumpled handkerchief and blew her nose. "I suppose you're going to tell me I should find myself a randy boy-toy, or were about to offer your own services, shopworn though they may be!"

The remark annoyed me. I said: "You're right. I'm a little long in the tooth for that caper. I also prefer blondes."

She whirled and lashed out at me. The back of her left hand caught me on the side of the head. I grabbed her by the shoulders. I pride myself that I have never struck a woman . . . except Amanda, the third time she slapped my face. But at that moment I was sorely tempted to spoil my record. I also recalled that Amanda forgave me, and that we made love afterwards, one of our better efforts. I said: "What the hell's the matter with you?"

"You shit!" she snarled. "I got the point! You were needling me about Shirley!"

"The hell I was!" I released her. The side of my face felt as if it were on fire. "You should see a shrink," I told her.

She covered her mouth with her open right hand. "I'm sorry," she said. "I really am. I lost control of myself."

"That's the second time today."

The telephone rang. I felt certain it was Evelyn, and I thought it would be better to pretend I wasn't home and call her back later.

"Aren't you going to answer the phone?" Pamela Collins asked in a low voice.

I crossed to the side of the bed and picked up the receiver. There was a long silence. Then a woman's voice came on the line. She spoke with a foreign accent. "I have a call for Mr. Robert Masters," she said. Then I heard Paul Levin's voice from what sounded like very far away.

"Robert, my boy! How the hell are you?" He was shouting, and then a second later he sounded as if he were in the next room.

"I'm all right. How are you?" I said.

"Couldn't be better. I'm in Lisbon. Am I calling you at a bad time? You sound distracted." I was watching Lady Collins as she crossed to the bathroom. She closed the door noiselessly behind her.

"No, I'm not distracted. Just surprised to hear from you. It's been a while. What are you doing in Portugal?"

"I'm on vacation. What else?"

"I thought you'd retired years ago. I didn't even know you were still alive."

"Yeah, you're right. I'm getting on. How old are you, while we're on the subject of age?"

"Thirty-nine," I said. "Or maybe sixty-two, I'm not sure."

"Sixty-two, eh?" He chuckled happily. "Lover-boy is sixty-two. So you finally caught up with me. Listen, this is not a very good line, so I'll make it short. I'm with a party of friends. They've chartered a yacht and we're on our way to Greece and Turkey. They tell me we might stop in somewhere near you, so we could meet up. What's the nearest port to your neck of the woods?"

"Gibraltar, Algeciras, Málaga. Take your choice. There's also a marina nearby if your yacht isn't too big."

"I can't remember all that," he said impatiently. "Have you got a fax?"

"No, I haven't."

"Okay. Then I'll call this number after I've had a word with the captain and see what he suggests. I'd like to catch up with you for a few hours."

"That would be nice," I said. "Call me early in the morning, or late at night."

"Will do," he replied, and hung up abruptly.

My guest emerged from the bathroom. I noticed that she had slipped on my sweater. I was trying to recall how many years my senior that Levin had been when we had first met in Beverly Hills. He was nearing eighty, I reckoned, but he sounded no different.

"Do you think I might have a drink?" Pamela Collins inquired in a low voice. "I feel I need one now."

"I guess so," I replied.

"I said I was sorry, for God's sake!"

I said: "Sorry is not enough," Evelyn's favorite phrase.

"You don't understand . . . I still love him. He's my whole life. I haven't even looked at anyone else for twenty years." Her eyes filled with tears. I didn't feel sorry for her, although tears have usually had that effect on me.

"I have some Scotch but that's about all . . . if you still want that drink."

"Please."

I went into the kitchen, poured half a glass of whiskey into a tumbler and added some water. On the way back into my room I glanced into the mirror over the chest of drawers. There was a bright red mark on the side of my face. I handed her the tumbler. She emptied it and put it down on the windowsill.

"I don't know where to go," she said. "I can't face Cecil tonight. He can be violent at times. He has been in the past."

"I guess it runs in the family."

"He doesn't want a divorce, either," she went on. "He's quite happy with the status quo. He can keep his floozy on the side, and whenever he feels like a change, he can give me a bang. It makes him feel *macho*." She dabbed her eyes with her handkerchief. "Could you lend me some money? I came out without my handbag and I'll need a few thousand pesetas if I decide to check into a hotel."

I took a five-thousand-peseta bill out of my wallet and handed it to her. "That's the best I can do," I said. "But you can stay here for an hour or so more if you like. Collins will have cooled down by the time you get home, I should think. Then you can tell him what you told me. He's not going to beat you up because you tried to scare his girlfriend. And if he does you'll have even a better case against him."

"I hope you're right," she said. She put the money down on the windowsill next to the empty glass, then crossed to the bed and sat down. "I'm hungry," she announced next. "I haven't eaten anything all day."

"I'll go get something," I told her. There wasn't much in my fridge except a couple of oranges and an old loaf of sliced bread.

"You don't mind?" she asked.

"No, I don't mind. Why don't you just rest for a while."

"I think I will," she said. She stretched out on the bed and closed her eyes. I covered her with the cashmere blanket I use for my siestas, checked to make sure I had my house keys, and left her there. Once I was out on the street I decided I'd better call Evelyn before she called me. There was a public pay phone on the corner. Down the street there is a small market that sells barbecued chickens. I ordered one from the man in charge, then walked back to the pay phone. I dialed Evelyn's number, and she answered after the first ring.

"I was wondering what had happened to you," she said. She sounded cheerful enough.

"I just got home," I told her. A kid on a motorbike went by. I covered the mouthpiece of the phone with my left hand, but the boy on the bike made a U-turn and passed the booth again, leaning back and pulling on the handlebars to make the front wheel spin in the air.

Evelyn said: "About a hundred years ago we made a pact never to lie to each other . . . remember?"

"I remember."

"So from where are you calling?"

"The pay booth on the corner. I stopped in at Arturo's for a beer."

"Well, are you coming by for dinner, or shall I call Kathy?"

I glanced at my wristwatch. It was a quarter past eight. "Call

Kathy," I said. "It's late, and I'm not particularly hungry. I'll drop in later but I'll call first to make sure you're there."

"Whatever you say," she replied, and hung up without saying goodbye.

I put a coin in the slot and dialed her number again. The line was busy. I guessed she was calling Kathy, and even if they were planning to dine together I knew that it would be a long conversation. I retrieved my coin and walked back to the market. I had to wait for the man to wrap up my chicken, and it was dark by the time I arrived back at my flat. When I opened the front door I noticed that my pullover was draped over the back of the chair facing the window. Fergy was stretched out on my siesta blanket at the foot of the bed.

The bathroom door was ajar, and I stepped inside. The hand towel, neatly folded in half, was lying inside the washbasin. I glanced up at the mirror. Pamela Collins had scrawled a message for me across the glass with her lipstick. "I won't bother you anymore," she had written. I felt relieved. I crossed to my bed, picked up the telephone and dialed Evelyn's number. There was no reply. I could only guess that she had gone out to dinner with her friend, a small revenge she knew from past experience would irritate me. Kathy was a night owl who liked to stay up until the early hours of the morning. Well, I thought, Fergy and I will be dining on roast chicken in lonely splendor. It was not the worst way to end a bad day.

Part II

How old would you say you were if you didn't know and they were to ask you?

—Satchel Paige, in conversation

15

LOOKING BACK, I had what I realize now was a premonition concerning my appearance at the *cuartel* of the Guardia Civil the morning after Pamela Collins's unexpected visit. And had I followed my instincts I would undoubtedly have been better off not going. But as a foreigner I felt it was necessary to heed the summons of the most efficient paramilitary police force in this country, although in all probability they would not have come looking for me. Nor, I figure, would Collins have bothered to pursue the matter. So I disregarded what I assumed was nothing more than lethargy, got into my car and drove into the adjacent town, arriving at the neat brown brick building only a few minutes late.

The Bentley was parked in front of the place in the zone reserved for official use, and Collins and Leahy were waiting on the concrete steps that led into the main entrance. They were both dressed for golf, Sir Cecil in his pale blue windbreaker, Leahy in the same outfit he had worn the previous afternoon. "I hope this won't take too long," Collins said. "We've got a starting time at Las Brisas at twelve-fifteen."

"We should be able to make it," Leahy remarked. "That's almost two hours from now."

"You don't know Spain," I told him.

Collins said: "It's a shame you can't join us, Robert. It's a perfect day for golf." He was looking off in the direction of the armed sentry inside the portico, and I noticed the words TODO POR LA PATRIA on the concrete slab above the archway.

A portly Spaniard in a dark suit emerged from the building to join us. Collins introduced him and we shook hands. "Señor Sánchez is the manager of my bank," he said. "I thought it might be helpful to have him along."

Sánchez smiled. "They have made an arrest," he said, in well-schooled English. "It seems the people at the golf club have had a previous encounter with the suspect. What is needed now is for both of you to identify him."

"Well, that's good news," Collins said. "Let's go in and get it over with."

Sánchez seemed hesitant. "You realize what all this will lead to, Sir Cecil," he said. "If they've got the right man you will have to sign a *denuncia,* and both you and Mr. Masters will ultimately have to appear in court."

Collins looked over at me. "What do you think, Robert?" he asked. "It would be a shame to let this chap get away with stabbing you, don't you agree?"

"Yeah, I do," I replied hesitantly. I wasn't looking forward to appearing in court and taking part in a lengthy trial.

"What do you say, Bill?" Collins asked Leahy.

The lawyer scratched his head. "We're here now," he said. "Be difficult to cut and run."

"All right, then let's proceed," Collins said.

Sánchez led the way into the building. The place had the familiar look of a brig, spotless floors and bare walls. We entered the office of the *teniente,* the lieutenant in charge. He was a man in his early thirties, clean-shaven, with glistening dark hair. He reminded me of the Marine shavetails serving aboard ship, dressed as he was in a well-ironed light green shirt and creased green trousers. There was a photograph of the King of Spain in uniform on the white wall behind his desk. Introductions followed without the usual hand-shakes.

The lieutenant spoke rapidly in Spanish to the banker. The suspect, I gathered, was being held in an adjoining room. Collins and I were to go with the officer to have a look at the man. The window through which we would be looking was equipped with a special glass that made it impossible for the suspect to see us. Sánchez translated the instructions for the benefit of Collins and Leahy, and we followed the lieutenant out of the office and down a corridor into another room.

There was a curtain on the wall facing us, which the lieutenant drew. Seated on a bench was the *bolero*. He was dressed in the same torn jeans and yellow shirt he had worn on the golf course. His cap lay on the bench beside him. He was handcuffed. "That's the chap, all right," Collins said.

The lieutenant glanced over at me, and I nodded. "You're quite certain?" he asked.

"He's even wearing the same clothes," Collins said.

The lieutenant knocked on the one-way glass and the *bolero* looked up. He had a narrow lined face with long straggly hair that covered his forehead. He had the look of a hunted animal, fright-ened and yet defiant. *"¿Están seguros?"* the lieutenant asked again.

I said: *"Sí. Seguro,"* and one of the guards drew the curtain. The entire process had lasted less than three minutes. Without another word the lieutenant led the way back into his office, and we all sat down facing the photograph of the King.

Sánchez did the translating during the brief scene that fol-lowed. If we were certain that this was the man who attacked us, all that was needed was for both Collins and myself to sign a *denuncia*. This document would then be forwarded to the *juez*, the judge who would later hear the case. Prior to a trial we could withdraw our *denuncia.* That was apparently how the law worked. Without a *denuncia,* the man would be released.

Collins turned to Leahy. "What do you think, Bill?" he asked again.

"It's up to you and Masters," the lawyer replied.

Collins turned to Sánchez. "Would you ask the lieutenant how long all this will take. For instance, how long before the man is brought to trial?"

"Not more than two weeks," the lieutenant replied in Spanish. We would both be asked to appear. Collins would be required to sign my *denuncia* as a witness, and then make a *denuncia* of his own.

"Then we might as well go ahead," Collins said.

Sánchez translated Sir Cecil's reply, and the lieutenant nodded. If we didn't mind waiting ten minutes, he said, the formalities would be taken care of, the clerk was out having a coffee break at that moment.

Collins smiled and said: "Fine. We'll go out for a coffee ourselves. Right, boys?"

There was a café down one of the narrow streets that ended in the square, and Sánchez led us there. He excused himself, he had to get back to the bank, and the three of us took our places at the small bar. Three plastic trays full of *tapas* were arranged to tempt us, covered by a protective glass: hard-boiled eggs in mayonnaise, Russian salad, and filets of anchovy in vinegar. The Russian salad was being visited by a shiny blue fly. I ordered three *cafés con leche.* "That was a rather strange identification procedure," Leahy said. "Wouldn't hold up in a British court of law."

"Maybe that's one of the things wrong with our country," Collins remarked.

"I'd like to be the attorney appointed by the court to defend this man," the lawyer continued. "Even if the identification were to prove acceptable, I think I could make things difficult for the prosecution. In the first place, you, Cecil, speak no Spanish, so how could you be certain the man's intention was to rob you. He might just as well have wanted to sell you some used golf balls."

"Well, that's what he did at first. Then he threatened me with a knife."

"True enough. But I would still plead the whole thing was something of a misunderstanding," Leahy said. "He might have taken out his knife for other purposes."

"Bollocks," Collins said. "What other purposes? Is your man going to plead he was intending to peel me an orange, or perhaps carve our initials in the trunk of a tree? I never heard such rot!"

Leahy remained unruffled. "I would argue that when Robert here attacked with his seven iron, my client merely defended himself as best he could—"

"I still want to know why he took out his knife!" Collins interrupted. "Was it to clean his fingernails?"

"Well, he might have intended to do a number of things with it . . . cut some kindling for his fire, make a slingshot?"

"Oh, come on, Bill. You'd be laughed out of court with that kind of defense," Collins said in a somewhat calmer tone of voice.

"Even if he was threatening you, Cecil, Robert's attack was unprovoked. At least he should have waited for an explanation."

"What's the point you're trying to make?" Collins asked. "You think it's a mistake for us to proceed?"

"Not necessarily. I just want to warn you that a smart lawyer could complicate matters. Don't you agree, Robert?"

"There's always the chance of that," I said. "In any court of law."

Collins said: "The man's a thug. He should be put behind bars."

"I agree with you," Leahy replied. "But don't forget, you fellows will always be outsiders."

Our coffee had arrived. The barman added hot milk from an unsavory pitcher. "If anything," Collins muttered, "you've made me even more determined to see this thing through. Unless, of course, Robert, here, has a change of heart."

I said: "No, I'm with you." I couldn't get the face of the *bolero* out of my mind's eye, the narrowed eyes, the chiseled features that reminded me, strangely enough, of the face of one of the thieves in a painting of the crucifixion I had seen during one of my visits to the Prado.

"I know this may sound pompous," Collins said, "but if a respectable citizen is unwilling to back up the forces of law and order, anarchy will soon prevail." He downed his cup of coffee. "Shall we go back, boys? I'll take care of the tab."

Leahy and I sauntered out into the street. "What was that all about?" I asked him. "Were you trying to talk Sir Cecil into backing down?"

"No, not really," the lawyer said, and smiled. "I only wanted to warn him that this whole thing was going to complicate his life. He has a lot on his plate, you know."

Collins joined us. "I must learn their bloody language," he said. "I can't even go into a pub unassisted."

"Did they try to overcharge you?" Leahy inquired with a grin.

"I don't know," Collins replied. "Finally I just gave the chap a thousand pesetas and told him to keep the change. That's approximately five quid for three cups of miserable coffee."

16

THE UNSMILING LIEUTENANT HAD DEPARTED, we discovered, once we had returned to the *cuartel*. "Probably gone off on a drug bust," Collins said. "Isn't that what they call that sort of exercise in your country, Robert?"

"More likely he had an earlier starting time at your club," Leahy commented. "Almost everybody's caught the golf bug these days."

A stout man wearing a small black pistol came into the lieutenant's office and introduced himself as Sargento Andrés. He had been put in charge of our *denuncias*, he declared, and wanted to know who should go first. Collins suggested politely that it should be his turn, but that turned out to be impossible as there was no one in the building who could serve as a translator, Señor Sánchez having returned to his bank. Collins asked if he could come the next day, and the sergeant left the room to inquire if this would be possible. He returned half a minute later to agree to a postponement for Sir Cecil, and Leahy and he rose from their chairs. "Sorry to leave you holding the bag, my dear fellow," he said. "No use our hanging about. Incidentally," he added, "we're giving a small dinner for my solicitor here, and it would be nice if you could join us. Bring a lady, if possible. Pamela likes to have an even number at her table."

"Things must be more peaceful at home," I said.

"An armed truce," he replied. "Come see for yourself."

I told him that I would let him know, but he insisted, saying that I should come alone if bringing a friend on such short order would turn out to be difficult. Once the two Englishmen had left I was ushered into an adjoining office where I was joined by a clerk, an elderly man with glasses and a sparse head of hair. That he was not overly fond of his job was apparent from the moment he sat down in front of his ancient typewriter.

The recording of the facts concerning the "act of aggression" on the golf course turned out to be a lengthy procedure. Halfway through the deposition the clerk suddenly tore the paper out of the machine and we started all over again from the beginning. He had made a mistake that he didn't bother to explain, and it was nearly one o'clock once the two-page document had been completed. I was free to go, the clerk announced, and I left the small office. As I reached the main hallway of the building, the *bolero* (his name was Pedro Fernández, I had learned during my deposition) was being led to another part of the *cuartel*. He glanced over at me, and our eyes met. There was no sign of recognition. He merely stared at me, then raised his manacled hands to scratch his nose and continued on his way.

It occurred to me that it was not the first time Pedro Fernández had found himself in custody. Yet I suddenly found myself regretting my *denuncia*. It was a feeling in part of pity, although I told myself the man deserved none. My wound had healed, Collins had only suffered a slight inconvenience, and what was more important, we would undoubtedly become involved in a long legal process that would cause us to waste a lot more time. To what profit? If the man went to prison for a year or two would he be reformed when he got out? The argument that our failure to back up the police would promote a state of anarchy didn't seem realistic either, I concluded and went off in search of a pay telephone.

I found one within fifty yards of the *cuartel* that hadn't been vandalized. I dialed Evelyn's number, and she answered at once. But the freeze was still on, I realized. "How was your evening?" she asked.

I said: "Quiet. Dead quiet."

A long pause. Then: "Who did you have dinner with?"

"A natural redhead. Her name's Fergy."

"Very funny."

"Would you like to have lunch?" I asked.

"What? Today?"

"I'm sorry to call so late," I said. "I know you must be very busy."

"I'm washing my hair," she said defiantly.

"Okay. Then what about dinner? We've been invited by Lord and Lady Collins."

"I haven't got anything to wear." A familiar cry.

"Then let's forget it," I said cheerfully.

"No, wait a minute," Evelyn said. "I'd like to meet the Lady Pamela. She sounds interesting, and you say she's attractive."

"Yeah. Sort of attractive."

"And it's a free meal, right?"

"Are we down to that?"

"Well, close," she said. "What time, and what's the uniform of the day?"

"I don't know," I said. "I'll have to check. I was going to cancel out."

"Call me later and let me know what you decide," Evelyn replied, and hung up.

17

I THOUGHT I'D BETTER FIND KIKO and inform him about everything that had happened. I knew that he wouldn't be at his office during the lunch hour, so I decided to call in on the *tasca* he usually went to when he was alone. I wasn't hungry after my session at the *cuartel*, but I felt like a glass of beer and a *tapa* that hadn't been picked over by the local flies. I found my way to the new highway that had been opened during the last summer, and fifteen minutes later I was in San Pedro de Alcantara. The new highway is one of the principal improvements this coast has been blessed with, although it now serves as a proving ground for the speed demons in their Japanese motorcycles and the latest models of European cars.

It was two o'clock by this time and the place was fairly crowded, but there was no sign of Kiko. I stood at the bar and drank a glass of Cruz Campo to wash down the piece of Spanish *tortilla* I had chosen from the selection of appetizers on display. I was just about to leave when my son-in-law arrived and I joined him at a corner table that had just been vacated by two truck drivers. He ordered a plate of the *guiso* that was the *plat du jour* and a glass of red wine, a more wholesome meal than the lunch I had consumed. "Things have changed," I told him as he dipped a piece of bread in the brown sauce before attacking his lamb stew.

"I know all about it," he said, sipping his wine. "I had a visit from your friend, Lady Collins, this morning."

"Did she want her money back?" I asked him.

"No, not at all. She informed me that you were out of the picture, and wanted to know if I had someone else to assign to the job."

"She *still* wants her husband followed?" I asked, surprised.

"That's what she said. It seems that she's thinking of a divorce now, and she wants to document her husband's fooling around with this other woman. She wants it all in English, she told me, because the case will be heard in the UK."

"Fair enough," I said, "as long as she really understands I'm out of the whole thing."

He nodded. "You ought to try this *guiso,*" he said. "It's the best." He has always had a habit of chewing with an open mouth, a lack of manners that Susan must have overlooked during the initial phases of their romance. "What happened with the Guardia Civil?" he asked. Apparently he had been well informed about Collins's morning activities.

I told him without going into detail but added that Sir Cecil's *denuncia* had been put off until the next morning. "So far I'm the only heavy," I added.

"That figures," he said.

"You think it's all a mistake?"

"I don't know. It wasn't just your average mugging. The guy attacked you with a deadly weapon."

"What'll he get if he's convicted?"

"Five years. Maybe more. But he'll be out in nine months on good behavior. The jails are overcrowded."

"Will he try to get even?"

"Not a chance," Kiko said. "He's a petty criminal. He'll go back to peddling drugs or stealing radios out of cars. It's lucky you missed him with your seven iron. If you'd maimed him, or broken his jaw, the family would be after you. Probably make you pay the hospital bill. This way you're the victim. That's a lot better."

"What's happening with you and Susan?" I asked him.

"Nothing much . . . it's business as usual. She's still seeing her *señorito,* I guess. We don't talk much."

"I suppose that's all to the good. Well, I'll see you tomorrow."

"I hope so," he said. "I want to hear all about the big party tonight. Don't worry. I won't quote you. I know that you're no longer on the payroll, *abuelito.*" *Abuelo* was bad enough, but the diminutive made me want to throw up.

I said: "Don't you forget it, *muchacho.*" Calling him kid was a mild attempt to put him in his place.

We shook hands. "Good luck with finding a new tenant for your house," Kiko said with a faint smile. "Holy Week is coming up soon."

I stepped out into the bright sunlight. It made my eyes ache. I put on my dark glasses, but that didn't help much. I couldn't remember where I had parked my car, so perhaps the term *abuelito* was justified. I felt I needed a siesta, needed one badly. Before arriving on this coast needing a nap usually meant I was coming down with a cold.

My telephone was ringing when I arrived outside my front door. It stopped before I had let myself in. I closed the shutters, lay down on my bed and pulled the cashmere blanket over me. It smelled slightly of Pamela Collins's perfume. I would have to air it out before Evelyn's next visit, I told myself. A long siesta was a luxury I had had to do without for several days, so I slept soundly for an hour and a half. Then I woke up, set the alarm for six-thirty and went back to sleep. It was then that I was visited by a dream that is perhaps worth recording, although it is not really pertinent to this story.

Paul Levin was the central character of my dream. He had grown a beard that made him look like an elderly chimp. We were both in a small office on Sunset Boulevard that belonged to an independent producer, one of the King brothers. That was considered to be the last step down in the business. The producer looked like an Italian gangster. He had his feet up on his desk and was smoking a cigar. He was talking to Paul Levin as if I weren't there. He had read in the trade papers, he was saying, that my option had not been taken up. So he had thought about offering me a part in the movie he was about to make. But then he had changed his mind, he explained, by way of an apology.

Paul Levin interrupted him. "You're trying to tell us we've been blacklisted," he said. "That's it, isn't it?"

The man laughed. "You know what Jack Warner said," he replied. "He was talking about not hiring the Commies in the business. He said: 'There is no such thing as a blacklist. All I have to do is pick up the telephone.' "

That was the end of the dream. Once awake, I remembered that Naomi's father had told me the story about Warner many years ago in Paris. So much for the vagaries of the mind. I went into the bathroom and brushed my teeth. I needed a beer, but there wasn't one in the fridge so I thought I'd drop in at Arturo's for a *caña*. On the way I passed my car where I had left it on the side street. Someone had stuck a piece of paper under the windshield wiper, I noticed, and thinking it was an advertisement for one of the new shops in town, I pulled it free.

At first it looked like a blank piece of paper, but when I turned it over I saw that a single word had been scrawled across it with a red felt-tipped pen: ¡CHIVATO! For an instant my Spanish failed me. Then the meaning of the word came to me: Informer! Stool pigeon!

My first reaction was that it was a bad practical joke, something Kiko might have thought of because I had asked him if there was any chance of my assailant wanting to get even once he was released from jail. But that seemed most unlikely. No matter how much our relationship had changed recently, he would not permit himself to go that far. Yet he was the only person who knew I had made a *denuncia*. My thirst had vanished, and I hurried back upstairs and knocked on the door of his office.

He opened it himself an instant later, but he was not alone. Alberto, the ex-foreign legionnaire was seated in a chair in front of his desk. He got to his feet as I entered. I said: "Could I have a word with you in private," and Kiko dismissed the man with a curt jerk of his head. Once he had left, I handed Kiko the scrap of paper.

He glanced at it, then held it up to the light on his desk. "Where did you get this?" he asked.

I told him that I'd found it under the windshield wiper of my car. "I thought maybe it was your idea of a practical joke," I said.

"Come on, don Roberto," he said. "That's not my style."

"Nobody else knows about my *denuncia*."

He scratched his head. "I'll tell you how these things work in this country. The Guardia Civil, once they have decided to hold a suspect, is obliged to call an *abogado de oficio* . . . a public defender, you'd call him in the States. That's because your man Pedro-the-Thief undoubtedly doesn't have his own lawyer. Then the suspect is informed of the charges against him. It's quite possible that this took place later in the day. The suspect is also informed of who made these charges. So there's just a chance Fernández was visited by a member of his family, and they got the idea that a few threats might keep you from ratifying your *denuncia*. That way Pedro will go free."

"What do you think I should do?"

He shrugged. "There's nothing much you *can* do," he said. "Usually the next step is to call you on the phone in the middle of the night. If they use that tactic you can go to the police."

"And what will *they* do?"

"Sweet fuck-all, probably. But you never know."

"Collins still hasn't signed *his* complaint," I said. "We could just drop the charges."

"Sure, you could. If you're that scared."

"I'm not scared," I said. "Not yet. I just wonder if it's worth all the trouble."

"That's for you to decide. I wouldn't let them get away with it." He got up from his chair and refilled his pipe. "Why not move back into your villa? I doubt they'll find you there. And I can get Pepe or Alberto to move in with you, free of charge. I got you into all this, remember?"

"I remember," I said caustically.

"Well, talk to Collins tonight and see what he feels. They'll be after him, too." He lit his pipe. *"¡Que país!"* he added, rolling his eyes.

"It's your country, not mine."

"From what I read in the papers," he said, "yours is no better."

18

THAT EVELYN WAS THE PRETTIEST WOMAN at the party was apparent at first glance. We had arrived late due to her last-minute change of wardrobe, proof of an insecurity that only surfaced occasionally, so that the evening was already in full swing, with the library filled with guests enjoying champagne cocktails, French champagne, I noticed. Nor was Evelyn's plea, as we rang the doorbell, not to abandon her necessary, it turned out, for Sir Cecil took her arm as soon as I had made the introductions and guided her through the room. I made my way to my hostess and kissed her hand. "You're late," she said, "but you're forgiven because you wore a tie. Cecil refused."

Collins was wearing a golden-buttoned blazer with a pink shirt open at the neck that made him look even more handsome and made him stand out among the other men, most of them his seniors. "I'm sorry," I said, "but the traffic was heavy in town," a polite lie Pamela Collins dismissed with a shrug.

"We'll be going in to dinner soon," she warned me, "so get yourself a drink. There's whiskey if you don't fancy champers."

Collins had already supplied Evelyn with a glass of Moët et

Chandon, so I made my way over to the table on the far side of the room that was being used as a bar. While the butler was filling my glass, Señor Sánchez, the banker, joined me. I greeted him formally, and he corrected me, asking me to call him by his first name, which he informed me was Julio. He recalled that we had met that morning at the *cuartel* of the Guardia Civil, adding that he and Collins had made a second trip there late in the afternoon since it would have been impossible for him to go there the next morning.

"Then Sir Cecil signed his *denuncia*," I said.

"*Sí, claro*," he replied. "That was our understanding, wasn't it?"

"Yes. I suppose so."

Sánchez looked closely at me, as if he sensed that I had had a change of heart. "Do you regret having done so?" he asked.

I said: "No, not really. Although I expect there'll be a few complications."

"Complications? I don't understand."

"Well, we'll have to go to court," I replied. "That's never much fun."

"Fun, no," he said, and turned away. I watched him as he made his way to the side of a heavy-set, dark-haired woman I guessed was his wife.

Collins came over to me. "How's the arm?" he asked.

"Better," I said. "Almost healed."

"We missed you today," he remarked. "I got my own back with Leahy. Took a hundred quid off him. I'm going to London tomorrow but we'll have a game as soon as I get back." He lowered his voice. "I was going to ask you to come along," he went on. "It looks as if a divorce is in the offing . . . so I might have to ask you to make a deposition."

"I don't follow you," I said. "What kind of deposition?"

"Well, the little incident outside the club the other day. It could have some bearing on the case. If things get nasty, that is."

"I hope they won't," I said.

"So do I," he replied. "Come along now. We're going in to dinner."

To my surprise, I was seated at my hostess's left, and down at the other end of the glittering table Evelyn had been placed on Collins's right, a last minute reshuffling of the place cards, I reckoned. Sánchez was on Pamela Collins's right. The rest of the guests were all English, I soon discovered, gray-haired men and their bleached-blonde wives. Bill Leahy was by far the youngest of the group, and he was seated on the other side of Evelyn. On my right was Sánchez's wife. Her name, she told me, was Lucilla. "You're an actor, I understand," was her opening gambit.

"I was," I said. "A long time ago."

"And now you're retired?"

"More or less."

"You live here?"

"I have for a long time."

"You speak very good Spanish for an Englishman."

"I'm an American."

"Forgive me. I should have known. But I never go to movies," she added apologetically.

That was pretty much the end of our conversation until the main course arrived. I noticed that Leahy and Collins were making a great fuss over Evelyn, and that she appeared to be having a good time. Pamela had noticed it too. She leaned over toward me. "I've decided to take your advice," she whispered.

"Yes? In what department?"

"As soon as Cecil comes back I'm going to London and retain a solicitor. Cecil says I don't need one, but *I* think I do."

"It can't hurt," I said.

Sánchez was staring straight ahead on her other side, not talking to his neighbor on his left. Pamela said: "We'll talk later." Then she turned to the banker: "Is the peseta going to be devalued soon?" she asked him with a seductive smile.

"I wish I knew," he replied, and laughed loudly. "The country is in bad shape. This government has been a disaster for the economy."

"Ours hasn't done too well, either," Pamela Collins replied. "The world's in a mess."

The butler had appeared, bearing a large platter of roast beef with Yorkshire pudding. My hostess indicated to him in pantomime that he should serve Evelyn first. A maid carrying a large salad bowl had taken her place behind him. "Help yourselves from both sides," Pamela called out to her guests. "It's very plebeian but it saves a lot of time."

For some strange reason I found myself thinking about Pedro Fernández. I suppose it was the sight of so much food being offered to people who were accustomed to being well fed, but suddenly the image of the starved face of the *bolero* crossed my mind's eye. Then I recalled the title of a book I had seen in my father's library many, many years ago, that I had glanced at often enough but never ventured to read. *Beware of Pity* was the name of the book, a warning that had stuck in my mind. But pity, it occurred to me at that moment, was the only thing those of us who have managed to escape misery had to offer.

"I hope you like roast beef," my hostess said with a smile.

"I do," I replied. "Rare, if possible."

"That may be asking too much," Pamela Collins said. "My chef is a Spaniard, and you know how hopeless they are about timing anything."

The meal was enjoyable despite the overcooked meat, and after a final course of fresh raspberries served with vanilla ice cream the ladies retired from the table, leaving the male guests to their port. Before leaving the table Lady Collins announced that coffee would be served in the living room. "That is, after all of you have finished telling your off-color stories."

There was a brief pause and then a red-faced, portly man addressed me across the table. "Aren't you the chap that was attacked on the first nine the other day?" he inquired. "The par-three hole."

I said: "Yes, that's right," and glanced over at Collins, who seemed not to be listening to the conversation.

But he had overheard the question just the same. "Robert came to my defense," he said. "I was about to be robbed, Colonel."

The colonel then went on to relate that there had been several incidents of the same nature on other golf courses in the region. Most of them had involved women who had had their purses snatched, although there had been one case where an elderly Swede had been threatened with his own five iron and had been forced to surrender his wallet.

"A bad scene," the colonel said. "They should bring back the birch, although I suppose they never flogged criminals in this country."

"In Franco's time it wasn't necessary," Sánchez said.

"They've arrested the culprit," Collins announced, "and they were damn quick about it. He'll be brought to trial in no time, I've been told."

"In Franco's time the police committed the crimes," I couldn't help saying.

Sánchez glared at me from across the table. "That's not entirely accurate," he replied. "In any event I get the impression that you're not convinced that you and Cecil should press charges."

Bankers were adept at reading people's minds, I realized, due probably to years of practice. I said: "My only worry is that Cecil and I will be involved in a time-consuming hassle that will involve court appearances and cross-examinations."

"Fair enough," Collins said, coming to my rescue. "I've worried about that aspect of it myself."

"Well, I hope you don't let this chappie off the hook," the colonel said. "Pass the port, please."

The conversation soon returned to a less contentious subject: golf. The many new American clubs were discussed, the disadvantages of using carts, which, although they speeded up the game, deprived it of what little exercise the sport had to offer, and the negative impact of all the "new players" who didn't know the rules and had no manners. Finally Collins suggested we "join the ladies," and we trooped into the living room. Sánchez hung back, as I did, and fell into step beside me.

"I was never a great admirer of the past regime," he said, by way of appeasing me. "But there was a lot less delinquency."

I agreed with him and muttered the usual cliché about the high price of democracy, a statement that was rewarded with a brief smile. Evelyn was standing near the fireplace, warming herself. "Are you having a good time?" I asked her.

"Not bad," she said. "I haven't been exposed to this many of my own countrymen for years."

Pamela was taking the orders for coffee or herb tea, and having finished, she stepped over to us. "Would you like to see the garden?" she asked.

"What? At night?" Evelyn asked, a little too sharply, or so it seemed to me.

"We have floodlights, my dear. We're very *moderne,* don't you know!"

"It's too cold outside for me," Evelyn replied, and went off to collect her glass of herb tea.

"What about you?" Pamela inquired. She lowered her voice. "I *would* like to have a brief word," she added.

"Lead the way," I said bravely, as I had noticed that Evelyn was watching us.

"I'm just going to show Robert the garden, darling," Pamela called out to her husband.

"That's a good idea," Collins replied affably. "He might want to take a dip in the pool."

Their exchanges throughout the evening had been too friendly to be genuine, but then I was probably the only guest with the exception of Bill Leahy who was conscious of the underlying tension. Pamela pulled open one of the sliding glass doors, and I followed her out onto the marble floor of the covered terrace. She touched a white button and the grounds before us were bathed in light. At the foot of each of the numerous palm trees, floodlights had been installed to illuminate the spacious grounds. At the end of the sloping lawn lay the swimming pool, a large pavilion adjoining it, complete with barbecue and changing rooms for the guests.

I said: "Disneyland." Pamela Collins ignored my wisecrack and moved to the far end of the terrace. I followed her. She was wearing a long black skirt with a gilded bodice that showed off the upper part of her figure. Through the tall windows of the living room the evening's festivities were visible, a lively pantomime that was more entertaining seen from a distance, a long-shot from a silent movie. "It seems Cecil is going to take his toady's advice," Pamela said quietly. "Last night when I got home he told me that a divorce was probably the only civilized solution to our problems." She paused. "He said he still loves me and that I will always be 'the woman of his life.' Those are his words."

"And what was your reaction?"

"I didn't know what to say. I was upset, of course. After everything that had happened. I felt humiliated. Because I lost control and struck you, more than anything else. I *am* sorry about that, you know."

"Not to worry. A private eye has to expect these small setbacks." I was tempted to mention that Kiko had told me she had retained his services but thought better of it. I didn't want to get involved again.

"You're a nice man," she said, "I realize that now. In any event, I feel I must prepare myself for the worst. Cecil wants to keep this house. He said it was too big a place for a woman on her own. We'll have to see about that. I don't want *her* living here. But I didn't say so. That's for the lawyers to settle. Don't you agree?"

"Absolutely."

"But I *did* want to apologize again for last night."

She was a changed person, calm and self-controlled. I wondered if she had taken a sedative. "We all say things we come to regret," I told her.

She nodded. I sensed that there was more on her mind. She held out her hand. "Friends?" she asked.

"Friends," I replied, and kissed her on the cheek.

She said: "I think I'd better get back to my guests. The thing Cecil has always admired in me is that I'm a good hostess. I don't want him to forget it."

19

EVELYN SIGNALED THAT SHE WANTED TO LEAVE, and I went to say goodbye to Collins. "Are you off?" he asked. "I'll see you to the door." He glanced quickly around the room. "Pam must have gone upstairs for a minute," he said. "I'll call her."

"Don't bother," Evelyn said. "We don't want to break up the party."

We had arrived in the front hall. Collins put his arm across my shoulders. "I know how you feel about pursuing all of these legal complications," he said. "But for the time being I think we should let this fellow rot in jail. I've had a word with Sánchez and he tells me we still have plenty of time to withdraw our accusations. Not ratify our *denuncias,* and that will end the matter. I'm of two minds about it, but you're the one who's suffered most . . ."

"Let me think about it," I said. "As you say, we don't have to decide anything for the time being. Let's wait until you get back from London."

"Perfect," he replied. "We'll make up our minds in a week or so." He turned to Evelyn. "I was delighted to meet you," he said. "I hope it's not the last time."

"Unfortunately, I don't play golf," she said.

He laughed. "We could have a meal, lunch or whatever."

"That would be nice," Evelyn replied, almost too politely.

Pamela came down the marble stairs with another woman. She excused herself to her guest and came over to join us. "You're leaving already?" she asked.

I said: "It's pretty late for an elderly gentleman."

"Oh, come off it," she said. "You're a mere stripling." She turned to Evelyn and the two women shook hands. "Do come again," Pamela crooned falsely.

Collins held open the front door, and he and Evelyn stepped outside. They were out of earshot for a moment, or I thought they were. "Say hello to your nice cat," Pamela said, offering her cheek to be kissed.

Collins was waiting in the driveway. "Can you get out all right?" he asked. "Where did you park?"

"No problem."

We had been the last to arrive. I unlocked the door on Evelyn's side and she got in without a word. She made no effort to unlatch my side for me, so I had to open the door with my key. I started the engine, and the radio came on as soon as the motor was running, the local British station that broadcasts popular music all night. A raspy woman's voice was complaining that she was not getting enough lovin', repeating the same phrase over and over again to only a very slight variation in the melody.

"Do we have to have that?" Evelyn inquired.

I cut the singer off in the middle of her song. It had started to rain—big, fat drops that splattered on the dusty windshield. "What's the matter?" I asked her.

"Nothing," she replied calmly. "Would you drive me home, please?"

"That was my plan," I said. It was better not to say anything, I thought, and let her start the quarrel I knew was coming, so we drove on in silence through the rain like a couple that has been married for years and doesn't have any more to say to each other. Finally I thought I would try to defuse the time bomb, we were very nearly at her house. "Did you have a good time?" I asked.

"Yes. For a while. He has good manners, Collins," she said. "Which is more than I can say for his wife."

"What did she do to upset you?"

"Nothing, really. Except that she treated me as if I hadn't been invited . . . and then asking you if you wanted to see the garden! How *cursi* can you get?"

"She asked both of us."

"Oh, come off it, Robert! She wanted to talk to *you*. She knew I wasn't going to step outside to spoil the fun. Then her last little jibe . . . 'Say hello to your nice cat!' What was that all about?"

"Nothing. Just a chance remark."

"When did you have her up to the apartment? Was that last night? You were lying to me, weren't you, when you called to tell me that you were too tired to have dinner? Because she was with you. That was the reason, wasn't it? How else did she know you had a cat?"

"She met Fergy last Sunday morning when she stopped by Kiko's office. I told you about all that." It was a half-truth, but I knew that admitting that she had come to see me would only make matters worse.

"Why do you lie?" she asked. "I can tell by the way she talks to you that you've seen her more than once."

"Well, I have," I said. "Collins insisted I come back to his house after the incident on the golf course. And she drove me back to where I'd left my car. We've been through all that."

We had arrived at El Refugio. I turned down the narrow street that leads to her house. It was raining even harder when I stopped in front of the entrance. "I know you're lying," Evelyn said. "I hate that. It's demeaning."

"And I hate your stupid jealousies," I replied angrily. "I'm an old man, for God's sake! And I'm not interested in anyone except you. You ought to know that by now! Besides, you think a woman like Pamela Collins would waste her time flirting with a penniless, retired actor? Wise up, will you? And have a little confidence in yourself . . . as well as in me!"

She said: "I have plenty of confidence in myself. But I know *you*. You've never changed. You can't help it. Any female who's even mildly attractive turns you on. I've watched you. You have to flirt with them all . . . why, I'll never know!"

"You're out of your mind!"

"No, I'm not. I think *you* are!" She started to get out of the car, but the rain stopped her. "I think we should have a long rest from each other," she added. "Beginning right now!"

"Anything you say!"

She wrenched open the door and ran off through the rain. I sat watching her as she searched for her house key in her handbag. For a moment I thought of going after her, but once she had stepped inside she slammed the door behind her with a finality that was convincing.

It wasn't the first time we had had a scene of that kind. By the next morning she had usually calmed down, so I drove off. Pamela Collins had obviously wanted to make trouble, there was no doubt about that. But I couldn't quite figure out why, except that in her present state of mind she had come to resent any pretty woman that her husband made a fuss over. Well, I had only myself to blame. I could easily have declined her invitation to visit the garden, but I would have felt like a fool if I had. Her final remark, "Say hello to your nice cat," was undoubtedly intended to stir things up some more.

But I had other things on my mind. The news that Collins had signed his *denuncia* troubled me more than the bitchery of his wife, although he had indicated that there was still time for us to back out of the whole thing. I drove on through the rain, wondering how long he intended to stay in England. I parked my car on the street behind the apartment block, slipped the radio under the seat on the passenger side and locked both doors. It was unlikely that anyone would be waiting for me in the dark, but I felt a certain apprehensiveness as I made my way down the wet sidewalk.

Once I had arrived in my flat I hung up my blazer near the electric fire to let it dry out, sat down on the edge of my bed and took off my shoes and socks. The telephone rang, and thinking it might be Evelyn, I picked up the receiver. I could hear what sounded like heavy breathing, then a man's voice said: "Señor Roberto?"

"*Soy yo,*" I replied.

There was a long pause. *"Ten cuidado, viejo,"* the voice said. The busy signal followed as it always does after a caller has hung up.

I glanced at the alarm clock on my night table. It was one-thirty in the morning. "Be careful, old man" was not a particularly disturbing message, but the threatening tone of voice was unmistakable. I waited for the telephone to ring again, then dialed Evelyn's number. She had put on her tape and I waited for the beep, then said: "It's me. Please call me when you wake up."

Maybe Kiko was right, I thought—it might be a good idea to move back into my villa, although my telephone number was listed in the directory. But at least there I could switch my line to the *contestador automatico* that the telephone company had installed more than a year ago. I didn't feel really frightened. At that moment I was more concerned with Evelyn and the tone of finality that had ended our disagreement. Facing the loss of one's female companion this late in life was not unlike premature widowhood, a disturbing prospect.

I had the feeling that everything was going wrong at the same time. *Una mala racha,* as they say in this country. I got into bed and pulled the covers up over me. Fergy seemed to sense my mood. She jumped up on the foot of my bed and came slowly toward me. I knew she was intending to curl up beside me, to lie with her back against mine, as she often does on chilly nights, but this time she insisted on squatting down on my pillow and gazing intently at my face. I let her stay there for a while. Sleep was out of the question anyway—for the time being.

20

It was *una mala racha,* all right—what I didn't know at the time was that it was just starting. The telephone rang again at seven-fifteen. The same voice asked: *"¿Estás dormiendo, viejo?"*

I had been awake for most of the night, so the call was only a minor disturbance. *"¿Quien habla?"* I asked.

"¿Que te importa, cabrón?"

In a controlled voice I said: *"Cobarde,"* a fairly mild reply to one of the most common insults in the Spanish language. In Mexico men draw knives or pistols if someone refers to them as *cabrón,* which in literal translation only means the male goat. The inference, however, is cuckold, which in Spain is somewhat less offensive, although certainly not flattering. The usual reply is *"Me cago en tu madre,"* which the caller did not give me time to say.

I replaced the receiver and got out of bed. It was still dark outside but I decided to get up and prepare myself for the day. Fergy was watching me with an expression on her face that indicated quite clearly that she thought I had lost my mind. I don't think that I'm more cowardly than the next fellow, nor am I under the illusion that I am more courageous by nature. Still, the feeling that someone I had never met disliked me enough to call me repeatedly in order to insult me was disquieting to say the least. I went into the bathroom and turned on the shower, and the telephone rang again. By this time I had had enough. I grabbed the phone and shouted: *"¿Que quiere?"* in my most intimidating tone of voice.

There was the sound of a number of coins being deposited in a metal box, and a familiar voice said: "Did I wake you, Daddy? I'm sorry."

"No, you didn't," I replied. "What are *you* doing up at this ungodly hour?"

"I'm at the airport," my one-and-only daughter informed me. "I had to call you this early because my plane is taking off in twenty minutes."

"Your plane? Where the hell are you going?"

"To Madrid . . . and then on to California. I told you I was thinking of leaving, remember?"

"Yeah, I remember. But I thought not until this summer."

"Well, I changed my mind."

I could hear the water running in the bathroom. I said: "Hold on a second. I have to turn off the shower." Susan was still on the line when I returned. "Where did you get the money to buy your ticket?" I asked her.

There was a pause, then she said: "A friend loaned me three hundred thousand pesetas. But don't worry, Daddy. I don't have to pay him back right away."

"What about Tommy and Isabel?"

"I'm taking Isabel with me. Tommy will join us once his Easter vacation begins."

"Then you're not coming back, is that it?"

"Of course I am," she said. "After *Semana Santa.*"

"What about Kiko? Did he agree to all this?"

"Well, not exactly. I was going to tell him, but I haven't seen

125

him for two days. He's been staying at his office, or somewhere. I just couldn't handle all the arguments anymore."

"That's great," I said. "So you're counting on me to deal with him."

"He doesn't speak to me anymore. Chances are he'll listen to you."

"What makes you think so?"

"He'll have to, won't he?"

I took a deep breath. "Happy days. What a mess!"

"Don't worry, Daddy," Susan said. "Everything will work out in the end." I could hear the loudspeaker at the airport droning on in the background. "I have to go now," she added after a brief pause. "I love you."

Declarations of love, it seems, are always forthcoming at moments like these. I said: "Yeah, well, have a good trip, and call me when you arrive."

"I will. I promise."

"Give my regards to your mother."

Susan laughed. "I sure will," she said. "I'll be back soon."

"I hope so," I replied. "I can't handle this alone." The Spaniards say that when your children are small they're so cute you want to eat them, and once they've grown up you're sorry you didn't. Poor Kiko, I found myself thinking, remembering how happy he had looked on the beach at Almería the day I had reluctantly agreed to his and Susan's plans for the future. Well, everybody is happy in the beginning—there's no doubt about that. Even Phyliss and I had spent a few weeks of marital bliss before I had been shipped out to the South Pacific. Although Amanda and I had known right from the start that we were both making a mistake.

I felt weary. I stepped over to the window to open the shutters. It was just getting light. The sky was clear but there was a thick bank of clouds on the horizon hanging low over the sea, promising rain. It was as if even the day had an ulterior motive. Life was supposed to get easier as you near the end, I thought. It was almost comical. I returned to the bathroom and turned on the shower, hoping the warm water would revive my spirits. It did. I dried myself and shaved. In the shaving mirror the circles under my eyes had deepened from loss of sleep.

I got dressed without turning on the lamp next to my bed in order not to waken Fergy. If Kiko had spent the night in his office it would be wiser to have breakfast in town, I reckoned, so that I could avoid him until after he had read Susan's farewell note. I closed the front door as quietly as possible and hurried down the stairs. The street lamps shut down the moment I stepped out into the chilly morning air. The wind was from the west and there were whitecaps far out at sea. Then as I turned the corner of the Paseo Maritimo I noticed that a small yellow Seat was parked behind the pay telephone booth. A man in jeans and a tattered bomber jacket was struggling to load a folded-up wheelchair into the hatchback of the yellow car. He was holding on to the rear door with one hand, apparently not strong enough to remain upright on his crippled legs. I stepped over to him, picked up the wheelchair, and placed it inside. A woman's scarf, I noticed, was lying on the rubber matting.

The man glanced over at me, muttered something unintelligible, a curse or a reticent thank-you, I wasn't sure. He had long, unwashed dark hair combed straight back from a narrow face, and as I stepped back he slammed shut the rear door of the Seat. My unasked-for assistance had annoyed him, it seemed, and I retreated to the sidewalk. You don't do a good deed for the thanks you expect to get, I reminded myself, and stood for a minute or two while the man made his way slowly along the side of the car. He dropped into the driver's seat, then lifted his legs inside with both hands. The starter-motor sounded as if there were a few teeth missing in the flywheel, but the engine caught finally and the man drove off.

Then as I walked on to where I had parked my car I caught sight of a piece of paper stuck under one of the windshield wipers. I pulled it free. "YANQUI," had been scrawled across it, "VETE A TU CASA. ¡Y A LA MIERDA!" I stood rooted in place, flushed with anger. My nemesis, it seemed, was a cripple, a pitiful *desgraciado,* probably a relative or a friend of Pedro Fernández!

His insulting message dated him. "Yankee Go Home" had been the usual graffiti sprayed on walls while Franco was still in power. Yet the fact that he was aware of my nationality seemed to indicate that he knew who I was and that he had probably recognized me. It was not surprising. I had lived in these parts for years, and a great many of the residents knew me by sight even if they didn't know my name. I pocketed the piece of paper and unlocked my car. Tomás, the caddymaster, or one of the guards at the golf club who had been instrumental in Pedro Fernández's arrest, would probably know if the *bolero* had a crippled brother or friend, and if they were willing to identify him I could soon put a stop to his nightly telephone calls and nasty little messages.

I sat there for a few minutes to collect my thoughts. Before making another *denuncia* I had to make sure I had the right man. There was a slim chance that the cripple had been there by accident. After my conversation with Susan I had showered, shaved and gotten dressed. I glanced at my watch. It was eight-fifteen. It seemed odd that it had taken the man with the wheelchair almost a full hour to return to his car. It was most unlikely that he was waiting for me to appear. The faded woman's scarf on the floor of the Seat indicated that he may have had an accomplice. Together they might have planned to confront me in my apartment and then had changed their minds.

It was getting late. I had wanted to drive to El Refugio after breakfast and attempt a reconciliation with Evelyn. Well, breakfast would have to wait, as would calling on my girlfriend. First things first. I turned the ignition key and drove off in the direction of Collins's golf club. I wasn't enjoying being cast in the role of the detective in real life—not that I'd ever had a chance to play that good a part in Hollywood.

21

AT THE FIRST TRAFFIC LIGHT I changed my mind, and as it was still early, I decided to drop in on the office of Ramon Galvan, a golfing friend and a lawyer. Galvan, who was born and raised in Madrid, was one of the first lawyers to move south, anticipating the real-estate boom that came to the coast in the late fifties. Beside giving me occasional advice on my taxes, he has been kind enough to play golf with me, a hacker who is not much in demand when it comes to players with a single-figure handicap. Ramon is also one of the rare local professional men who is at his desk at nine o'clock in the morning, which is where I found him after knocking on the door of his office.

"*Bueno . . . vamos a ver,*" he said, very well, let's see, words with which he always began an analysis of any problem I have presented him with in the past. "After making your *denuncia* you have been disturbed by a number of telephone calls, correct?"

"That's right," I said.

"Any threats?"

"Not any specific ones."

"*¿Insultos,* nothing more, *verdad?*" Ramon speaks fairly correct

English, but occasionally adds Spanish words to make his point. "That is nothing unusual," he continued, lighting a cigarette. He put it out at once, remembering that he is trying to stop smoking. *"Vamos a ver,"* he said again. "A few years ago I had a client, a Spanish businessman whose son was robbed on his way home from school. The *chorizos,* the delinquents is the right word, were apprehended. The bicycle and the boy's wallet were found in their possession. My client decided to prosecute them, signed a *denuncia* with the police. Then, as in your case, he began to receive threatening notes and telephone calls. He was worried about his son's welfare. He came to me for advice."

"Just as I have."

"Correct. He wanted to go to the police for help. Did I think that was a good idea? he asked me. Well, I turned the problem over in my mind. I knew that if I advised him to disregard the calls and the threats, and then some harm came to his son, he would blame me, and himself, of course. So I told him to drop the charges against the two boys who had committed the crime. Now your case is a little different. Your daughter, you say, has left town. It is only you who are in jeopardy. Correct?"

"That's right."

"Are you frightened?"

"Disturbed," I said. It was an understatement.

"I see. Then wait a few days. Until the threats become more specific. Be on guard." He paused. "You cannot apply for a permit to carry a gun because you are not a resident."

"So I hear . . . That's the law, isn't it?"

"It is," he said. "But you can carry a stick, a cane, a cane with a sharp point. Or your seven iron." He grinned. "That is all you can do. Later you can always decide not to ratify your *denuncia.* Or if you are sure it is the crippled man who is threatening you, you can report him to the police. But you must be certain."

"I understand."

"Lo siento, Roberto," he said, which means: I feel it, I am sorry.

"Lo siento mas," I replied.

He sighed. "When your arm gets better we can play nine holes whenever you have time."

"I'll call you," I said. I didn't feel reassured. I could see myself fighting off a group of thugs, thrusting and slashing like D'Artagnan. Ramon walked me to the door. "If I wound one of the *chorizos* with my cane, he can bring charges against me, isn't that right?"

"Absolutely," Ramon said. "Unless you can prove that your life was in jeopardy. We live in a democracy."

22

THERE WERE TWO FOURSOMES WAITING on the first tee, and a tall Swede in Bermuda shorts was practicing his swing while waiting for the group of players on the fairway in front of him to hit their second shots. His wife, a plump woman with round white calves, was waiting eagerly off to one side of the red markers of the ladies' tee. Tomás, in charge of the heavy traffic, was standing off to one side holding a clipboard with the day's batting order. He said: "Ball!" in an authoritative tone of voice, and the group on the smooth grass behind him became silent. I waited until the tall Swede had sent his missile into the air, then stepped over the starter.

Tomás acknowledged my *"buenos días"* with a brisk nod. I explained the purpose of my visit, and he listened politely, his eyes on the Swedish couple who had set off down the fairway. Then he shook his head. He had no knowledge of Pedro Fernández's family circumstances, he told me, nor had he had anything to do with the *bolero*'s arrest. Carlitos, the *guarda jurado,* was the man I should question about Pedro. Unfortunately he was out on the course and would probably not be back until ten o'clock, the time allotted to him for his morning break.

I thanked him and walked back to the office of the caddy-master in order to use the pay telephone located there. I punched out Evelyn's number but she had not as yet turned off her tape. It was a quarter to nine, and I decided to have my belated breakfast. I felt hungry, no doubt because of my lack of sleep. The club bar was open to nonmembers, and I knew from past experience that I could get a cup of coffee and a croissant there. I pulled open the sliding door, and to my surprise there was Cecil Collins, seated alone at a table near the bar. He nodded, and waved for me to join him. "What brings you here?" he asked. "Have you got a game?"

It seemed to me that he sounded less friendly than usual so I saw no point in telling him my long story. Anyway, I didn't want to involve him in my amateur sleuthing. Instead, I told him that I was missing a club out of my bag and was merely checking if I had left it behind the day we had played together. "What about you?" I asked. "I thought you were off to London today."

"Late this afternoon," he replied. "Leahy is joining me at nine-thirty for a last walk in the sunshine. And nowadays breakfast here is more peaceful than at home."

I thanked him dutifully for dinner and he nodded. "She's a very attractive woman, your friend," he said. The waiter came over to our table, and I placed my order. "I'm glad for the chance to talk to you," Collins continued, once the man had left us. "Pamela and I had a rather stormy discussion after the guests had departed. Not a very pleasant way to end the evening."

I said: "I'm sorry to hear that. I thought you had come to some sort of an agreement."

"So did I, but that turns out not to be the case." His eyes narrowed. "Among a few other things she divulged last night was that you were spying on me that fateful rainy morning."

I blushed, a habit since puberty I have never managed to get rid of. I said: "I was planning to tell you myself—when the right moment presented itself."

"But it never did, did it?" Collins remarked acidly. "I thought something rather strange was going on when Pamela offered to show you the garden. I know her pretty well. She doesn't play games—like some wives do when they've had a little too much to drink."

I didn't know what to say. I thought it was better to let him finish and then try to explain about Kiko and the rest of the stupid mess I'd blundered into. The waiter arrived with my coffee and croissant, a welcome interruption as far as I was concerned.

"So what are you doing here this morning?" Collins asked. "Continuing the exercise? As well as seeing no harm comes to your employer's husband?"

"No," I said. "Last Tuesday was my one day of glory."

"It's turned out that way, has it?"

I told him about Kiko, and how he had pushed the job of tailing him off on me. Collins nodded. "You must have been fairly desperate," he said. "Evelyn hinted that you had some financial problems, but I had no idea they were that serious." He was still polite, detached, sarcastic. "Of course, your coming along to England with me must have seemed comical to you. If anything, you'll probably turn out to be Pam's star witness."

"No. Not Pamela's and not yours," I said. "I don't want any part of your hassle."

"Do you expect me to believe that? Then what *are* you doing here this morning?"

I told him about the telephone calls and the poison-pen notes that had been left on my car and my discovery of the suspected culprit. He appeared only vaguely interested, interrupted me to warn me that my coffee was getting cold. I went on to tell him that I was going to speak to one of the guards to confirm my suspicions, and if they turned out to be accurate, go to the police again.

He nodded. "Well, I'm tempted to say that you're only getting what you deserve, but I won't." He smiled, pleased with his little jest. "At the same time I can't help recalling your good offices. They almost cancel out your perfidy. Almost, but not quite."

Leahy came into the bar and strolled over to our table. "Ah, Roberto," he said, squeezing my shoulder. "Are you joining us this morning?"

"No," Collins informed him. "Our friend is here in his capacity of private detective."

Leahy raised his eyebrows. "I don't follow you," he said. "Anyway, we'd better get started. There's a crowd of angry Swedes on the first tee."

Collins said: "Not to worry. We have a starting time." He got up from the table. "Can you take care of our breakfast, Robert?" he asked. "Charge it to Pamela's account."

"That won't be necessary," I told him.

I watched them leave. Then I finished my coffee and croissant and went out to find Tomás. I had to wait on the first tee for a quarter of an hour until Carlos, the guard, arrived on his motorbike. He was a heavyset man with glasses and a ruddy face. He wore an official-looking cap on his round head and had a tarnished brass badge on his windbreaker. A sturdy German shepherd accompanied him. Tomás explained what I wanted to know, and the guard looked dubious. He asked me to follow him to the parking lot so that we could talk without disturbing the golfers.

It turned out that he knew me by sight, he lived in San Pedro not far from Kiko's office. He was acquainted with Pedro Fernández's family, he said, had known them for a good many years. I asked him whether Pedro had an invalided brother, and he shook his head. *"Primo,"* he said, cousin, correcting me. The man had been a bricklayer until he had been injured in an accident on a building site some years ago. I showed him the note that had been left on my car, and he shrugged. Had I seen the man do it? he asked. I told him that I hadn't, but that the handwriting could be verified by the police in case I made a *denuncia*.

He seemed even more doubtful. Pedro also had a sister, he informed me, which explained the woman's scarf in the back of the

Seat. It was possible that she had written the note. But a *denuncia,* he added, might be premature. *"Son gente peligrosa,"* dangerous people. It might be more prudent, was the way he put it, to talk with them first.

"Talk with them!" I made no attempt to hide my astonishment. "You just said they were dangerous people."

He sat astride his motorbike, looking down at his dog. *"Sí,"* he said, nodding. But they were *"una pobre gente también. Desgraciados."*

Poor people or not, the man had attacked me with a knife, I told Carlos.

"No sé," came the reply. It could also be that the man was only defending himself.

I recalled what Bill Leahy had said—that Collins and I would always be considered to be outsiders. Wasn't it information supplied by the guards that had resulted in Pedro Fernández's arrest? I asked. Carlos became even more reticent. Several other *boleros* had been under suspicion. Fernández was the only one among them who had a criminal record, which was why the Guardia Civil had arrested him.

What was the point of talking to these people? I asked. To warn them, he replied, so that they would stop molesting me. Would he come with me? I asked. Again Carlos hesitated. He was willing to show me where they lived, he said, and we agreed on a place to meet late that afternoon, a café near the old lighthouse in the center of town. El Tropical was the name of the place.

He went off on his motorbike, his dog trotting after him. Collins was right, I was only getting what I deserved. I wasn't at all sure that calling on the Fernández family was a good idea but going back to the Guardia Civil was an equally dubious course of action. They would be reluctant to arrest Pedro's *primo* on such a flimsy complaint, would issue a warning, which with Carlos's assistance I could do myself. It was worth a try. I would ask Kiko to accompany me, which might be enough to frighten them and put a stop to the nuisance calls and threatening notes. I had the rest of the day to think it over. In the meantime I had a more pressing problem to solve.

23

IT WAS A QUARTER TO ELEVEN when I got to El Refugio. I stood for an instant outside Evelyn's front door, remembering the countless times I had arrived there in the past as a friend and later on as a lover. In the spring and summer the smell of the *damas de noche* in her garden had never failed to increase my feelings of pleasant anticipation, and in the wet weather of winter there had often been the smell of the wood fire burning inside her living room. On this day there was only the cool wind of late winter that I couldn't help feel was a warning that I had begun to take her friendship for granted. Hesitantly, I knocked on the door with the brass knocker.

Kathy Vernon stood facing me, the customary cigarette in her mouth. "It's Robert," she called out by way of a greeting. "How are you this morning?" she asked as an afterthought.

"As well as can be expected," I said, and kissed her cheeks rather reluctantly. Evelyn came out of the bedroom. She was dressed in jeans and boots and a cashmere sweater I had given her as a Christmas present.

"Good morning," she said briskly. "I wasn't expecting you."

The faded jeans reminded me of my youth, like so many things do nowadays.

"I came by to tell you that I'm sorry about last night," I said.

"Shall I buzz off?" Kathy asked with a little smile. "Isn't that what you expect me to say, Roberto?"

"We can go into the bedroom," I replied.

"Oh, don't bother. I have a few chores to take care of before I leave town. So I might as well go now." She crushed her cigarette in the ashtray. "See you, Ev," she added. The door fell shut behind her.

I muttered: "Cunt," before I could control myself, and because I'd wanted to say exactly that before.

Evelyn looked pained. "That kind of remark is not particularly endearing," she said. "Today of all days."

"I'm not running for sheriff," I replied.

She crossed to the fireplace. "Kathy and I are going to Marrakech for ten days," Evelyn said. "I need a rest."

"Are they working you that hard at the china shop?"

"No. I just want to get away for a while."

"From the rain, or from me?"

"A little of both," she said. "You agreed last night, remember? That we needed a vacation from each other."

"I was pissed off."

"What an elegant way to put it."

"I apologize. Where are you planning to stay?"

"We don't know yet. I'll send you a postcard."

"That would be nice." I was upset. "Well, have a good trip. Call when you get back."

"I will." She sounded reluctant.

"What about Hercules?"

"He's going to a kennel."

"Poor Hercules."

"He'll be all right. So will you, I'm sure."

"I'll do my best," I told her, and that was the end of our conversation.

I noticed that my hand was trembling slightly as I unlocked my car. A sign of age, no doubt, of not being able to cope any longer with a lovers' quarrel. I drove to my house. The sky had turned gray and the wind had subsided. The rain was about to return. I noticed that the shutters on the upstairs windows were open. Maria, my maid, had returned to duty, I discovered, once I had climbed up the flagstone steps and walked through the open front door. She smiled and greeted me warmly, looking pretty and rested after her week's holiday.

I listened to her complaints about the Belgian tenants, to her account of how hard she had been forced to work. She hoped, she said, that I would never rent the house again. I told her that I would have to, because of the crisis—and wrote out a check for her last two months' wages. Yes, the crisis, she agreed, it was affecting everyone. Many people were out of work in the *pueblo,* and shops were closing every day. I told her that I might be moving in for a couple of weeks while the agent I had used before was looking for new tenants.

I left her to her hoovering and unlocked the door of the spare bedroom where I had stored the things I didn't need to take with me when I had moved to Kiko's apartment. The first suitcase I opened turned out to contain some of the old photo albums I had started many years ago and never finished. There were a few stills from my earliest movies, a portrait of Phyliss by a Beverly Hills photographer that showed her smiling mysteriously, probably inspired by the Mona Lisa, as well as a few shots of both of us taken while I was still in uniform. It was a reminder of the distant past I could do without at that moment, but I went on to open the second warped album, which turned out to be slightly better value.

There was a picture of Sue Wilson standing in front of my shack in Trancas, taken on one of our illicit afternoons and which proved women's hair styles had come the full circle, one or two snapshots of Harry Lessing and myself on a duck-hunting trip in northern California that made me realize how much my tastes had changed the thought of shooting anything having become abhorrent since the end of the war. There was also a yellowed photograph of my father's bookshop on 4th Street in Santa Monica, the old man standing in front of the shop's awning. I also came on a photograph of Naomi standing on the steps of the Prado in Madrid, and one of her in a bathing suit on the terrace of a café in St. Tropez, and a few blank pages beyond, a couple of faded pictures of Amanda and myself about to enter the bullring in Ronda during the early days of our unhappy marriage.

By that time I had had enough of old memories, and I put the albums back into the suitcase, locked the door of the spare bedroom, having decided to leave everything as it was until I moved back into my house should that prove to be necessary once I had gone to see Pedro Fernández's family later that afternoon. Maria came upstairs to tell me that she had to leave early but would be back in the morning to continue her cleaning. I said: *"Bien, hasta mañana,"* which was the usual password on this coast, and she went off in her ancient car.

I was in no mood for a solitary lunch. The weather was deteriorating rapidly, the sea already a dark gray all the way to the horizon, so I decided I would try to find Kiko and get that unpleasant matter over with as well. I picked up the telephone in my bedroom but the line was dead, the Belgians having failed to honor that obligation as well. I knew that Pepe would not be making an appearance because of the threat of rain, so I closed the shutters on the upstairs windows and set off for San Pedro. It was a quarter to one, and I knew my son-in-law would still be in his office. Later on I planned to drop in on the real-estate agent who had rented my house to the Belgians in order to find out if there was a chance to recuperate the rent they owed me, as well as look for more dependable clients.

Kiko was in the process of double-locking the door of his office when I arrived. A small black dog on a leash stood behind him, wagging its tail. Kiko said: *"Hola,"* and reversed the key on his double lock. "Come in for a minute," he added in a surly voice. I followed him inside. The television set was on, an extra precaution my son-in-law favored against a possible break-in. "Your daughter has flown the coop," he said, securing the dog's leash to the leg of a chair.

"I know all about it," I told him. "She called me from the airport."

"Did you give her the money for the trip?" he asked, staring at me with sullen, bloodshot eyes.

"You know me better than that," I said. The dog had managed to approach me, pulling the chair with it. I leaned down to pet it.

"Sit, Susie!" its master commanded without success. "I got her yesterday from the pound. To take the place of the bitch that left me," Kiko explained, "Only I'm going to have this one fixed—so she won't come in heat all the time."

"I'm her father . . . remember," I said, a mild warning.

He seemed not to have heard me. "I suppose her boyfriend supplied the cash for her air tickets," he said. "That would be just like him, the shit."

"Nobody ever steals anybody's girl. Most men seem to have a habit of driving their women away."

"You think it's normal for a woman to run out on her family?" he asked rhetorically. "She should see a shrink."

"She'll be back after Easter."

"As far as I'm concerned she can stay away," Kiko said. "It's hard on Tommy but he'll get over it. He's crazy about the dog. And Isabel . . . well, if she takes after her mother I might as well get used to living without her, too." He shook his head. "What about you?" he asked. "Are you going to move back into your house?"

"Probably. I haven't decided yet." I told him about the man with the wheelchair, and he listened, looking bored.

"So you won't need protection, is that it? A cripple! What the hell! That's no threat! Anyway, I can't spare one of my boys right now."

"Collins is going to London today, and Lady Pamela has confessed all . . . that she hired me to follow him. He insinuated that I behaved like a shit, and I couldn't argue with him."

"Well, there are plenty of the other jobs around," Kiko replied. "Crime is still booming." He lit a cigarette. He seemed nervous. "You want to have lunch?" he asked.

"Thanks, but I think I'll pass," I told him.

He shrugged. "You know what they used to say about women," he went on. "If they didn't have a pair of tits and that thing between their legs, there'd be a bounty on them. People would be out gunning for them, like vermin."

He was a male chauvinist pig, my son-in-law, a charter member of the club. I didn't laugh. I'd heard the remark before. I got up, patted the dog and left. What had taken Susan so long to leave him? I wondered, and crossed the hallway to my apartment and cooked myself a couple of fried eggs and bacon, a lunch high in cholesterol that I felt I could somehow manage to survive. Stress is more harmful than animal fat, I have been told, and a meal with Kiko in his—and my—present state of mind was bound to be damned stressful.

24

AFTER I HAD FRESHENED FERGY'S SANDBOX and straightened out my bed I decided to take a brief nap. I lay down on top of the covers and discovered that my heartbeat was more audible than usual. Cleaning up after Fergy and making my bed had not been a strenuous chore, so I was alarmed. As I am not a hypochondriac, I realized at once that my scene with Evelyn was probably the cause, but at my age any irregularity of the ticker is not a thing a man should disregard. I checked the audible pulsations against the second hand of my watch but lost count at my first try. Then on my second attempt I found that my heartbeat was only slightly quicker than normal. Somewhat reassured, I lay there, and after a while took up the count again. Ninety has always been a normal number for my heart, and after setting the alarm on my bedside clock for four o'clock, I dozed off.

I awoke at ten to four, put on my sneakers and set off for Cecilia Roberts's real-estate office. Before meeting Evelyn I had dined occasionally with Cecilia, dates that never progressed beyond a platonic friendship, mainly because she was at that time living with a young deckhand who worked on a rich Arab's yacht anchored more or less permanently in the local yacht harbor.

Cecilia's appearance had not changed much since our last meeting two years ago. She was a little plumper but still pretty, although she had changed her hairstyle to the frizzy look that she assured me was more practical than the way she had worn her hair before. Black women were straightening their hair, and blondes were choosing tight curls, it occurred to me as I sat facing her in her small office, a cubicle in the local marina where her sailor is employed.

He was still living with her, she confided in me, and all was well in the "romance" department. Then I asked her about the Belgians. She was astonished, admitted that she had not checked on my tenants lately and went to her files to look for a possible address in Brussels they might have given her. Did I mind waiting? she asked. I told her that I had plenty of time and wandered to the window to look at the yachts at anchor outside.

She would write them a firm letter, she said, returning to her desk, although she was not hopeful that it would produce results.

"Did they leave a deposit to cover breakage and the telephone bill?" I asked her.

"They were meant to," Cecilia replied, "but I don't think they ever got around to it. My fault, I'm afraid."

"That's great . . . so what do we do now?"

She spread her white hands, which I noticed were adorned with a great number of golden rings of all sizes. "I really don't know," she said. "I'll write them, and we can only hope for a positive answer."

"Which will probably not be forthcoming."

"They seemed like such a nice couple."

"So nice they didn't think it necessary to pay the maid, *or* the phone bill."

She said: "I *am* sorry, Roberto."

"You can make amends by finding me some even nicer tenants

for *Semana Santa*," I told her. "The kind that will pay in advance." I got up to kiss her well-powdered cheeks.

"Of course. We always do that on short rentals." She smiled. She had nice teeth. "How's Evelyn?" she asked.

"Fine. How's your beau?"

"Still swabbing the rich Arab's decks," she said, and shrugged. "It's a job. How's your golf?"

"No better." I had reached the door. The west wind was making the riggings creak on the sailing yachts moored in the vicinity. "Have you got the phone number of my flat?" I asked Cecilia.

"I'm sure I do."

"Well, call me if you find a sucker."

She laughed daintily. "We might have dinner some night," she said.

"Anytime," I told her. "I'm as free as a bird . . . an elderly bird, unfortunately." I closed the door firmly to secure it against the breeze.

25

It was a quarter past five when I arrived at El Tropical. Carlos was standing on the sidewalk outside the café. He was still wearing his windbreaker, but had abandoned his cap and badge. I waved to him and he crossed the street and got into my car. *"Buenas tardes,"* he said politely. Did I mind if he smoked, he asked once he had settled himself in the front seat next to me. I told him I didn't mind and asked him where we were going. He would direct me, he told me, and we started off. The first raindrops had appeared on my windshield as we drove through the town.

"Mal tiempo," Carlos observed.

I agreed. When I was a young man an older and wiser friend warned me that if I continued smoking I would lose my sense of smell. I paid no attention to him for many years, and he turned out to be wrong. My olfactory powers seem to have increased, which I am conscious of only too frequently. My companion's windbreaker, I reckoned, must have weathered many a storm and sudden heat wave. Ignoring the light rain, I cranked down the window on my side of the car once we had turned off into the old part of town. Carlos indicated a parking place in the square opposite the oldest

147

church in the *barrio,* and we continued on foot down one of the narrow streets that can accommodate only one vehicle proceeding in the posted direction. My companion was breathing heavily, proof that he had become too dependent on his motorbike.

We passed a small bar with the usual beaded curtain in the entryway, and Carlos suggested we stop in for a *café con leche.* We were a little too early, he told me—for what I couldn't guess. As I followed him inside a youth on a powerful Japanese motorcycle came roaring down the empty street, heading the wrong way. Carlos shook his head. *"Los chorizos,"* he said. They do what they like, they have no respect for the law. Spain had changed. Everything had gotten worse. People had no manners. Everything was deteriorating. He glanced up at the yellowed bullfight posters over the bar. There were no brave bulls anymore either, no *toreros.*

A pretty girl appeared to take our orders. Carlos asked for an *anís seco* to drink with his coffee. I declined to join him. The girl went off for a fresh bottle. Her bottom half was enclosed in tight exercise pants, we both noticed. The only thing that has improved in Spain are the women, Carlos stated. *"Y mucho,"* he added with a grin.

It was getting dark outside. Why were we too early? I asked. Because, Carlos explained, Pedro's sister would probably still be in bed. She was a dancer and worked all night in a flamenco club. It would be better to arrive once she was awake and dressed. Then after a long pause he went on to say that he would indicate the house we were looking for but would not join me in my meeting with Rafael, the *primo.* It would only cause more trouble if he stayed on. I regretted not having asked Kiko to accompany me, but given the mood he was in, he would probably have refused to join me.

We sipped our coffees. Carlos consulted his watch, then tossed off his *anís. "Vámonos,"* he said. He insisted on paying the bill, and we stepped out into the rain. Together we walked up the narrow street. The low white houses, one exactly like the other, looked less picturesque seen from close quarters, rabbit hutches with peeling, whitewashed walls. Here and there an attempt to decorate a dwelling had been made, a green door, a pot overflowing with geraniums. It was a cheap housing project from another time, but still better than the new high-rise tenements.

We turned a corner. Another narrow white street lay ahead. Number twenty-three, Carlos informed me, fifty yards on your right. *"Hasta otra día,"* he said, turning back.

I thanked him for his help and continued on alone. Number twenty-three had a scarlet door that looked as if it had been recently repainted. There was no doorbell so I knocked on the rough wooden planks with my knuckles. There was no reply. I waited for a minute or two and knocked again. The rain was falling steadily and I was about to leave when the door was pulled open. A woman in a faded blue dressing gown stood facing me. She had dark hair that fell in loose strands to her shoulders. Her pale, oval face was unlined. Her dark eyes looked me up and down with hostile suspicion. *"¿Que quiere?"* she asked in a deep voice.

I said: *"Buenas tardes,"* and told her that I was looking for Rafael, who I believed was her cousin.

"No está," she replied.

"But he lives here, doesn't he?" I asked.

She shook her head. "He comes here sometimes," she said in English, with only a trace of an accent.

"You speak English?" I asked, surprised.

"Doesn't it sound like it?" She frowned. "I worked in London," she said. "For two years. You are the American," she added, "who lives in San Pedro."

"Well, one of them," I told her.

She didn't seem to appreciate the attempted joke. She shivered and pulled the dressing gown tightly around her thin body. "When I see Rafael I will ask him to telephone you," she said. "What is your number?"

"He knows it," I said. "That's why I've come here. I want him to stop calling me."

She pressed her lips tightly together until they formed a straight line. It didn't improve her looks. "I will tell him you were here," she said. She stepped back. "I'm Pedro's sister," she added, and closed the door in my face.

I stood there in the rain like a rejected Fuller-brush salesman. For an instant I was tempted to pound my fist on the red boards directly in front of my nose, but I knew it would be useless. A battered beige Lada, an early model of the Russian four-wheel-drive vehicle, came slowly down the street. Its driver, a gray-haired man with a broad, bearded face, stared out at me, then increased the Lada's speed, splashing an old woman dressed in black who had appeared in the doorway behind me. *"Cabrón,"* she said, and spat into the muddy rainwater flowing past her slippered feet. I was in enemy country.

26

I TOOK THE OLD ROAD HOME. I had plenty of time, and I knew that way I would have a better chance to dry out, because the heater in my car was more effective than the electric fire in my flat. It had been an even more enervating day than the day before, a waste of time and emotion. I felt depressed. I turned on the car radio to block out the scraping of the windshield wipers. From six to eight the British-run local radio station plays jazz and old favorites, a welcome relief from hard rock.

The first song that evening took me back to the war, the good times you remember once you have blocked out the bad. "Don't sit under the apple tree with anyone else but me!" a trio of girls' voices chanted, a suitable lyric for the time, even if you had been a fairly active sailor like myself. Popular music was capable of stirring up all kinds of memories, producing instant nostalgia. Would the currently popular music be capable of producing a similar effect for the poor bastards who were young today, I wondered, the senselessly repeated phrases of songs that barely had any melody? Or was nostalgia a thing of the past, along with romantic love? You are getting to be a surly old man, I told myself. Watch it!

I made my way back to my small apartment. The sky outside my rain-splattered window was black. I fed Fergy the remains of a can of cat food which she devoured in a matter of minutes. Then I crawled into bed, and went to sleep almost immediately.

The telephone woke me. Another nuisance call, I reckoned, and was tempted not to pick up the receiver. I noticed that I had forgotten to switch off the lamp on my night table. It was a few minutes past midnight. I had slept more than five hours. The telephone rang on and I reached out for it, ready to give Rafael, or whoever else was calling, the full blast of my rage at being disturbed.

Before anyone came on the line I heard Spanish music, a *buleria* punctuated by the clicking of castanets. *"Soy Carmen,"* a woman's voice whispered huskily after a while.

A wrong number! *"Equivocación,"* I snarled.

"No . . . no!" the woman insisted. "You came to see Rafael . . . this afternoon."

"And who are you?"

"Pedro's sister," she said. "It was impossible for me to talk, so I am calling you now."

"Why was it impossible?" I asked angrily.

"I was not alone. But if you have time now we can meet."

"It's late!"

"Sí. I know." She paused. "I am at Marisa's. *El tablao flamenco.* You know the place?"

"Yes, I know it." Marisa's is a tourist trap in the old part of town, a flamenco club that stays open all night.

"I can meet you in the bar, if you want," the woman said.

"I can't come now," I said. "I'm in bed."

"As you like."

She hung up. I sat up. I was wide awake. I pulled the covers up around my shoulders and turned off the light. There was a sharp, metallic sound, as if someone had shot a pellet at my window. I turned on the light again. I had forgotten to close the shutters, I noticed, and got out of bed to do so. A sudden burst of wind blew the curtains back into my face, made them billow out into the room. It was like a scene in a cheap suspense movie, the kind you don't believe but that make you nervous just the same. I latched the shutters into place. I was becoming paranoid. Shivering from the cold, I climbed back into my bed. Fergy arched her back and stared at me with black frightened eyes. Her tail looked as if it belonged on the cap of Davy Crockett. I took the receiver off its cradle. Then it occurred to me that Evelyn might call to tell me that she missed me. She had done so before, not that many years ago. As a precaution I returned the reassembled telephone to its usual place. Sleep was out of the question.

I got up and slipped into my clothes. Marisa's was a public locale. Nothing much could happen to me if I went there, I felt certain. So I collected my golf umbrella and put on a dry pair of shoes. But I was less than relaxed once I stepped out into the dark street. I got into my car and drove through the empty town. There was more traffic when I arrived in Marbella. A few bars were still open for business in the old quarter. I found my way to the small square and stopped in front of Marisa's club. Paco, the parking attendant, recognized me. *"Muchos años,"* he said with a smile as I handed him my keys. *"Sí, Paco."* It had been years since I had been there, I agreed. I had been a frequent customer in the days before the place had started catering exclusively to tourists.

The bar near the entrance was crowded with local hangers-on that preferred to watch the show without being seated at one of the small tables. A young gypsy in black trousers and a white shirt was doing a *zapatéo* to the music of a guitarist. Marisa got up from her chair near the dance floor and came over to embrace me. She had gained a lot of weight, was bulging out of her red-and-white polka-dot gypsy costume. "Roberto!" she exclaimed as I leaned forward to kiss her glistening cheeks. I was alone, I told her, and would prefer to stand at the bar, to which she agreed somewhat reluctantly.

153

I ordered a vodka and tonic and wedged myself into a place near the door. The young gypsy was concluding his frenetic routine, urged on by the staccato handclapping of the troupe of entertainers seated behind him on the small stage. There were three women, and two men dressed in black, with two guitarists off to one side of them. The boy was good, graceful and passionate, but the seated audience, made up mostly of tourists, responded with only mild applause. The men beside me at the bar were more supportive, contributing a few muted shouts of *olé*, which was probably what they were there for, a claque of locals who were supplied with cheap drinks for their efforts.

I surveyed the dimly lit room, searching for Pedro's sister. Marisa had moved out onto the dance floor and was clutching a microphone. I knew what was coming, her Sinatra imitation of "Strangers in the Night." It earned her spontaneous applause. She curtsied, picked up her skirt, and joined me at the bar. "Ay, Roberto," she sighed. "How is my English?"

I said: *"Fantástico!"* and she chuckled happily.

One of the female dancers had ventured out onto the dance floor, her thin body encased in a bright red dress.

"This one is good," Marisa confided in me. "Velly, velly good. Not so young anymore. Like me."

The woman in red had started to dance a *buleria*. I studied her face. Marisa ordered a whiskey and water. "Watch her," she whispered. *"Se llama Carmen."*

It was Pedro's sister, I realized. She looked totally different. Her dark hair was pulled straight back, and she wore a red carnation in the knot of hair at the back of her head. There was a fierce beauty about her as she danced, her arms high in the air, her hands executing the classic flamenco movements. Her girlish figure, swelling slightly near the top of her dress, expressed a voluptuousness that was startling, more startling even when I recalled how she had looked in the faded blue dressing gown not that many hours ago.

Marisa, standing beside me, had lit a cigarette that dangled from her mouth as she clapped her pudgy hands, producing a sound like repeated pistol shots. Her *olés* rose above the noise she and the others of the troupe were making. Her enthusiasm was genuine, persuasive. "Does she dance here every night?" I asked.

Marisa shook her head while continuing her *palmas. "La chica tiene una vida complicada,"* she replied.

That the girl had a complicated life didn't surprise me. I sipped my drink. The *buleria* seemed to have reached its climax, but then continued. The carnation was catapulted to the back of the stage by a violent movement of Carmen's head. Her hair cascaded down. She flung it back. She wasn't called Carmen for nothing, I found myself thinking. The young gypsy had gotten up from his chair to dance with her; with her and around her, but only rarely touching her with outstretched arms. The beat quickened, the dancers climaxing again and again, until finally the end came, the movement and the clapping stopped and dissolved into a wave of wild applause. Carmen dropped her head to acknowledge the ovation, then scooped up her hair and knotted it into place again. One of the old guitarists retrieved the carnation and handed it to her with a solemn bow. She dropped her head and curtsied, then went off quickly to the right, returned once more an instant later and trotted off to join Marisa, who had stepped forward to welcome her. They exchanged kisses. Then together they moved to a place beside me at the bar. I was still applauding when she recognized me. "Will you have a drink?" I asked her.

She nodded, turned to the bartender and mumbled something in Spanish. "You changed your mind," she said, and managed a brief smile.

I said: "Yes, and I'm glad I did."

"But I can't talk now," she informed me, still breathless. "Will you wait until after the show?"

"I might as well now that I'm here," I said. I didn't mean it to sound impolite, but the young woman looked puzzled, then turned quickly to the bartender. He handed her a tall glass of water, which she drank thirstily. The guitarists had resumed their efforts. I recognized the music, a *Sevillana,* and Carmen went off to join the other dancers of the troupe in the innocent, lovely patterns of that, probably the most charming of Spanish dances.

Marisa had joined the group. She waved to me. *"¡Roberto! ¡Ven!"* she called out, probably because she remembered that years ago I had joined one of her *Sevillana* classes at the house of a Spanish friend whose wife had been eager to improve her limited talents. I shook my head and blew Marisa a kiss. I didn't feel like making a fool of myself. I hadn't had enough to drink yet.

27

ONCE THE *Sevillanas* HAD ENDED one of the other gypsies ventured out onto the floor to dance an uninspired *buleria*. Her frenzied efforts seemed forced. She was a blonde and she had thick ankles and square knees, none of which helped. Her male partner was less graceful than the boy who had danced with Carmen. Throughout the number Carmen sat at the back of the stage with the other performers, clapping her hands mechanically and adding an occasional shout of encouragement that was barely audible. But most of the time she stared off into the distance, giving the impression that her mind was elsewhere, well outside the confines of the noisy room. Was she remembering better days, I wondered, when as a young dancer full of illusions and dedicated to her art she had appeared with a more talented ensemble in front of a more knowing audience? Or was she considering the trouble her brother had gotten into, although I suspected that by this time she had become accustomed to his encounters with the police. That there was a near-tragic quality about her appearance was undeniable. Despite the red gown and her slicked back dark hair she looked as if she had been treated pretty harshly by life, a victim of poverty that her inborn talent had not made it possible for her to escape.

Then it was once again the turn of the young man who had danced the *zapatéo*. He sang now without a microphone, a *soléa* that was moving enough but well outside the ken of the audience he was facing. There was mild applause, and Marisa rose, full of animated chubbiness, while the music changed to a *rumbita* that was more to her public's liking. The usual procedure of singling out a spectator to dance with her followed. An elderly Englishman was dragged out onto the floor, an embarrassing spectacle. The other two women in the troupe followed their boss's lead, which led to general hilarity and the raucous shouts of the wives and friends belonging to the inept and, for the most part, unwilling participants in the fun.

Carmen had remained seated, was still clapping her hands mechanically, looking down at the floor. Marisa shouted to her, urging her to join in the dancing. The tall Englishman she had chosen as her first victim had escaped and returned hurriedly to his table. Undaunted, Marisa danced off in my direction, leering happily at me. I knew what she had in mind and retreated to the far corner of the bar. I resisted her for a few seconds, then was dragged out onto the dance floor. I did the box step that I had learned almost half a century ago, raising my right arm and twirling the fingers of my hand. *"¡Muy bien, Roberto!"* Marisa shouted. She looked off to her left, noticing that a new party had entered the locale. Once again she shouted a command to Carmen and went off to greet new customers. I started to follow her, but was intercepted by Carmen.

"¿Bailamos?"

I couldn't tell if it was an invitation or a command. Not that it mattered. It would have been *mal-educado* to refuse. It was part of her job to entertain the customers. Her face was expressionless, her thin body erect. Only her feet and arms moved to the rhythm of the *rumbita,* the dance that by the purists is considered to be a modern bastardization of true flamenco. Then after a few more steps she executed a graceful spin and, taking my arm, danced me back to my place at the bar, making it look like a perfectly executed exit.

We stood facing each other for an instant, and I leaned forward to kiss her cheek. She recoiled, and I felt foolish. She must have known that I wasn't coming on to her. I could only guess that dancing with me for even a minute or two had seemed to her to be a betrayal of her brother, or something like that. I was annoyed. My coming to meet her at Marisa's had been her idea. I watched her go off to join the others at the back of the stage. The guitarists were putting away their instruments, and the dancers were chatting among themselves, sauntering toward a side door. It was the normal intermission. The two waiters, whose job it was to serve the seated guests, were already taking orders for a second round. I signaled the barman and asked for my check. Marisa came over to me, mopping her face with a handkerchief.

"*¿Te vas?*" she asked. She looked down at her wrist. She wasn't wearing a watch. "*¿Tan pronto?*" I recalled that it was her favorite little joke.

I told her that I had to get up early, and paid for my drink. It took a while for me to retrieve my umbrella. Then I stepped outside into the deserted square. It had stopped raining. Paco, the parking attendant, was nowhere to be seen. My car was boxed in by a Mercedes with Sevilla plates. To no avail I yelled for Paco, waited for a little while, then started back toward the club. From a distance I noticed someone was standing in the doorway. It was Carmen. She had draped a black shawl around her shoulders, which made her look like a character out of a play by García Lorca, except that she was smoking a cigarette.

A car came slowly up the street, a yellow Seat coupé, the same year as Fernández's cousin's car. For an instant I thought I had been set up, after all. Then I realized that the driver was an elderly woman with blonde hair and a heavily made-up face. "You like girl?" she called out to me.

I said: *"No gracias, señora,"* and she gave me the finger, probably because the word *señora* had offended her, although she was clearly no *señorita.*

I started back toward the club. Carmen hadn't moved, the light over the entrance shining down on her dark hair like a stage spot. "I finish in an hour," she said in a low voice, tossed her cigarette into the gutter and went inside. Paco appeared from nowhere. I was annoyed with all of them.

"Mis llaves," I called out to him.

"Los tiene la jefa," he explained. Why he had given my car keys to Marisa he didn't bother to say. An American limousine pulled up and four Arabs got out. Paco got into the oversized car and drove off. Cursing to myself, I followed the party of Arabs back into the club.

The barman was busy making drinks. I noticed that Carmen had returned to her chair. Marisa was standing center stage, getting ready to launch herself into one of her songs. She glanced back in my direction.

"¡Mis llaves!" I called out to her.

She smiled, snapping her fingers to the beat of the music. Then she reached inside her bosom and held up my key ring for an instant before dropping it back inside her dress. *"Luego,"* she shouted, *"más tarde."* She was convinced that she was being adorable, *muy flamenca.* "Espain is different!" she chirped in a high voice.

There wasn't anything I could do. I would have to wait until she finished her rendition of "Granada," another of her favorite numbers. I turned back to the barman and ordered a third vodka and tonic. Paco, the missing parking attendant, had come into the bar. He grinned at me and pointed to Marisa, then spread his hands in a gesture of helplessness. I didn't feel tired anymore. The beat of the *palmas* and castanets was echoing inside my head. For the first time in years I knew that Evelyn would not be expecting me to call in the morning.

28

A COLLEAGUE DURING MY DAYS IN ALMERÍA, a Spanish actor who had been a bullfighter in his youth, once told me an anecdote that I recalled now as I stood listening to Marisa sing. After one of his triumphs in the bullring during the spring *feria* in Granada, he and his *banderillero de confianza* had ventured into one of the caves where flamenco is performed by the local gypsies. Recognizing him as the hero of the day, the leader of the gypsy band had ordered the door to the cave to be nailed shut, making an early exit impossible. It turned out, so the anecdote went, that it was all a plot arranged by one of the girls in the troupe who had fallen in love with my actor-bullfighter friend and was making sure that he would not escape until dawn.

Was I being detained in a similar manner? I found myself wondering—had Carmen enlisted Marisa's help, it being her intention to do everything possible to get her brother out of jail? It seemed unlikely, but it was a possible explanation. I *was* getting paranoid, I decided. Or perhaps the vodka and tonics were merely taking their toll.

Marisa finished her number with a flourish, curtsied, beamed at the table of Arabs and sat down on the narrow bench near the bar. She fanned her neck and cleavage and patted her chest with her small handkerchief. Then she motioned for me to join her on the bench. *"¡Que calor!"* she whispered, and sighed. She searched for my key ring that had slipped down inside her dress, found it, giggled and handed it back to me. "A yoke," she explained. "You must stay. *Un ratito más.* Now I buy you a drink."

It was the turn of the blonde woman to dance again. The young Arabs amused themselves at her expense. Marisa frowned. She hissed for them to be quiet. In Spanish she informed me that all *Moros* believe that any woman who danced for a living was a *puta,* and that was probably true in their country. They were her least favorite clients. *"¡Ay, Roberto!"* she sighed. *"Que vida."* She called to a passing waiter and ordered a *whiskycito* for herself and another vodka tonic for me.

A brief intermission followed. Then the entire ensemble danced *Sevillanas.* The troupe appeared to be enjoying themselves, performing the less strenuous routine that children learn to do at an early age. Once they had all returned to their chairs, Carmen rose from her place, and after waiting for her audience to settle down, she began a *soléa* that once again showed off her exceptional talent.

She was a star. There was no doubt about that. It seemed to me that it was strange that she had come down to performing in this kind of a place. But then she was no longer in her prime, no longer had the flashy good looks of the young women who were in demand in Seville and Madrid. Beauty and talent were expendable in her profession. There were always plenty of Andalusian girls who knew how to dance; perhaps not as expertly as their seniors but they had better bodies and smoother skins, *más guapa,* that seemingly most important attribute a young woman could possess in this country.

Carmen danced on, oblivious to her surroundings. Despite her thin figure she was able to transmit a sensuality that held her audience in awe, even silenced the Arabs in their navy blue suits and slicked-down black hair. I reckoned it made them dream of possessing a woman with Carmen's energy and dynamic grace. Nor were they alone in this, I felt, looking around at the other tables where men sat with their overweight wives, golf companions, but not what their husbands craved for in their erotic fantasies.

Carmen's *soléa* was having an effect on me, too. Was that the secret reason she had asked me to come there? Again I recalled how she had looked earlier in the evening—in her blue bathrobe, with her hair undone, shivering in the damp air. She was no longer the *bolero*'s sister, she was establishing her identity, as she did every night. Only tonight, I began to suspect, she had a special reason. She wanted to demonstrate to me who she was so that she could meet me on an even footing.

I couldn't help thinking of Pamela Collins and the sheltered existence she had enjoyed once she had married Sir Cecil. I knew that the comparison was not a legitimate one, but it was inevitable at that moment. After all, it was the ridiculous circumstance of our chance meeting that had brought me here. And Evelyn basking in the desert sunshine hundreds of miles to the south, with Kathy, the well-provided-for divorcée. Was I falling in love? I asked myself as I sat watching the final flourishes of Carmen's *soléa*. My mind was anything but clear.

She acknowledged the applause that rewarded her performance with a deep curtsy and returned to her chair. Then once she had repaired the damage to her hairdo, she resumed her minor function of clapping her hands, *palmas* that were meant to sustain the mood and help encourage whatever act was to follow. But the intensity of her *soléa* seemed to have ended the evening. Now there was a general restlessness in the audience, people calling for their bills and getting up from their chairs.

Marisa rose from her place on the narrow bench beside me, still fanning herself, and made her way to the bar. I joined her there. It was a quarter to four in the morning. *"Se acaba la fiesta,"* she said, the party is over.

Carmen's chair at the back of the stage was empty. I noticed that Paco had left the bar, probably to devote himself to his chore of disentangling the vehicles parked under the trees outside. I asked again for my check and the barman held up his hand, pleading for patience while he took care of the scraps of paper the two waiters had handed him in order to collect from some of the other customers. Half an hour later I was at last able to settle my account. I kissed Marisa's glowing cheeks and shouldered my way through the crowd at the door. It started to rain again as I stepped outside, and I realized that I had come away without my umbrella and went back to get it.

I waited in the shelter of the doorway, then walked over to where my car was parked. Paco was busy shouting instructions to the various drivers who were attempting to leave without damaging their cars. I unlocked the door on the driver's side, and as I did so became aware of someone standing behind me. It was Carmen. She was wearing jeans and a Navy pea jacket that had seen better days. *"¿A dónde vas?"* she asked me.

"Donde tu quieras," I told her. Wherever you want to go.

29

"¡RAFAEL!" SHE WHISPERED and slid down into the space in front of her with the same ease with which she had lifted herself into the passenger seat after getting in on my side of the car. She sounded angry rather than alarmed.

I caught a glimpse of a man on crutches moving down the sidewalk on the far side of the square. He lowered his head as we passed. I turned down a narrow street, and Carmen sat back in her place beside me. A small dog chased us for half a block, barking furiously at my Fiesta's rear wheel, which didn't help calm anyone's nerves. As we reached the intersection of the main road the light turned red and I stopped. A blue-and-white police car had come to a halt on the other side of the junction. I glanced up at the rear-view mirror. A motorbike was coming slowly up the street. Its rider pulled up on our right, stopped and sat gunning his engine. "You do not have to worry about Rafael," Carmen said. "He has no car."

"I saw him in a yellow Seat," I told her.

In Spanish she said: "That's my car. I let him use it some-times."

"Like early yesterday morning."

She nodded. "He took me home," she said. "But the car is with the *mecánico* now. It wouldn't start this afternoon."

"Is he your *novio?*" I asked her.

She shook her head. "He's a friend of Pedro's," she replied, switching back to Spanish. They had all grown up together, she explained.

"Is he in love with you?"

She shrugged. *"Quizás,"* she mumbled. Perhaps. "Where do you want to go?"

"How about El Tropical? We can get something to eat there if you're hungry."

"I prefer El Rodéito."

I knew the place, it was a few miles out of town on the main road to San Pedro. I'd been there a couple of times with Evelyn—it was a Castilian restaurant that was open twenty-four hours a day and did a brisk business with the *juergistas,* the all-night crowd of revelers.

"Is it too expensive?" Carmen asked.

"Not if we go Dutch."

She smiled, finally, and reached into the pocket of her pea jacket. "I have two thousand pesetas," she said, holding up one of the new bills.

"You prefer El Rodéito because Rafael can't follow us there, is that it?"

She nodded, and we drove on in silence for a while. There was very little traffic on the main highway, only a few of the big refrigerator trucks starting their journey to Madrid from Algeciras. But there were half a dozen cars parked outside the restaurant. I pulled up in front of the entrance and let her out so she wouldn't have to walk across the muddy parking lot in the rain.

"It is better we speak English now," she said, looking at herself in the mirror over the counter of the bar where she was waiting for me.

"If you prefer."

I followed her into the main dining room, where the head-waiter led us to a corner table. The only people near us were a young man and his girl who were holding hands. All the other customers were not much older, well-dressed young Spaniards fin-ishing a long night. The men stared at Carmen once we were seated, maybe in part because of the difference in our ages. It made me edgy.

The headwaiter came over to our table and nodded to us, too tired to bother with any kind of verbal greeting. Carmen ordered an omelette and a green salad, I ordered fried eggs with bacon and toasted bread.

"*¿A beber?*" the man asked curtly.

"A glass of cold milk," Carmen said in English.

"*¿Y el caballero?*"

I ordered a beer, the man nodded and went away.

"He's not very *simpático*," Carmen said.

"He's tired. It's been a long night."

"I am tired, too." She slipped out of her pea jacket and let it drop over the back of her chair. She was wearing a white turtleneck sweater that outlined her girlish bosom and her straight shoulders. Now a good many of the people seated at the other tables were staring at us. Carmen stared back. "They will get tired of watching us after a while," she said, turning back to face me.

"A young woman and an old man," I said. "An unusual sight at this time of the morning."

"*Vieja la ropa,*" Carmen said; the clothes are old, a stock reply I had often heard before. Yet it was the first time she had aban-doned her indifferent manner. The waiter returned to deposit a small dish of olives on our table.

"Why did you ask me to come to Marisa's?" I asked. "To see you dance?"

She smiled and shook her head. "I wanted to talk," she said. "It was not possible at our house."

"Because of Rafael?"

167

"No. I live with my mother." She took an olive, ate it and deposited the seed in an ashtray. "Is it important to you that my brother goes to prison?"

I hadn't expected her to be so direct. I hesitated. "Important, no. But he committed a serious crime." I paused, pointedly. "He threatened a man with a knife. He was intending to rob him."

"The Englishman?" she asked. "Was he your friend?"

"No, but what difference does that make?"

"I thought that was why you came to help him. The Englishman . . . he is a very rich man."

"You think it's all right for the poor to rob the rich?" I asked her. "Is that it?"

She shook her head. "The rich rob the poor," she said. "Pedro only wanted to frighten him."

"Look," I said, "this isn't the first time your brother has been in trouble."

"Not like this," she said quickly. The waiter brought us our food. My fried eggs were underdone but I didn't complain. Carmen was impatiently waiting for him to leave. "If my brother goes to jail it will ruin his life," she said quietly.

"He almost ruined mine."

"But he didn't."

"He might have."

She sat staring at her food. "So there is nothing to be done," she said gloomily.

"Mine is not the only *denuncia*," I told her. "The Englishman signed one, too."

"You could talk to him."

"Well," I said, "let me think about it. There's also the Guardia Civil. They will think it strange if we drop the charges."

"They can do nothing if you do not ratify your accusations. It happens every day."

She was pretty well informed about the legal proceedings, I

168

thought. "Why don't you eat your *tortilla*," I suggested in Spanish. Her milk had arrived, and my beer.

"If you help my brother you will be helping me."

"He broke the law, Carmen."

"The laws are made by the *señoritos.*"

"Maybe so. But if we don't live by them we'll all be back in the jungle. Rich and poor."

She still had not touched her food. *"No soy una puta,"* she said. "But I have nothing else to offer you. If you help me I will spend the night with you."

I laughed. "There isn't much left of the night."

Her eyes narrowed. "Do you know how desperate I must be to make you such an offer?"

I apologized. "I would have to be desperate to accept it," I told her. "An old man, desperate for a woman." I felt sorry for her. "Don't try to buy your brother's release," I said.

"You said you would consider helping me."

"And I will. Maybe you're right. Maybe sending him to jail will serve no purpose. But I will have to discuss all of this with the Englishman. And the Guardia Civil."

"Will you promise to do so?"

"I promise."

She began to pick at her food. "I have a child," she said. "A girl of five. Her father left us two months after my daughter was born. Pedro tried to find work as an *albañil*, a bricklayer, because I was unable to dance for a while. But the crisis came and he lost his job. We had no money to buy food or to pay the bills for water and electricity. Rafael, Pedro's cousin, had only the compensation from his accident. So Pedro went out to look for golf balls he could sell. I went back to work a month after my child was born but I was able to dance no more than three nights a week. Marisa paid me as much as she could. My mother has only a widow's pension. My father was a fisherman. He died eight years ago. So we managed to survive the summer. At the start of winter I was strong enough to work five nights a week. But in the winter business is bad for Marisa. She closes her place in January and February. Now she has opened the *tablao* again because soon the tourists will come back for *Semana Santa*. Then this happened. Oh, I am sure you have heard many stories like this. Because life is not easy for everyone on the Costa del Sol. *¿Verdad?"*

We ate in silence. I could have told her my own tale of disaster but I didn't. It would have sounded less than convincing and hardly comparable. "I'll do what I can," I told her.

She nodded and drank her milk. "Can you understand now why men are made to rob?" she asked, putting on her pea jacket.

I said: "I'm not an idiot, or one of your *señoritos*. I've lived in this country for many years."

She nodded. "I know," she said. "Now will you take me home?"

I signaled to the waiter that we wanted to leave.

"Do you need my two thousand pesetas?" she asked.

"Not this time," I told her.

30

LONG BEFORE WE HAD ARRIVED back in the old part of the town where she lived I had made up my mind not to ratify my *denuncia*. And while we drove back through the steady rain I rehearsed to myself just what I would say to Collins to justify my decision. I didn't anticipate much resistance from him. He had indicated that going ahead with the case was pretty much up to me. But then our relationship had changed since his and Pamela's dinner party. It might well be that he would be less accommodating now that he was no longer disposed in a friendly manner toward me.

I found my way through the narrow maze of white streets and stopped at the corner of the lane closed to automobile traffic. We had hardly exchanged a word until then except to comment on the dismal weather. Before saying *adiós* I offered to lend her my umbrella for her short walk home. "You can drive up to my door," she said. "At this time of the night there is no one to complain."

I put the car in first gear and released the clutch. The beam of the headlights lit up the narrow road. In a doorway ahead of us I caught sight of a black umbrella and a pair of crutches. "Go back," Carmen said.

"Rafael?"

She nodded. I put the car in reverse and backed into the road behind us. It seemed incredible that the man had been waiting there all this time. I glanced at my watch. It was five o'clock in the morning. "What do you want to do?" I asked. "Walk home?"

She shook her head. "I don't want to see him now. Tomorrow I will tell him that I spent the night with Marisa."

I managed to turn around in the narrow street. "Are you scared of him?"

"Sometimes. Sometimes he can be violent. Especially if he has been drinking."

"Do you want me to take you to Marisa's house?"

"No. She will be asleep."

"Then where do you want to go?"

She didn't answer at once. She turned in her seat to face me. I had started back to the main road. "Where do you live?" she asked finally.

"In San Pedro."

"Marisa said you lived in a villa behind the town."

"I used to," I said. "I rent the place now. But my tenants have left."

"Can we go there and sleep for a while?"

"We could," I said. "But the house hasn't been lived in for weeks."

"And the apartment?"

"There's only one room."

She shrugged. "Does it matter?"

"What about your mother? She'll worry, won't she?"

"She never comes into my room until late in the day. She dresses my daughter and takes her to school. Then she goes to the market. I can take a taxi back before she returns home."

"And Rafael?"

"He will get tired of waiting and go somewhere to sleep." She lit a cigarette. "Do you sometimes regret feeling pity for another person?" she asked.

I laughed and said: "Yes. Once in a while."

"For your wife?" she asked in Spanish, abandoning the familiar form she had used before, perhaps to establish a more formal relationship now that we were about to spend the night together.

"No," I said. "For my son-in-law."

"You, too, have a daughter?"

"Yes, but she doesn't go to school anymore." Briefly I told her about Susan and her flight from marriage. She listened quietly.

"Spanish men," was her only comment once I had finished my story. "Or all men," she added. She once had an American *novio*, she told me, *un extranjero* who used to come to Marisa's club every night for many weeks. He was a dancer, at least that was what he told her, and he was interested in flamenco. He was *muy guapo*. For a long time he made no advances and she was beginning to think he was gay. Then ultimately the inevitable happened and they became lovers. The relationship only lasted a fortnight or so. Then he said he had to return to his country. He promised to come back in a few months but he didn't. She never heard from him again.

"Did your husband find out?" I asked her.

"My husband?" She laughed. He had left her long before all that, she said without a trace of bitterness.

"And now? Is there anyone else in your life?" I asked.

"My daughter," she said. *"Y nadie más.* What do I need a man for? To make scenes? To question me? To come home drunk and threaten me and my child?"

I said: "We're not all like that, *guapa*. There are exceptions to the rule."

"Quizás . . . but why take a chance? I am very well the way I am. Do you mind if I smoke another cigarette? I have noticed you do not like it."

"I don't, but go ahead."

"No, I will wait then. Until we get out of the car." She slipped her package of Ducados back into her coat pocket. "You always live alone?" she asked.

"Most of the time."

"And you have many women friends?"

"Not many. Just one."

"And where is she now?"

"On her way to Marrakech. She felt she needed a rest from me."

She smiled. "So it will not be dangerous for me to finish the night in your apartment, *¿verdad?*"

"Verdad," I replied. "Not dangerous in any way."

"It would be more flattering if you were a little less certain."

It was her first, even mildly flirtatious remark. I glanced over at her. We were driving along the coast; the amber street lamps on both sides of the highway were barely visible in the driving rain. A car passed us at great speed, engulfing the windshield with muddy water. *"Ten cuidado,"* Carmen warned me. I had strayed too far from the right lane.

In English I said: "Just for the record . . ."

She looked puzzled. "For the record?"

"So that there can be no misunderstanding—long before we saw Rafael waiting near your house I had already made up my mind not to press charges against your brother."

"And the Englishman?"

"I'll do my best to persuade him to abandon his *denuncia,* too."

"Te lo agredesco," she said in a low voice. I am grateful.

"I hope I'm not making a mistake."

"I hope so, too." She paused. "My mother will be very happy."

We were approaching San Pedro. I turned off the main road and drove into the center of the town. At that hour of the morning it was easy to find a parking place near the front of my building. Together we climbed the concrete stairs. I unlocked the door to my apartment and followed her into the room. I had left the bedlamp on and she stood for a moment looking around her. The bed was just as I had left it. Fergy was asleep in her usual place, curled up on a pillow.

"So you don't live alone after all," Carmen said smiling.

31

I CROSSED THE ROOM to open the shutters, knowing that the daylight would waken me. I didn't want to sleep too late so that Carmen could arrive back at her house before noon. Then I took the receiver off its cradle and locked the front door.

"You expect someone to call?" she asked.

"It's possible."

She had taken off her pea jacket. "I will sleep in the chair," she said. "I am used to it. Before I went to work at Marisa's place I often worked in Sevilla and slept in the bus on the way back home."

"I'll sleep in the chair," I told her.

"No. It will make the cat unhappy," she replied, laughing. She turned the armchair around so that it did not face the window, then carried the straight-backed chair on which I usually hung my windbreaker across the room and placed it to face the armchair. "Have you got a spare blanket?" she asked.

I gave her my siesta rug. She wrapped it around her legs. "It smells nice," she said. "You have had a visitor here before."

"Only to ask advice," I said.

"Your *novia?*"

"No. My *novia* has a place of her own."

"Ah, she is rich."

"Not really. Would you like a glass of milk, or some water?"

"No, gracias." She hesitated. "Will you help pull off my boots?" she asked.

She was wearing *botas de campo* under her jeans, the knee-high leather boots men and women wear in the country that have become popular in the towns. She sat down in the armchair and I helped her shed them. "Who does this when you're alone?" I asked her.

"I manage," she said. "Usually they are not as wet as they are tonight." Her feet had been naked inside her boots. She tucked them inside my siesta blanket and stretched out on the two chairs. "Sleep well," she said in English.

"You, too. Do you want a pillow?"

"No. I'm fine. Please put my jacket here on the floor next to my bed," she said. "It is always colder before dawn."

She had left it on the wooden chest that stands near the front door, and I brought it over to her. In Spanish I told her that I would leave the light on in the bathroom after I had finished there, and leave the door ajar.

"As you like," she replied.

I went into the bathroom, washed my face, brushed my teeth and put on my pajamas. The vodka had worn off and I felt surprisingly sober. It was a strange way for the evening to end, I thought as I crossed to my bed. My guest appeared to have fallen asleep—at least her eyes were firmly shut, I noticed, before I turned out the lamp next to my bed. Carmen had undone her hair so that it covered the lower half of her pale face. Fergy still had not moved. Now as I pulled the covers up over me, the cat stretched, uttered a lazy sigh and went back to sleep.

I lay back on my pillow and stared up at the ceiling. Evelyn had undoubtedly arrived in Marrakech by now and I wondered if she might call. Well, if she did, I could tell her that I had taken the receiver off its cradle because of the nuisance calls. I disliked lying to her but I knew I couldn't tell her the truth. Then I began to wonder if she had ever lied to me. She had always been completely honest in the past, which made me feel worse. Then I started to worry about Collins. He might insist on going ahead with his *denuncia,* although once I had failed to ratify my complaint the charges against Pedro would probably be dropped. Still it would have been better if I had waited to tell Carmen of my decision.

I closed my eyes and turned on my side. I must have fallen asleep because when I opened them again the sky outside my window was a light blue. It had stopped raining. I glanced over at the armchair and saw that it was empty. I sat up in bed. Carmen, I discovered, was lying beside me, and Fergy had settled down in the narrow space between us. For a brief moment I was tempted to reach out and touch her, rest my hand on her back, on the small triangle of white sweater that was not covered by the blanket, gently, not with any carnal purpose, although I must admit some notion of that kind had crossed my mind. My impulse was merely to reassure her that I found her to be attractive and that it was not all that undangerous for her to spend what had remained of the night with me. It would not come as a complete surprise to her—I felt certain of that.

The moment passed. I made no move toward her. I sat with my head resting against the metal bedpost, recalling that for nearly all of my life women had made the first signal that a physical advance would be welcome, and that only in a few instances had I made the first move. Then it occurred to me that as the years passed, the most noticeable change in one's character was an unwillingness to take risks, even the minor risk of being rejected, which was less minor if the object of desire was at least more than twenty years younger. It was a cowardice that was understandable, I consoled myself, although looking back on the moment, my lack of daring was something I soon came to regret.

The first rays of the sun touched the western headland some

ten miles away. Carmen turned slowly to face me and opened her eyes. She said: "Good morning. I was cold in the night but I didn't want to wake you to ask for another blanket so I came to be with you and the cat. Will you forgive me?"

"Sure," I said. "But I can't speak for the cat."

She laughed, and sitting up, stroked Fergy with her right hand. "What do you call her?" she asked.

"Fergy."

"Like the English duchess?" She dropped back on her pillow. "What time is it?"

"Eight-twenty."

"You slept like a stone," she said. "You didn't move when I got up from the chair."

"I was tired."

"*Mea culpa* . . . I kept you up all night."

"I wouldn't have slept at all if you'd come to bed right away."

She smiled. "My mistake." She turned on her side and touched my shoulder with her right hand. "You're a nice man," she said.

"Too nice, sometimes."

"*Quizás.* Will you look away?" she asked. "I took off my jeans when I came to bed, and left them hanging in the bathroom."

"I'll close my eyes."

It was safe for her to be flirtatious now, I thought. I could hear the shower starting and pulled the blankets up over me. It was cold in the room, colder than before because the weather had changed. After a while I got up and got a clean pair of slacks, a fresh shirt and jockey shorts out of the chest of drawers. I would have to wait for her to finish in the bathroom before getting dressed, so I went into the kitchen and opened a can of cat food for Fergy. Her sand-box was in the bathroom, and I worried that she might have used it during the night. She didn't, as a rule, but she just might have this once. I doled out a small portion of the tuna mix and put the tin plate down in front of the stove. Fergy wandered over to sniff it, then ate a few bites. She was accustomed to being fed later in the day. She followed me into the main room, watched me switch on the electric heater, then went slowly back to her food again.

I was standing by the window looking out at the sea when Carmen reappeared. She had put her hair up in a bun at the back of her head, the way she had worn it at Marisa's. "Was I long?" she asked. "Your shower was too tempting. I wanted to take one when we arrived but I was afraid to ask."

"Did you find a clean towel?"

"Clean enough." She hesitated for an instant. "I have a confession to make," she said. "I used your toothbrush. I held it under the hot water for a long time afterwards."

"And before, I hope."

"Yes, of course," she said, and laughed. "I would have done so even if we had been lovers."

"But we weren't. Unfortunately."

"*¿Quizás?*"

That seemed to be one of her favorite replies. I had looked up the word in my dictionary long ago—when I had first heard Nat King Cole sing the song of that title. Its meaning was "perhaps," but it could also mean "I dare say." I hummed the tune, and she sang a few of the opening bars, dancing gracefully toward me. I said: "You're in a good mood today. Is that because you've escaped a fate worse than death?"

She looked puzzled. "I don't understand."

I explained. Which took quite a while; there was no Spanish equivalent, probably because they didn't consider rape worse than death. "It was meant to be funny," I added.

"It was you who escaped," she said, laughing.

"*¿Quizás?*" The shower and the few hours' sleep had had a startling effect on her appearance. In her white pullover and her skintight jeans she seemed to have shed fifteen years, was young again, young enough to make me feel old. For the second time that morning I was tempted to reach out for her, but didn't probably because Evelyn had only too recently exited from my life. Then, too, I was still in my pajamas, unshaven with unbrushed teeth.

"Don't be too sure that *you've* escaped," I told her, and she laughed what sounded like a forced laugh.

In Spanish she said: "I will wait. Right now I will wait for you to get dressed, and then if you have time, we can have coffee. Later I will go home and wait for whatever is my fate." She used the word *destino,* which sounded less ominous.

"*Our* destiny," I said, a remark that might have sounded more challenging had I not been facing her in bare feet so that in her boots she was an inch taller than I was, as well as neatly dressed in her *vaqueros* and sweater, her face clean and shining, without make-up. It was that, I realized, which had made her appear to have shed all those years.

It isn't often that I wish I were younger. I know that it's pointless, but that didn't stop me that morning. I looked at my face in the bathroom mirror for quite a while. Then I brushed my teeth without first rinsing my toothbrush in hot water, my first and only act of daring.

32

WE WENT DOWN TO ARTURO'S PLACE for coffee. I had squeezed two glasses of orange juice before leaving the flat and she had told me more about her life, how her mother worked afternoons as a daily for an elderly English couple to help make ends meet. As a rule she slept until four in the afternoon and then collected her daughter from school. On Sundays she would try to sleep most of the day and then help her mother make dinner. After that she would take Alicia, her daughter, for a walk in the park. It didn't seem like too much of a life.

We were standing at the counter waiting for Arturo to finish opening a fresh cardboard container of milk. There was no one else in the place. I heard the street door behind us being pulled open, and turned to face Rafael. He was leaning on his crutches. He shouted: *"¡Puta!"*, just that one word, and propelled himself forward. I stepped in front of Carmen.

Arturo yelled: *"¡Que se vaya!"*, the best translation of which is "Get the hell out of here!" and dropped the container of milk. Out of the corner of my eye I saw him start toward the open end of the counter. He held the scissors in his right hand, raising it like a dagger.

Rafael stopped, whirled and made a rush for the street. I went after him. I have no idea of what my intentions were—grab him, I suppose, and shake him, although I was angry enough to go well beyond that. He beat me to the door. Once outside he turned to face me. I stopped and for a split second we stood glaring at each other. He said: *"Cabrón,"* and lashed out at me with one of his crutches. I stepped back and bumped into Arturo. By the time I had turned around Rafael was hurrying down the sidewalk at an astonishing pace. He passed the telephone booth and stepped out into the main street. A car came around the corner, braked to avoid him, and continued on its way, the driver looking back and cursing as he passed me.

Arturo said: *"Es un loco."* He had seen "the crazy" hanging around for days. We should call the police.

And what did he expect me to tell them—that the fellow had attacked me with a deadly weapon? We went back inside the café. Carmen was buttoning up her pea jacket with nervous fingers. She asked Arturo to call a taxi.

"I have to get home," she told me.

"Finish your coffee," Arturo said. "The taxi will take ten minutes to get here." He went to the telephone at the end of the counter.

"I should never have asked you to come to Marisa's," Carmen said in a low voice.

"It's too late to worry about that now." "You're sure he's your brother's friend and that's all?" I asked her.

"I know what you think. But you have no idea what they are like. Any woman who refuses to sleep with them and stays out all night is a *puta*. You don't know Spain so well after all."

I said: "I guess not," and regretted that I had doubted her. "Forget it," I told her. "It's not important."

"It is to me," she replied. "I have no need to lie."

"I know." I covered her hand with mine. "Do you really think your brother will change once the Guardia Civil has released him?"

"I said I don't know."

"Well, we'll soon see."

The taxi arrived. I paid for our coffee and got in the back of the cab with her. She insisted that it wasn't necessary for me to come along but I told her that I would see her home. "Like a gentleman," I said with a smile.

"Is that what you always do?"

"I usually drive myself home."

"Yes. Of course. I'd forgotten. Your *novia* has her own villa."

"That's right. And she doesn't have a *loco* spying on her all night." I noticed that the driver was taking an interest in our conversation. "Speak English," I said.

"Of course! We're on the Costa del Sol!" She pinched my leg. "I will call you tonight from the *tablao,*" she said. "Will you be at the apartment?"

"Sure," I said. "Where else would I be?"

"Have you still got the number?"

"I've memorized it." She told the taxi driver to stop at the corner of the street. I kissed her on both cheeks before she got out of the car. "Try to sleep . . ." she said, slamming the door behind her.

I watched her run up the narrow lane in her boots and pea jacket. A stray dog barked at her. Twenty yards before she arrived at her front door she turned back and waved. I sat back on the plastic seat covers. "Where to now?" the driver wanted to know.

"Back to where you picked me up," I told him.

Kiko was standing in the hallway when I reached the top of the concrete stairs. "Your telephone has been ringing all morning," he said. "Finally I let myself in to answer it." He crossed to my door and opened it with his key. "I thought maybe it was Susan."

"There's a nine-hour time difference. It's two-thirty in the morning, California time."

"I didn't stop to figure all that out," he said grumpily.

"Well, who was it that called?"

"Some guy who said he was an old friend of yours—Paul something or other."

"Levin?"

"That sounds like it. He told me that he was on a yacht that would be arriving at Banus this afternoon. Wait a minute. I've written it all down." He went across the hall to his office and was back in less than a minute with his notebook. "The yacht is called *Penelope*. She'll be docking at the first pier. This Levin said he wanted to invite you to dinner. At seven-thirty sharp. And not to bring a date. They're overbooked with ladies, was how he put it. Oh, and yes. She flies a Panamanian flag, wouldn't you know."

"Did he give a number where I can call him back?"

"Hell, no. He's on the high sea. You're going, aren't you? It sounds like a very posh deal."

"If I feel up to it."

"Yeah . . . you do look beat up. What have you been up to now?"

"Nothing much. Chasing cripples," I replied. I didn't want to tell him about Carmen.

"By the way," Kiko said, "Lady Pamela has gone off to London with his lordship. *¿Fantástico, no?* If they get back together I'll have a hard time collecting my fee."

"Stranger things have happened."

"You should have let that druggy mug him and then split the take with the sport. It would have saved time."

I said: "Tell me about it." I crossed to the door. "If you don't mind, I think I'll crash for a while."

"A good idea," Kiko said. "But if you want to get some rest I'd suggest you take your phone off the hook."

"I may just do that," I told him, and shepherded him out into the hallway.

I didn't feel tired. I knew why—a sudden infatuation had always had the same effect on me, bringing on a euphoria I had experienced even in my teens. That and the lack of sleep were probably responsible for my agitated state of mind, I decided, as I sat staring at the notes Kiko had scribbled down on his notepad.

The thought of seeing Paul Levin again was probably a contributing factor. A good many years had gone by since our last meeting in his Beverly Hills apartment when he had hosted my farewell party, a last friendly act. I found myself wishing that my present status was not quite as desolate but there was nothing I could do about that. Dinner on board a luxurious yacht would require an improvement in my wardrobe, I realized, but before collecting my best blazer and a pair of gray slacks up at the villa I thought I'd better pass by the bank for some cash. I didn't want to appear like a penniless senior citizen in the eyes of my old friend. After dinner Levin might well ask to make a tour of the town.

The young man in charge of foreign accounts consulted his computer, then handed me a narrow slip of paper with my balance. My net worth, it turned out, was 66,455 pesetas, forty thousand pesetas less than the sum I had scribbled in my checkbook, the bank having paid the telephone bill my Belgian tenants had neglected to pay. My euphoria fading fast, I started toward the street door. Before I reached it, I was intercepted by Señor Sánchez.

I recognized him at once from our previous meeting at the cuartel of the Guardia Civil and at the party. Although I had been a client for at least twenty years I had no idea that he was the branch manager, nor that Collins was a fellow depositor. My account had obviously never been important enough for him to have introduced himself in the past. After the customary greetings he took my arm and led me into his office. "I happened to see you at the counter," he said, "and thought I might take the opportunity to inform you that I've had a fax from our mutual friend, Sir Cecil Collins."

"He's in London, I believe," I said.

"That's correct." Sánchez was shuffling through the papers on his desk. He found what he was looking for and smiled. "Among other things," Sánchez said in a confidential tone of voice, although we were alone, "Sir Cecil has informed me that he wishes *not* to proceed with his *denuncia*. He feels that it would be time-consuming and meaningless in the end. He has asked me to advise you of his decision and I was about to dictate a letter to you at your home address."

"You think he's doing the right thing?" I asked.

Sánchez shrugged. "He probably is. The courts in this country are most unreliable—as they are in England, I daresay."

"I guess there's no use in my proceeding on my own, is there?"

"I cannot advise you on that."

"Well, I'm not all that eager to go ahead," I told him. "Will you inform the authorities?"

"I will indeed."

We shook hands. So that was that. You always worry about the wrong thing, I thought as I stepped out into the bright sunlight of the main street. Carmen would be delighted and Pedro would soon be back out on the golf course again, a lot sooner than I.

The fields on both sides of the road were a bright green once I had turned off the main highway, with here and there a rubbish dump to remind you that you were in Andalusia, but the steeper meadows near the summits were brown and bare. They stood out like a fake backdrop against the clear blue sky. Now that the sun was out the countryside had more of the appearance of the paradise it was advertised to be. Pepe had cut the weeds on both sides of the driveway, making the place look quite acceptable now.

Maria had left a note on the freshly waxed tiles of the hall so that I would be sure to see it. The *señora de la agencia* had called, she had written in her childish handwriting. I dialed the rental agency's number and a secretary answered. After a long wait Cecilia came on the line. "I've been calling and calling," she said. "Don't you ever stay home?"

"I've had a busy morning," I said. "So what's new?"

"I have some people who want to rent a house. Is yours still available?"

"It is indeed. What nationality are they?"

"You won't believe this," she said with a giggle. "They're Belgians. They plan to arrive next Wednesday. I'm going to show them your place first."

"For how long a rental?"

"Three months . . . until the middle of June. They have two children and a nanny."

"Okay," I said. "Two thousand five hundred dollars a month, payable in advance."

"That's more than the other people paid."

"Not the way it turned out. Anyway, that was my winter rate."

"Actually this couple was hoping to have the rent apply to a predetermined sale price," Cecilia said. She sounded reluctant about that part of the proposition.

"I don't want to sell unless, of course, they make me an offer I can't refuse."

"Well, let's not worry about that now. I'll do what I can, Roberto. Call me early Wednesday morning to confirm an appointment. It's hopeless for me to call you."

She hung up. I put down the receiver and went up to my bedroom. Maria had made the bed, I noticed as I proceeded to the guest room. Beyond it is the small dressing room I had kept locked up so as to be able to store some of my clothes. The key was still under the chest of drawers in a special hiding place. I opened the closet under the eaves of the roof and got out my blazer and a pair of gray flannel slacks. The shoulders of the jacket were covered with dust but otherwise it looked okay. I went back into the master bedroom, opened the shutters and hung the blazer and trousers out to dry in the sun.

Then I went downstairs and built a fire in the living room. I was getting hungry but I thought it better to stay on until late afternoon so that the house would dry out a little. The sun was already quite strong, and I went out on the terrace to sit in one of my disintegrating wicker chairs. The view never failed to bring back my attachment to this part of the world. Where the hell would I go if staying on became impossible. Back to California? And what was a price I couldn't refuse? Two hundred and fifty thousand dollars? Or maybe three? Three-fifty? Maybe before the crisis. The safest investment on three hundred thousand, at the going rates, would provide twelve thousand dollars a year, barely over the poverty line. I could rent a flat in the Valley for maybe eight thousand a year, and try to live on my social security. The rub there was that I hadn't paid in enough during my acting career. I had visited the U.S. consul's office in Fuengirola the day after my sixtieth birthday, and the woman in charge had informed me that a nonresident earning more than ten thousand dollars a year was not entitled to social security until he or she had turned seventy.

The good news was that I would qualify someday, since I had always declared the cash I had received for leasing my villa. It all resulted in a simple, logical conclusion. My best bet was not to change my lifestyle, as precarious as it was. Strangely enough I had never thought of myself as a loser, except at golf. Perhaps I had been deluding myself for three decades. Then I recalled the words of a chief petty officer in the Seabees who had been shipped out to the Pacific on the same day as me. "No matter how bad things get, there are always a lot of mates worse off than you." It was simple logic but it applied, I thought, and went back to the house to lock up.

Although it was nearly five in the afternoon the sun was still high above the horizon. The sea lay like a golden sheet inside the curve of the bay. Paul Levin and his rich friends would have a smooth passage all the way from Gibraltar to Banus no matter what size their chartered yacht. Knowing Paul, I reckoned it would be about the size of the *Normandie*. That dates you, pal, I muttered to myself, the *Normandie* was hardly the first transatlantic liner that anyone less than sixty would use as a point of reference.

33

KIKO'S GUESS HAD BEEN ACCURATE for once. A limp Panamanian flag
hung from a varnished mast on the *Penelope*'s fantail. I joined the
crowd of Saturday night tourists who were gaping at the festivities
on board. A young sailor in a white shirt and black trousers was
standing guard alongside the roped-off gangway. Behind him, in
the spacious stern, a cocktail party was in progress. There were
about eight guests, all dressed in sport clothes, white trousers and
sweaters hung carelessly around their shoulders, so that I felt over-
dressed in my necktie and blazer. On the raised superstructure of
the stern two speedboats rested in wooden cradles, covered with
white tarpaulins. The yacht *Penelope* looked to be about a hundred
and fifty feet in overall length with a fat smokestack amidships. She
was not the most modern-looking vessel, had probably been built a
couple of decades after the end of the war, my war, but she had
been kept in immaculate trim, her steel hull covered with a smooth
coating of white paint. On the flying bridge well forward I could see
two officers in white uniforms and navy blue shoulder tabs gazing
out at the crowd below.

A husky German tourist was taking a photograph of his wife

and son who had positioned themselves at the foot of the gangway and were smiling for the camera. I waited until the man had taken his snapshot, then moved past him to address the sailor on guard duty. "I've been invited on board by Mr. Paul Levin," I told the man.

He looked me up and down, then unhooked the rope behind him. I moved slowly across the gangway, feeling like an ensign reporting for his first tour of duty on a battle cruiser. I wondered whether I was expected to take off my shoes before stepping down on the teak deck, but as I had remembered to wear my cleanest tennis shoes I felt confident that I wouldn't be called to order. All of the other guests, I noticed, wore rubber-soled shoes, although some of the ladies were shod with stiletto heels. I looked down at the steps at the end of the gangway, making sure not to fall, and when I looked up I found myself facing Paul Levin, who had come out onto the fantail to welcome me.

He hadn't changed as much as I had expected, was still the neat, compactly built man I remembered him to be. He was dressed in a gray flannel suit that quite obviously had not been bought off the rack. To my relief he wore a necktie, a conservative blue polka dot, not one of the garish designer jobs favored by television announcers. His hair, which I recalled as being dark brown, was now white, and went well with his evenly tanned face. Only the wrinkles on his neck above his collar betrayed his age, as did the brown blotches on the back of the hand he held out for me to shake. "Robert Masters," he said, as if he were announcing my arrival at the end of a long footrace, "I can't tell you how pleased I am to see you!"

"Me, too," I said. "It's been a hell of a long time."

"Reunion in Málaga," he said. "It sounds like the title of an old-fashioned novel."

I put my arm around his shoulder for a brief moment, and he led me forward to meet his rich friends, who were in the midst of an argument that our presence had failed to interrupt. The point of contention, I grasped at once, was how long to stay on at their present mooring. "A ship of fools," Levin muttered. "Let me introduce you. This," he continued in a louder voice, "is one of my oldest pals."

I passed from one person to the next without making an effort to remember all of their names. I gathered that they were all "private people," which was how we all used to refer to anyone not in our business. I had just finished my tour when a blonde woman stepped through the varnished entryway with glass windows that led to what was obviously the main cabin. She looked to be the same age as most of the others, maybe a year or two older, but she was well conserved, had a good figure, the result, no doubt, of aerobics.

"Last but not least," Levin announced, "the *pièce de résistance*, an old friend of yours, Sue Wilson, our cohostess aboard this tub."

The woman opened her well-rouged mouth, then clapped her right hand over it. "I don't *believe* it!" she exclaimed. She turned to Levin. "You little bastard," she said. "If I'd only known . . ."

"What would you have done?" Levin demanded. "Jumped overboard?"

"No! Certainly not!" Sue Wilson said, laughing shrilly. "But I would have worn my Sunday best!" She stepped forward and embraced me. I kissed her pale cheeks. She was the only untanned member of the group, having apparently learned somewhere along the way to stay out of the sun. Probably once she had decided to become a blonde.

"My God," she said. "You haven't changed all that much."

"But you didn't recognize me."

"I would have, given a little more time. How are you, Bobby? Pretty well, it seems, from the looks of you. You're a sight for sore eyes."

"So are you. Unchanged, except for your hair."

"Yeah, well . . . there you are. It all helps."

Levin was standing off to one side, enjoying the scene. Sue

said: "I knew you lived somewhere around here but I had no idea . . ."

"I told you that I had a nice surprise for you," Levin said, and chuckled happily to himself.

"Is this your yacht?" I asked.

"No, of course not," she replied. "Janet and I chartered her. Her old man bought the studio and is about to sell it for a neat profit. He plans to join us in Turkey once he's made his deal."

"Heavy bread," Levin put in.

"You're always talking about money, Paul," Sue Wilson told him. "Haven't you learned it's vulgar?"

A slim man with dark hair and a mustache had stepped over to us. "Have you met Raoul?" Sue asked me.

The man nodded. "That's all been taken care of," he said coolly. "We were wondering how long you and Janet were planning to stay here?" he asked, ignoring my presence. "One or two nights?"

"We haven't made up our tiny minds," Sue told him. "We have to go back to Gib tomorrow to take on provisions, and then maybe come back here for another day. That is, if the weather holds up. There might be some fun people about."

"Eurotrash," a gaunt woman wearing dark glasses called out to Sue.

"I don't know about that," Levin said. "No worse than where you come from, dearie."

"How would you know, Paul?" the woman replied. "Anybody who lives in L.A. can't be too fussy."

"Where are we going to dine?" the man Sue had introduced as Raoul asked. "I'm starving."

"Well, you'll just have to wait," Sue Wilson said. "Canapés are on the way up from the galley." She turned to me. "Do you know a place called La Meridiana? We've been told it's the best food in town."

"It's good," I said. "Although I don't go there very often. It's expensive."

Raoul had withdrawn, had wandered off and dropped into a deck chair. "Who's he?" I asked Levin.

"Some South American asshole-friend of Janet's," Sue answered for Paul. "He's on the make for me, hoping to feather his nest. Gosh, it's good to see you," she said, squeezing my right hand, which she had not released. "Come over here and sit down."

I followed her over to a wicker couch on the starboard side of the covered deck. I felt out of place. I thought of Carmen in her tiny house and wondered if she was all right. Sue asked one of the stewards for a glass of champagne. Across from us Levin was leaning against the port railing talking to a tall, gray-haired woman in a green dress. I guessed she was important . . . Paul was listening instead of talking, which I recalled was unlike him. A heavyset man stood behind them, drink in hand.

"We've got so much catching up to do," Sue Wilson said. "I don't know where to start."

"Do you still play tennis?" I asked her.

She laughed. "Heavens, no. I go to a gym three times a week. I hate it but it keeps me in shape.

"So I see."

"What about you? I heard you got married some time back."

"It didn't take."

"Any kids?"

"A daughter. Your namesake."

"Oh, really? That's touching."

"Did you remarry after Eddie died?"

"No, no, no," she replied, shaking a forefinger. "Once was enough."

"It lasted quite a while, didn't it? So it couldn't have been all that bad."

"It wasn't," she said. "Eddie took good care of me. I know what you're going to say—that I wasn't crazy about him. But he was really a nice guy."

"No flashing lights, right?"

"I know all the old jokes," she said cheerfully. "That the three most overrated things in the world are home cooking, home loving and Texas. And that fucking your wife is like striking out the pitcher. But that isn't all that matters, is it?"

"Don't ask me."

A well-rounded woman, another blonde in a white pants suit, had come out of the main salon. She appeared to be about the same age as Sue. She wore her hair pulled back into a bun, which made her look more matronly. Sue's blonde curls made it seem she could spot the other woman half a dozen years. Sue said: "There's Janet," and waved.

Janet Slater came over to us and I got to my feet. Sue made the introductions. "I may have told you about this character," she added. "He was kind of my first beau."

"Well, not really," I said as we shook hands.

"I'm delighted you could join us tonight," the woman said, disregarding my remark. A steward arrived bearing a tray of glasses and a bottle of champagne wrapped in a white towel. Janet Slater shook her head. "I'm going to have a diet Coke," she said. "But never mind, I'll get it."

We watched her go off. "I know you weren't my first beau," Sue said reprovingly. "But I never got around to telling her the story of my life. She's from Kansas City!"

"I'm sorry. That slipped out."

"Fortunately she didn't hear you. She's a little deaf. But if she likes you, you've got it made. You could come home and start your own production company . . . and I'm not kidding." She laughed merrily.

"I won't be around long enough," I said.

Sue said: "Why not? We could pick you up on our way back from Gibraltar and you could join the cruise as my special guest."

"I don't think I'd fit in," I said.

"Oh, why not? Christ, you're still as straight as you were in

Palm Springs light-years back. You haven't changed, but it's about time, don't you think?"

"I'm Eurotrash," I told her. "And I don't have any fun clothes."

Levin had rejoined us. "How are things down memory lane?" he asked.

"You know what I was telling this idiot?" Sue said. "That he could join us on old *Penelope*. And you know what he said? That he didn't have the right clothes . . . There's plenty of room," she added, turning back to me. "You'd have a cabin all to yourself."

"He could bunk with you, too," Levin said, grinning. "Just for old times sake."

"Of course," Sue said. "Why not?" She seemed to be enjoying the joke.

"It's too late," I said. "We missed that boat a long time ago."

"That's not a nice thing to say," Sue replied, pretending to be hurt. "You better think about it."

Levin said: "He could bring a date."

"Nope. None of that. There are too many dames on board as it is. Organize the troops, Paul. We might as well go and have dinner."

"Do you know who Penelope was?" I asked Sue, once Levin had left us.

"Not a clue," came the not unexpected reply.

"She was Ulysses's wife. She waited twenty years for him to come home from the Trojan War."

"There you are," she said. "History always repeats itself, doesn't it?"

As if in a sudden frenzy, Raoul shouted: "¡A comer! Let's eat!" But no one paid any attention to him, and it was more than half an hour later that the "shore party" finally moved off.

34

LEVIN ANNOUNCED HE WAS GOING in my car and that we would lead the way to the restaurant with the others following in the minibus the captain had rented for the evening. On the way to the port parking lot Levin occasionally stopped to peer into the shopwindows we passed, and I urged him to hurry, since the others would be waiting for us outside the main entrance of the port. "Let 'em wait," he said. "It won't kill them." Then once we had arrived at my car he stood for an instant looking it over before he got in. It was obvious that the appearance of my Ford Fiesta bothered him, it wasn't the kind of conveyance he was used to.

"It's been raining for a couple of weeks," I explained, "and I haven't had a chance to have it washed. It's clean inside."

"That's okay," he said, getting in and adjusting the trousers of his suit so as not to spoil their creases.

I stopped at the roundabout outside the port and Levin waved to Raoul, who was at the wheel of the minibus, signaling him to follow us. Sue was in the back and blew us a kiss. "Don't go too fast," Levin cautioned me. "If we lose these characters we won't eat until midnight." He turned for an instant to look back, then folded his arms across his chest and stared straight ahead at the road. "When was the last time you had a job?" he asked. "Can you remember that far back?"

"An acting job?"

"Well, what else have you been doing? A little light pimping?"

I laughed and said: "I haven't stooped to that yet, Paul. They don't make many movies in Spain nowadays. So it's been a while."

"Then how do you make a living?"

"I manage," I said. It was not a completely accurate statement.

"Do you own a house?"

"Yeah, I've got a little place up in the hills. I bought it a while back when I sold my pad in Trancas."

"How much did you get for it?"

"A couple of hundred thousand. Maybe it was two-fifty, I don't remember."

"You know what those places are going for now?"

"I have a vague idea. A million or two."

"That's right. Before the storm, anyway." He paused and glanced back to see if the others were still following us. "Do you live here all year round?" he asked.

"I do now. I used to go skiing in the winter but since the recession I haven't. I rent my villa when I'm short of cash and move into a rented apartment. Most of the time it keeps the wolf from the door."

He shook his head. "You know I've often thought I gave you some bad advice after you got caught in the hay with Eddie what's-his-name's wife."

"Sue wasn't his wife then, and we didn't get caught in the hay. We were in a nice soft bed."

"Don't quibble. You know what I mean. I think now that if you'd hung on the whole thing would have blown over. We panicked. I panicked, that is. I thought Eddie would make things tough for both of us. But he had a lot of enemies in the business and one or two would have hired you just to bug him."

"Never look back. Isn't that what they say?"

"Yeah, I guess so. But when you get to be my age you can't help it. I wrote you, remember . . . and told you to come home."

"I didn't feel like it. I was having a good time, and whatever money I made was tax-free. That helped. I also thought that getting out of town would make things easier for Sue."

"She did all right," he said. "Old Eddie was pussy-whipped, and if she'd taken a stand he probably would have laid off you."

"Past history," I said. "Is she okay now? Financially?"

"Eddie left her all the stock he had in the company. She got that and the house and whatever cash he'd socked away. Then when Janet Slater's husband hit town and bought the studio she became one of the superrich."

"She deserves it. She's a nice lady."

"It's easy to be nice if you've got about twenty million dollars in the bank," he said, and paused to digest his own wisdom. "You know, if you're short I'd be glad to help you out. I can always write it off as a bad loan if I live long enough. And if I don't—what the hell, I've got nobody to leave my money to and you might as well get some of it."

I said: "Thanks, Paul. That's a nice gesture."

"I mean it, kid."

I laughed and said: "I know you do, pal." We pulled into the parking lot of the Meridiana, and the elderly attendant took over my car.

"You ought to think about Sue's offer to join us," Levin said, brushing off his suit. "You could stay on for a couple of days, get off in Monte Carlo and fly back here. You probably have a dame waiting for you, but by that time you might have impressed Mrs. Slater enough for her to mention your name to her husband. One phone call from him and you'd be back in the business. At least you could make a living."

"As a sixty-year-old featured player?"

"Who cares? You could play somebody's father, or grandfather, if necessary."

"Sue mentioned that he's selling the company."

"He'll buy another one, that's for sure. You can bet your ass he's not going back to making rivets in Kansas City."

"I'll think about it," I said.

"We might not stop here again," Levin warned me. "Make up your mind by tomorrow morning. Chances are we won't hoist anchor until eleven o'clock."

"Okay," I said. "Let's join your friends."

"Acquaintances," Levin corrected me as we trooped up the open-air stairway leading to the restaurant. The moon had just come up over the summits in the east, while the peaks of the mountains to the west reflected the last rays of the setting sun. A warm gust of wind swept down from the Sierra Blanca like a gentle caress.

The others had all entered the restaurant, but Sue stood waiting for us outside the door. "It's gorgeous here," she said. "No wonder you never made it back to smog-city."

"You should have been around yesterday," I told her. "Or all of last month. It never stopped raining."

"I bring sunshine with me everywhere I go," she said, and did a little soft-shoe number on the tiled floor. Then she rested a hand on Levin's shoulder. "*You* are in charge of the seating arrangement tonight," she said, "and if I'm not next to Robert here . . . I'll have the bosun cut your balls off. Or I'll do it myself."

"I'll take care of it," Levin said. "As long as I don't get the tab."

Everybody ordered drinks from the bar while our table was being set up. I asked for a whiskey sour on the rocks, thinking it would make the evening more bearable. The rest of the crew stayed with champagne, while Janet Slater remained true to her diet Coke. She turned to me and said: "Help me with this menu. My three years of high-school Spanish were too long ago."

I was standing beside her chair and was able to show her that by turning the page she would find the menu in English. Meanwhile, the smart chatter continued from nearby. I wondered why Mrs. Slater, who seemed like a nice, unpretentious woman, had chosen this group from her guest list, then reckoned that filling a big yacht for a Mediterranean cruise out of season might not be all that easy. The headwaiter came to take our order, and it was a full forty minutes later we were finally called to the table. I had finished my second whiskey sour by that time and was experiencing the strange sensation of not having any legs, of floating, like one of those lawnmowers that operate with an air cushion. If you're not used to drinking, I said to myself, it's a mistake to start after a long night without much sleep.

Paul Levin surveyed the elegant dining room and seemed impressed. Glass windows with plant beds outside, indirect lighting and a fairly good house were perhaps more than he had expected to find in what he undoubtedly considered to be a backwater at the entrance to the Med. Our party, with Paul's exception, were the least formally dressed customers that night, the clientele being mostly Spanish. "I'm glad you wore a tie," he said to me in an aside, then began to seat his fellow passengers with an authoritative manner.

He placed Janet Slater at the head of the table and stepped up to the chair on her right. I was assigned to her left, with Sue on my other flank. The rest of the unruly group sat down in their assigned places without comment, accustomed, so it seemed, to Paul being in charge. The silver base plates were removed by two waiters, and the first course was served.

"Sue has told me very little about you," my hostess began, "but I've gathered from other sources that you were rather a bad boy when you were young."

"Not really bad," I said. "Just easily tempted."

"Like me," Sue put in, and giggled.

Mrs. Slater said: "I get it. Two innocents in the Hollywood jungle."

"It wasn't a jungle in those days," Sue said. "It was a never-never land."

"Well, don't you think it's about time to come home?" Janet Slater asked, turning to face me.

"Home is here," I said quietly, and reached carefully for the glass of water in front of me, hoping to distill the two whiskey sours I had consumed much too quickly.

"But you're an American, aren't you?" Janet Slater said. "Do you really plan to live here forever?"

"Forever is not all that long," I replied.

"Listen, home isn't what it was," Paul intervened. "The weather has changed and so has the town. And the business, for God's sake, is in the hands of a bunch of money-grubbing kids. Everybody wants to get out of L.A. and you want my buddy to go back? The only people who want to live out there are a bunch of Latino wetbacks, or boat people from the third world. The fires and the floods and the crime don't seem so bad to them. But anybody in his right mind who's managed to escape would have to be a masochist to go back."

I was puzzled by his diatribe. Was he acting the part of the devil's disciple, or had he had a sudden change of mind during the last half hour. "Is it really that bad?" I asked. "You still live there, Paul."

"Because I'm too old to move," he replied. "And because my business is there."

"You could quit," Sue Wilson said, "and retire."

"I'd die if I quit," Paul replied. "But don't think I haven't been tempted. And I get out every chance I get, and so do you, Janet. You've got a place in Santo Domingo and in Vail, plus a private jet to take you there. But if you had to sit in L.A. all year round, I wonder if you'd be such a hometown booster."

"I'd like to go back for a visit someday," I said, in defense of my hostess.

"Well, if you do," Janet Slater said, "you must call us. I'll give you a welcoming-home party."

I said: "Thank you. That would be nice."

"Don't come back until somebody offers you a job," Paul crowed. I was beginning to understand his strategy. "Have your old man put him in a movie," he said to Janet.

"All right. I'll talk to him. He'll be calling tonight," she replied. "I've forgotten to order the wine," she added. "Will you do it, Paul? You know more about all that than I do."

"I've asked Robert to join us on our cruise for a couple of weeks," Sue said, leaning forward to be heard. "If it's all right with you?"

"That would be lovely, I hope you can make it." Mrs. Slater replied, turning full-face to me again.

35

LEVIN SUMMONED THE WINE-WAITER with a sharp cry of *"Sommelier!,"* and although it was the wrong language he got an immediate response. A portly man with a red-and-gray-striped vest supplied him with a leather folder. Levin produced a lorgnette with a silver handle out of his vest pocket and began to turn the pages of the wine list. I was impressed. He sure had come a long way since his early days of sitting in a small office hidden away in a back alley with a part-time secretary. He was a man of the world now, unafraid to voice his opinions to one and all. He closed the folder and handed it to me. "I don't know anything about Spanish wines, so you'll have to help me, Robert," he said. He offered me his spectacles as an afterthought.

"I don't need those yet," I said, a tiny triumph.

"Don't they have French wines?" Janet Slater asked.

"They do," I told her. "But the Spanish ones are good, too. And a lot cheaper."

"Oh, don't be silly," she replied.

"Let him choose what he wants," Levin said.

I did as I was told and selected a red and a white vintage Rioja.

Sue had observed the scene with a mischievous smile. She turned to me and, lowering her voice, said: "You're not doing so well right now, are you?" she asked.

"What makes you say that?"

"Paul's efforts on your behalf. It was quite a performance. You obviously need his help."

"There's a Spanish saying: *Dios apreta, pero no ahoga,* which means: God pushes you down, but doesn't drown you."

"I get the picture," she said. "And to think it was all my fault."

"Oh, come on," I said. "I'm a big boy now, and I was a big boy then. Everybody is in charge of his own fate . . . Or almost, anyway."

"Well, if you decide to come back to L.A. you could always stay with me. As a houseguest."

"That might be compromising."

"Why? I've got a big house and I'm unattached. I suppose you're not?"

"I am, as of right now," I told her. "That part of my life has hit a few snags recently, too."

"Poor you," she replied. "All alone in a foreign land."

"I've got a cat that keeps me company."

"You could bring the cat," she said. "And maybe get her into the movies if all else fails."

"She's an it," I said.

"All the better." She paused. "It would be fun, no? And maybe we could even get together again. After forty years that would be one for the *Guinness Book of Records.*"

I smiled. "Yeah, if it works."

"Why shouldn't it? You can still get it up, can't you? A guy who doesn't need glasses to read the menu! Or do you have your doubts about me? Listen, I've had a nip and tuck taken all up and down the line. And I haven't fooled around. I've made a couple of the usual mistakes after Eddie passed away. But out there's a bad place for a single lady. You know what they used to say: In Hollywood even Joan Crawford sits around waiting for the phone to ring. Well, it hasn't changed much in that respect."

I said: "I appreciate the offer, but it's just not the kind of decision you make at a dinner party."

She laughed. "You know, that's one of the things I like about you. You're still cautious about committing yourself. Like that night in Palm Springs. I made all the running, remember?"

"Not for long."

She bent over her plate and giggled. "That's about the only mistake I ever made that I didn't come to regret."

"Because it worked out all right for you."

"Don't be bitchy," she said. "Listen, I was between a rock and a hard place."

"I remember you said that going back to the chorus wouldn't be all that bad."

"What a memory you have! But don't forget what a girl says isn't always the truth."

"That goes for the guys, too."

"I guess so," she said. "But think about it. It wouldn't be difficult to keep you in the style to which you have become accustomed. That's for sure."

"Right on." I noticed that Raoul, seated at the far end of the table, was straining to overhear our conversation. "Cool it," I told her. "We'll talk later."

"Not too much later. We sail in the morning."

"I know. And your friend Raoul knows it, too."

"Fuck *him*, and the polo pony he rode up on," Sue said.

"I'd rather not."

The youngest male member of the group who was seated on Sue's left turned toward her. "You haven't spoken a word to me all evening, love. I'm deeply offended." I'd been told he was Janet's hairdresser, obviously an important member of this party.

Sue said: "All right. What do you want to talk about? The weather? It's gorgeous, isn't it? There's a full moon." She turned

207

back to me. "You know, when the votes are all in, all that matters is finding someone who speaks the same language. Don't you agree?"

"Like Eddie?"

"Yeah. Like Eddie. At least he knew what made me tick most of the time."

"I guess that is important," I said, suddenly remembering that Carmen had told me she would call me at midnight, and that I had said I would be home.

"It is to me," Sue said. She paused to finish the remains of her drink. "Do you believe in kismet, in fate?" she inquired, fluttering her eyelids and clowning. "Or a second chance? Does that sound better?"

"I'm not sure I do," I told her.

"Well, neither am I sure," she replied, and once again giggled.

She was as likable as ever, direct in manner, and never too serious. Still I could imagine what going back to California with her would be like, me an out-of-work actor playing the part of an aging gigolo. It would serve Evelyn right if I took off, I thought, but knew that that was not the way I wanted to end our relationship. If I wanted to end it. I was also sober enough to realize that Sue's proposal was talk, flirtatious banter.

The wine-waiter held out a glass of red wine for me to taste. I took a swallow and nodded to him. It could have been hemlock . . . by that time I wouldn't have known the difference.

"Where do you want to go after dinner?" Raoul called from his place further down the long table. "There must be a disco or a flamenco joint in this town."

"Ask Bobby," Sue called back. "He's our guide for the evening."

"There are about ten discos," I said, "but they don't get going until one-thirty in the morning."

"We have time," Sue said. "We're all on vacation. Personally I vote for flamenco. A drink after dinner and then off we go. Or have you got a late date, Robert?"

"I don't," I said.

"Then what the hell . . . you're not going to rat out on us, are you? We've only just met up again after half a century. Or are you going to be a party poop and spoil my evening?"

"I was never a night owl," I told her.

"Bullshit," she said. "I've heard about this town. It stays open all night. Discos and flamenco. That's our plan."

"I need to get my beauty sleep. And I hate discos."

"All right, then we'll skip the disco. Take us to a gypsy joint. Something typically Spanish."

I couldn't see myself going to Marisa's with this group, but I knew that if they insisted there would be no way out. I glanced at my watch. It was only eleven-fifteen. With any luck it wouldn't happen. Then Janet Slater said: "Oh, I'd love to hear some good flamenco. It's what I've always liked best about Spain."

ON THE LAST LEG OF MY GUIDED TOUR Sue insisted on riding with me. She made no comment on the appearance of my car, waited for the attendant to open the door and got in. We started out of the parking lot with the others in the bus following us. Sue shivered. "It's cold," she said.

I reached back, found my golf jacket on the rear seat and handed it to her. She spread it out over her knees. "A long time ago a friend of mine who had been in the Spanish diplomatic service told me that one is never as cold as under the palm trees," I told her.

"I can see his point," Sue said. "Anyway, to get back to my life . . . things didn't go all that smoothly for me after you left town."

"How so?" I asked. "Eddie and you got married, and that's what you wanted, wasn't it?"

"I did at the time. It took a year for Eddie to pay off his wife. He sold the house up on the hill and bought a new place in Bel Air. He wanted us to make a fresh start. So for the first six months I was kept busy furnishing the new place. Then one day I came home and I heard him talking to someone on the phone. He was trashing you, saying you were bad news, a womanizer and a Commie. That was all the rage in those days, the best way to keep people from hiring anyone, and I guess he thought saying you were a skirt chaser wasn't enough. I knew that you were never mixed up in politics, although we never discussed anything like that as far as I can remember. You weren't, were you? Or were you holding out on me?"

"No, but I had a girlfriend who was pretty far left," I said. "I met her on the boat to France."

"Yeah? And what happened to her?"

"She was too good for me," I replied. "We parted company after a couple of years."

She shrugged and said: "Well, to get back to me . . . after Eddie put down the telephone I really freaked out. I thought you had enough trouble without that kind of a tag being hung on you. So I let him have it. I said: 'Womanizer, okay, but all that other stuff is bullshit.' He said: 'Don't talk to me like that,' but I couldn't stop. I told him he was just sore because he couldn't make it happen for me, and that had never been my problem with you, and he hauled off and hit me across the mouth with the back of his hand. I really flipped then. Even the thugs I had known in New York had never done that. I picked up a poker that was hanging next to the fireplace, and swung at him. I hit him in the ribs, and it must have really hurt, because he staggered back clutching his left side even though I had hit him on the right. I was scared. I thought maybe he was having a heart attack, he'd mentioned that the doctors had told him to watch his blood pressure. It turned out that it was what they call fibrillation and it wasn't all that serious, but it really got to him. He had a bad habit of smoking about ten cigars a day, and he quit after that little incident. We made it up, sort of, but he stayed pretty scared. He was spooked of dying . . . he was fifty-five, just the right age for a major coronary. I apologized about a hundred thousand times, told him the only thing that could make me lose my temper was if somebody hit me, especially in the face. He apologized, too, but it was a pretty strange marriage after that."

She tossed my jacket onto the back seat; the car heater had finally started to work. I didn't say anything, and she went right on. "Talk about Jean Harlow and Paul Bern," she said. "That was kid stuff compared to Eddie and me. He was afraid to come on to me after that, partly because of what I had mentioned about his failure as a lover, and partly because he was afraid his ticker might act up again if we really went at it in the hay. Oh, we managed once in a while, but it was never right, not even for him. After a while we settled for a companionate marriage, and that was okay, but every night it was like a soap opera, both of us going to our separate rooms in our best pajamas. He made me promise to be faithful and I was! What the hell, he was really a nice guy and he took good care of me in every other way. Three years later he got prostate cancer. It was terminal. They did an autopsy on him, and as it turned out there was really nothing wrong with his heart . . . all of his worrying was for nothing." She paused. "Poor old Eddie," she added with a sigh. "He got a raw deal."

Tales of Tinseltown, I thought to myself. We had arrived at the small tree-lined square in the old town. There was the sound of castanets over the music of a *Sevillana*. I gave Paco the keys of my car, informed him that the minibus behind us belonged to our party and told him that we wouldn't be staying very long.

"I'm sorry I bent your ear," Sue said. "It's not a very nice story. I've never told anybody else about Eddie and me, but since you were in on it at the beginning . . . Not that it's such a big secret. All our friends knew that it wasn't a match made in heaven."

"Very few are," I said. The others had joined us on the sidewalk.

"So this is where you go at night," Levin said. "No wonder I couldn't get you on the phone."

We went inside. There were only about a dozen people seated around the wooden dance floor. Marisa's face brightened when she saw me. She left her partner to continue dancing by himself and hurried over to have her cheeks kissed. *"Roberto, mi amor,"* she said. "Howareyou?" She was showing off her English, making one word out of her greeting.

I didn't attempt to make the introductions. Marisa shook hands with them all and led us to a table. Then she rejoined the dancers, shouting: *"¡Ánimo!"* and clapping her hands with a newly found frenzy.

A waiter hurried over to our table and took our order for drinks. Carmen had noticed my arrival. She glanced quickly in my direction, then continued dancing. The *Sevillana* ended with a wild flourish. For a short while the ensemble devoted itself to *palmas,* the beat crescendoing. Then the young gypsy did his *zapatéo,* pounding the parquet with his black, high-heeled jodhpur boots. Sue leaned over to me. She had seated herself on my right. Janet Slater was on my left. "The guy who opens a Dr. Scholl's in this town need never look back," Sue whispered, and I laughed. Carmen was watching us from her chair at the back of the wooden floor.

Mrs. Slater seemed totally engrossed in the act. She applauded enthusiastically once the young gypsy had finished and was taking a bow. "This is wonderful," she said. "I'm so glad you brought us here."

I heard Raoul say: "Very typical," with his customary superior air. "Good, but not great."

The *palmas* took up their beat. Then Carmen ventured out onto the floor. I felt nervous watching her as she started her *buleria.* I wanted her to impress the others as much as she had impressed me the first time I had seen her dance. "She's the only pretty girl in the joint," Sue whispered to me.

I nodded and said: "Watch her. She's also the best dancer." I wanted to cut short the small talk. Only the most uninitiated tourists were ignorant enough to carry on a conversation while a dancer or a singer was on the stage, especially an artist who performed with the intensity of feeling that was so evident in Carmen. From the very beginning, the first movements of her hands and arms, the

213

expression on her face showed her concentration, her dedication to every detail of the *buleria*. Undoubtedly she had rehearsed it a thousand times, but that was only as a backup to her *duende*, the mysterious word that means more than temporary inspiration, requires the magic of the moment to influence the performer as well. The second-rate *torero*, they say, uses the absence of his *duende* as an excuse when he can't cope with a difficult bull, thereby provoking the abuse of his public. A second-rate dancer can blame a poor performance on an indifferent audience. But the really dedicated artist in flamenco dances or sings for himself as much as anyone, just as the truly great bullfighters shut out the spectators that are present in the bullring. The onlookers can occasionally inspire, and often believe they play a part, but they are outside the inner flame that ignites the artist. That is the only way he or she can transmit emotion.

"You're right . . . she's good," Sue whispered.

I didn't reply. I had been a performer, too, in a small way, but had never been able to forget my surroundings, the cameraman and the director and the crew, but I knew how important their undivided attention could be.

I need not have worried about Carmen. She had the ability to shut out the world when she performed, and so was able to transfer her emotion to her audience so that when she ended her dance there was a sudden pause before the applause exploded inside the low-ceilinged room. She bowed, swept her hair back into place and bowed again. I blew her a kiss and she smiled, then retired quickly to the bar. "Is that the girl who's giving you trouble?" Sue asked.

"No. Unfortunately not. Wrong number."

"I didn't think it was. She's too skinny. Unless you've changed brands."

I excused myself and crossed to the bar. Carmen was still out of breath when I kissed her on both cheeks. "More of your rich friends?" she asked.

"Just one or two of them. From long ago."

"I wanted to invite you to supper. If you can get away."

"Tonight?"

"Yes, tonight. Once I have finished. It's my turn to take you."

"Aren't you tired?"

"Of course I am. But I'll recover. You've brought me luck."

"How so?" I asked.

"I'll tell you later."

"What about Rafael?"

"Don't worry," she said. "He will be going off to collect my brother early tomorrow morning. When the Guardia Civil releases him."

"All right. If you say so. Where shall we meet? At El Rodéito?"

"No. Wait for me in San Pedro. In front of the church. In the main *plaza*. The mechanic has repaired my car."

"I'll be there," I said. "What time?"

"An hour after you and your friends leave. The others won't stay long once you go. I'll change my clothes here. To save time."

Marisa had moved out onto the floor. "*¡Vamos, vamos!*" she called out in our direction, making what sounded like pistol shots with her small, chubby hands. I returned to my chair between Sue and Janet Slater. "Arrange a late date?" Sue asked. "Of course I don't mean to pry."

"Not really a date," I replied. "A nightcap."

"I don't blame you," Janet Slater said. "She's just wonderful. You should bring her to L.A. I'd love that girl to dance at one of my parties."

"You'll have to bring the two guitar players as well," I told her.

"I don't mind. She's worth it."

Paul had leaned across the table to eavesdrop on our conversation. "Tell her I'll handle her. And I'll split the commission with you." He glanced at his watch. "Isn't it about time for us to get back to the ship?" he asked.

"Not yet," Janet Slater said. "Let's just stay a little longer."

"What about your beauty sleep?" Sue asked me.

"It'll just have to wait," I told her.

Inevitably Marisa had got up to do her Sinatra imitation. She only did one verse, then it was time for the *rumbita*. Marisa selected a tall Englishman for her first partner, then ordered Carmen and the other girl to join in. Carmen came over to our table, and Raoul rose eagerly from his chair. We sat watching them. "He's a good dancer," I said to Sue.

She gave me a sour look. "It's part of his job," she said.

"What does he do for a living?"

"He plays polo . . . and he dances. He's a reserve officer in the Argentine cavalry, and he's had two rich wives shot out from under him. Now he's looking to score a hat trick."

"Sue! Really!" Janet said, but smiled.

"You know what Eddie used to say," Sue replied. "That you can take the girl out of the chorus, but you can't take the chorus out of the girl."

She was a little tipsy, I noticed, had finished her second whiskey on the rocks. "Good old Eddie," I said.

"Yeah, I really miss him sometimes. It's not so great being on my own."

Raoul was all elegant movement, showing off his Latin birthright. Carmen's face was a mask. The music stopped and he kissed her hand, bowing from the waist. I noticed that his glistening hair had not moved throughout the *rumbita*.

"It's time I was in bed," Levin said. "I'm too old to stay out this late. Will you drive back to the ship, lover boy?"

"We're all going, Paul," Janet Slater said, "as soon as you ask for the check."

"Be glad to," Levin assured her.

Sue turned to face me. "Will you come by in the morning?" she asked. "For sure?"

"I'll be there at ten-thirty." Then, without thinking, I added: "I wish I could come along . . . really."

"What? You and Carmen?" she asked, and tossed off the rest of her drink.

"You have a good memory, too, dear girl," I told her.

"Yeah . . . well, some things you never forget."

I followed Levin outside into the square. Paco went off for my car and I tipped him after he had helped Paul get in. The rest of the group was just coming out of the club. "Wait for the rest of the team," Levin said. "They'll never find the way on their own."

I drove off far enough to clear the street in front of Marisa's, and stopped. Levin seemed glum. He sat looking down at his feet, his arms crossed over his chest. "I guess you've always had a self-destructive streak in you," he said after a while. "And you haven't changed."

"What makes you say that?" I asked, although I knew what was coming.

"Well, here this woman is ready to take you on with no questions asked, and you prance off and make a date with a gypsy broad."

"She's not a gypsy, not that it matters. And so what? Why shouldn't I?"

"Bad manners," Levin said. "Listen, if you had a little more tact you could have waited to take the lady out some other night. What the hell, Bobby, if you came along for a couple of weeks on the *Penelope*, like I said, you'd have it made. Janet likes you, and Sue is ready for a shipboard romance. It would have been good for both of you."

"Come on, Paul. Sue's no fool," I said. "She knows better than to try to pick up the pieces after thirty years. She's a little pissed tonight, that's all."

"Maybe so, but she's a lonely woman and you're broke, right? Anyway, forget it. Leave me your address and I'll send you a check. That way you'll at least be able to make it back to the Motion Picture Relief Home if everything else fails."

"That's not really necessary, Paul. But thanks anyway."

"It would make me feel good," Levin said. "You could consider it a loan."

"We'll talk about it in the morning," I told him. "How come you never got married?"

"I've always been too busy, and now it's too late." He glanced over at me and shrugged. I noticed that Raoul, at the wheel of the minibus, had turned on his lights and had driven off. Levin didn't say anything more to me until we had reached the port. I thanked Janet Slater for her hospitality and shook hands with the others.

Sue waited at the foot of the gangway until the rest of the party had gone aboard. "I'm glad we met up again," she said. "You look great. Whatever you're doing, keep doing it."

"You, too." We hugged. She took off her shoes to walk across the gangway. I watched her until she had entered the main lounge. I looked at my watch. I still had half an hour to kill before Carmen would be able to make it to our rendezvous. The warm wind from the mountains was ruffling the smooth water of the marina, a promise of spring. I didn't feel sleepy so I went for a walk to clear my head. The full moon was high in the cloudless sky.

37

THE YELLOW SEAT WAS PARKED in front of the church in San Pedro. I pulled up behind it and turned off my headlights. Carmen got out of her car. She was wearing her pea jacket, but I noticed that under it she had put on a black dress, a feminine signal that this was meant to be a special occasion. I told her that she was *muy guapa,* and she smiled.

"I called you at nine," she said, "but there was no answer. I guessed you had gone out to dinner so I bought a roast chicken for my supper, but we can share it if you're still hungry. The barman at the *tablao* gave me a bottle of wine."

"Where shall we go?" I asked her.

She looked up at me shyly. "We could visit your cat . . ." she said.

I kissed her on both cheeks. "Isn't that dangerous?" I asked her, thinking Rafael might be lurking in the dark street again.

She shrugged. "Where else can we go? Perhaps to your house. We could build a fire and dine there."

I said: "All right," and asked her if it was safe to leave her car parked there.

"No one will steal it," she said, and went to get a straw basket out of the back of the Seat. Then she locked the doors and we got into my car.

"What are we celebrating?" I asked her.

"My good fortune," she said, smiling, and went on to explain that a man from Madrid, an *impresario,* had come to see her that afternoon. He had asked her if she could make herself free to work with a theatrical company in the capital. Marisa had agreed to give her a leave of absence until the summer.

"When will you leave?" I asked her.

"Tomorrow night on the train," she said. "You could drive me to the station in Málaga. If you have time."

"I have time."

She took my hand and held it until we had reached the junction of the small country road that leads up into the hills. Then she sat looking straight ahead at the moonlit countryside. "Was it difficult for you to get away from the blonde lady who was sitting beside you?" she asked.

"No, not difficult at all." I stopped the car at the foot of the path leading up to the house and took my keys to the front door out of the glove compartment. She followed me in silence until we had reached the terrace.

"Does all this belong to you?" she asked, indicating the garden and the fields that were inside the low stone wall I had built years ago.

"Only two hectares," I told her.

She laughed. "It's a beautiful *finca,*" she said. "But why don't you live here?"

"I have for many years. Now I rent the place when I can. I need the money."

"Ah, money," she said. "Isn't it a bore?"

"Only when you don't have any."

"I know all about that."

I unlocked the front door and we went inside. It was less cold in the living room than I had expected it to be. I laid a fire in the fireplace and searched for a match. She came over with her cigarette lighter and lit the crumpled-up newspaper under the kindling. "I've forgotten our picnic," she said. "Stupid of me."

"I'll go get it."

"No, I will. We're in Spain, you know. Did you lock the car?"

"No. It's open."

She hurried off, and I went into the bedroom to open the shutters. The light from the moon flooded the cold room. I went back into the living room and, leaving the door open, tossed another log on the fire. She returned an instant later. "Where is the kitchen?" she asked.

"Through that door."

She scooped up her basket. "And the light?"

"I'll show you."

"Now you will have to wait," she said. "I will do the rest."

"You don't know where anything is," I said.

"I will find what I want."

I heard her opening the cupboard drawers. She had taken off her pea jacket when she reappeared. She was carrying two plates and some cutlery. "Will you open the wine," she said, putting the things she was carrying down on the coffee table in front of the fireplace. She went back into the kitchen. The wine bottle was cold, and after opening it I put it down on the table. "We can sit on the floor near the fire," she called out to me. "Do you have a carving knife?"

"It's in the drawer of the kitchen table."

"I've found it." She brought the chicken, neatly carved on a plate, and put it down in front of me. "Have you lived here with your *novia?*" she asked in English.

"No. Only with my wife many years ago."

"I always forget," she said, switching back to Spanish. "The *novia* has a villa of her own." She poured the wine into the glasses she had brought on her second trip. "Did you leave your wife?" she asked, "or did she leave you?"

"We parted by mutual agreement."

"Did you have children?" She sat down cross-legged on the rug under the coffee table.

"Luckily not with that wife," I said.

She frowned. "How many times have you been married?" she asked.

"Only twice."

"Only twice!" she repeated, astonished. "But you don't appear to be that kind of man."

"What kind of man is that?"

"*Un faldero,*" she said, a skirt chaser. "Two wives and a *novia* who has left you! *¡Vaya por Dios!*"

"God had nothing to do with it," I told her. "I've been around for a long time."

She laughed. "I don't think I will have two husbands and a *novio* who has departed by the time I am sixty," she said. She broke the bar of bread in half and handed me the longer piece. Then she raised her glass. "*¡Suerte!*" she said. "*Y dinero, y tiempo para gastarlo!*"

Luck, money and time to spend it—it was certainly a toast I could drink to. The chicken was still warm. It had been wrapped in aluminum foil, she explained. "Do you have music?" she asked.

I got up to turn on the radio. It was tuned to the local British station, the jazz hour. "Not that kind of music," she said. I turned the knob to the Spanish station that plays flamenco and the songs of Julio Iglesias, Maria del Mar and La Pantoja, the current favorites. "That's better," Carmen said. "So after dinner we can dance."

"Aren't you tired of dancing?"

"Not with you."

I asked her why she had called me that first night and invited me to meet her at Marisa's.

"Because I couldn't talk when you came to my house," she

said. "My mother was with me. She didn't know Pedro was in jail. But she knows now. Rafael told her."

"And Marisa?"

"She is like my older sister. She knows everything." She paused. "She thinks I should forget him but I can't."

"She may be right."

"*¿Quizás?* But I don't want to talk about it tonight."

We ate our chicken. She took a piece of bread and soaked it in the gravy, popped it into her mouth and took a swig of wine. "*¡Venga!*" she said, getting to her feet.

We danced. After the whiskey sours and the wine I found I could almost keep time to the music. Women make all the important decisions, I thought once again at least the women I had known, Carmen included. It was probably the fact that she was leaving that had decided her to be reckless. Well, it was my night to be reckless, too. She glanced up at me. She had been looking down at our feet. "When I return from Madrid," she said, "I will teach you how to dance."

I drew her closer, and kissed her. It doesn't matter how old you get to be, the first kiss is always different. For a brief instant I thought of Evelyn, and felt guilty. But not after the second kiss. "Come to bed," Carmen said.

"The bedroom is very cold," I warned her.

"It won't be cold for long," she replied. "You, a *faldero*, should know all about that."

38

SHE TOOK A SHOWER before coming to bed, and was delighted to learn that the solar heating I had installed some years ago provided the house with hot water after a sunny day. In the moonlight she shed the towel she had wrapped around her, and I noticed that despite her slim body she was surprisingly womanly. I took her in my arms. "Has it been a long time since you made love?" she wanted to know.

"A while. And you?"

"Much longer. Be gentle."

It was an unnecessary request—I felt tenderness for her at that precise moment, more than passion. Passion came soon after. "¡Cómo me gustas!" she whispered, how you please me, pleasing words that made me want to please her more. She sighed once it was over. I grasped her right hand and held it firmly in mine.

"I was not mistaken in you," she said.

I kissed her gently on the forehead. "Why do you say that?" I asked her. "Because you still think of me as *faldero?*"

She said: *"Imbécil.* It has nothing to do with that."

"Did you make up your mind that this should happen before we came here?"

"Of course."

"Why?"

"I have no idea why. Un *capricho*. No, that's not true. I liked you, and I wanted you to remember me. Even after I have gone away, and you are back with your *novia*."

"That may not happen."

"It will," she said. "You are not the kind of man women leave because they get angry. For other reason, yes. Because you have no money, *quizás*."

"They've all known that from the very beginning," I said. "I've never kept it a secret."

In Spanish she said: "Shut up. I don't want to hear about any of the others right now. I want to sleep beside you for a while. Then in the morning you can take me back to my car. We won't have breakfast together. Not today. Another day, perhaps. Then early in the evening, at eight, I will come back in a taxi so you can drive me to the railroad station in Málaga. So that we can say goodbye, like lovers."

"I'll be waiting for you. At eight. What time is your train?"

"At ten o'clock."

"Have you bought your ticket?"

"I will do so at the train station. Now go to sleep."

I got up to turn off the light in the bathroom. When I came back to bed she was curled up on the far side. Her eyes were wide open. "I hope God doesn't punish me for my sins," she said.

"Are you religious?"

"Not really. Not anymore. Although I still believe in God. Not in the devil, but in God."

"And how would He punish you?"

She turned to face me. "Oh, in the usual way," she said with a faint smile. "I was punished once before, you know. I thought of my daughter as a punishment before she was born. Although I

225

wouldn't mind having a child by you. They say older men make wise children. At least that's what they say. But it would make things difficult for me. To have two.

"You don't have to worry," I told her.

"How can you be so sure?"

"I am sure. That's all." I didn't want to go into my medical history. Not at that moment.

She raised herself up on one elbow. *"Pero tu te as muerto conmigo, no?"* she asked. You died with me, no?

It was a gentle, poetic euphemism I hadn't heard for a long time, not since my brief bachelor days in Madrid. "Of course I did," I replied in English. "But you still needn't worry. That danger no longer exists. I'll explain the technical details to you in the morning. Not right now."

"Very well," she said, and leaned over to kiss me. "I believe you."

39

I DROVE HER TO SAN PEDRO at nine-thirty. The weather had changed. The breeze from the Sierras had given way to the west wind. There was a dark bank of clouds on the horizon. After she had started her car I drove to the port. Paul Levin was seated in the main cabin having breakfast. "The others are all dead to the world," he said. "You look like you need some coffee."

The skipper, a young Englishman, appeared a few minutes after the steward had brought me some toast and a jug of coffee. "Be all right, Mr. Levin, if we get an earlier start?" he asked. "The sea will be kicking up in less than an hour and I want to get to Gib before it gets too rough."

"Any time you say," Paul told him. He waited until the man had left us. "Sue asked me to tell you goodbye," he said. "We might be coming back here but I doubt it."

"Well, thank Janet for her invitation," I said. "She's a nice woman."

"Yeah . . . well, she thinks you're charming, too. Her husband called when we got back last night. He was worried about her being out so late, so she couldn't mention having met you. You know what husbands are like." He grinned. "Probably just as well you couldn't join our cruise. You might have stumbled into the wrong cabin some night."

"You overestimate my charms, Paul."

"Maybe so." He put his hand inside the tweed jacket he was wearing. "Here's the check I promised you. It's for five thousand dollars."

"Forget it," I said.

He folded the check in half and put it down on the varnished table in front of us. "You don't have to cash it. Just keep it in case of an emergency. We're all of an age when you never know what might happen. And back home you're eligible for free medical care, right, so don't be an idiot. I can take it off my income tax."

"If you insist, Paul," I said, and slipped the check into my wallet.

"If you need more, my new address is on it," he said. He got to his feet and held out his hand. "I was real happy to see you again. If we do stop by here this evening, I'll call you."

"I'll be home at ten-thirty."

"Okay. Take care of yourself, my friend."

"I'll do my best. Kiss Sue goodbye for me," I added. "Tell her I'll give her a shout if I ever get back to L.A."

"Don't wait too long," he said. "We're none of us getting any younger."

Levin got up from his chair. We embraced. The captain had started the engines. I could feel the teak deck vibrating under my feet. A sailor in a T-shirt had moved to the foot of the gangplank and was waiting for me to go ashore. Levin waved once I had reached the quai. "Keep in touch!" he shouted.

I waved back. I didn't wait for *Penelope* to leave her mooring. I knew it would take quite a while for a yacht that size. I walked back to the parking lot. I had no regrets. As the result of what might be called an industrial accident I had run away from that world, and I knew that it would be a mistake to return now.

I drove back to my apartment. It was as if I was starting out on a new adventure. I began to fantasize about the future. Lack of sleep has often had that effect on me. I saw myself backstage in a Madrid theatre watching Carmen perform. My daydream was a Latin version of the *Blue Angel,* the much older man, me, in the role of the possessive lover. And how would the story end? Would Rafael finally plunge his knife in my heart? No, that was too melodramatic an ending. A less acute, and probably more drawn-out, finale was lying in wait for me. It was just a daydream. Watch the road, pal! I counseled myself.

Fergy was lying on the bed when I opened the door. She looked up reproachfully but forgave me as soon as I had filled her plate with cat food. The telephone rang. It was Evelyn calling from Marrakech. I could barely hear her. She said: "Hi. How's your weather?"

"A little better," I said. "How's the weather there?"

"Perfect," she said. "Kathy and I are going on to an oasis farther south. I suppose you don't miss me."

"I'm trying not to," I told her. "Are you coming back soon?"

"In a week or two. I worry about Hercules."

"Where is he?" I asked, glad that she had changed the subject.

"In a kennel," she said. "Poor Hercules. It's that place in Estepona. Would you mind going to see if he's all right?"

"Not at all. I'm very fond of him."

"Then I'll call you tomorrow. Will you be there?"

I said: "Probably. I might go out for lunch."

"All right. I'll call in the evening. Be good."

"You, too," I said, and hung up. Two weeks would give me time to feel less guilty. I shaved and changed my clothes. The sky was full of black clouds. I decided I'd better drive back up to the house to close the shutters before the rain started. I was also hoping to catch Maria before she went home to tell her the place needed a good cleaning in case Cecilia turned up with the promised tenants.

Kiko came out of his office as I was leaving. He was all smiles. "I've got some good news for a change," he said.

"Did you hear from Susan?"

"No, of course not. What would be good about that?" he asked. "You won't believe this," he went on. "Lady Pamela is back. She only stayed in London one day. She called this morning. She and Collins didn't work things out after all. They're going to the mat. She's suing him for divorce. It's back to square one. She's a client again!"

"That's good news all right," I said.

He ignored my sarcastic tone of voice. "You'll be asked to make a deposition. She's already told me that."

"I can't wait."

"What the hell . . . there's nothing to that. You'll be asked to swear that you saw Collins and his girlfriend at the golf club holding hands. Big deal."

"They weren't holding hands."

"Well, whatever. They were thick as thieves, right?"

"I don't recall."

"Aw, come on, *abuelito!* You're not going to fuck me up, are you? A deposition is no big deal."

"Let's wait and see what happens," I told him. "They may get together again. Stranger things have happened." It wasn't too late to catch the *Penelope* in Gib, I thought, knowing that it was just an idle threat even as the notion crossed my mind. Anyway, I had promised my temporary *novia* that I would drive her to Málaga.

40

FROM THE BEDROOM WINDOW OF MY VILLA I watched the white Mercedes taxi pull up and stop in front at the bottom of the drive. There were three passengers, I noticed, and went down to stand on the terrace and wait for Carmen. She was in her jeans and pea jacket again. She wore a blue baseball cap, a present from her former Yankee lover, no doubt. She smiled and said *"¡Hola!"*, and I kissed her cheeks.

"You're not alone," I remarked.

"My mother and my daughter are going with me," she replied. "They're only planning to stay a week and then come back here. Alicia has to go to school."

"Have you got a place to live?"

"My uncle lives in Madrid. We'll stay with him while I look for a place. It's all right, isn't it?" she asked. "The taxi would have cost six thousand pesetas. Alicia can sit in the back with my mother. She doesn't take up much room."

I went back into the house, got the keys to my car and locked the front door. The taxi driver had already unloaded the two suitcases Carmen and her mother had brought with them. The mother was a stocky woman with graying dark hair. Her face was heavily lined and she had a golden tooth that was noticeable even from a distance. Her eyes were dark and piercing as she studied my face.

"¿Usted es americano?" she asked after we'd shaken hands.

"Americano del norte," I replied.

"Alicia!" Carmen said sharply to the little girl. She was quite tall for her age, and thin like her mother.

She gave me her hand and did a little curtsy. She looked frightened. She said: *"Buenas tardes,"* in a voice that was barely audible.

I said: *"Hola,* Alicia."

The girl and the mother got into the back of my car while the taxi driver helped me load the two suitcases into the trunk. I paid the man and he drove off. Carmen got in beside me. It was hardly the lovers' goodbye she had promised.

She must have guessed what I was thinking. "I didn't want them to come but my daughter cried all day, so what was I to do? I hope you don't mind." She spoke slowly in English, her eyes on my face as we followed the taxi down the hill.

"Don't worry about it," I said. "I understand."

No one spoke for the first quarter of an hour of the drive. Carmen's mother sat very straight in the seat behind her daughter. I could see her in the rear-view mirror whenever I happened to glance back. Her face was expressionless. She would be well cast in the part of Pilar, the female leader of the guerrilla band in Hemingway's novel, if they ever decided to film a remake. It wasn't all that surprising that Carmen's husband had decided to defect. It was not a very charitable thought. The child directly behind me was studying her fingernails. Occasionally Carmen turned to check on her family.

Then once we were on the new highway, high up in the foothills above the sea, the old woman came alive. *"¡Que bonito!"* she exclaimed, and urged Alicia to take in the view. What a shame that the weather is cloudy, she went on to say.

In Spanish I asked her how long it had been since she had been to Málaga. Not for many years, she told me, long before Alicia was born. The people she worked for took her to the north with them to spend the summer. Then she rattled on about how everything had changed, hadn't gotten better, mind you, except maybe the highway. But even that wasn't certain, because now more people would be killed each year. Then as we turned off onto the old road she was silent and gazed out at the squalor of the outskirts of the town that she apparently felt no need to comment on. We encountered a huge truck loaded down with new cars. *"Coches y más coches,"* the old woman said, shaking her head, cars and more cars. It was a sentiment I could share.

We passed the abandoned cigarette factory that stands like a relic of Victorian England behind a metal fence, its red brick walls well maintained. There was a rumor that it was to be turned into a museum, and I asked Carmen if that was true.

She shook her head. *"Ni idea."*

"It was in a building like that one your namesake was supposed to have worked," I said in English. "That's according to the story that inspired the opera."

"Was that not in *Sevilla?"* Carmen asked.

"I'll look it up. I have the book of stories at home. I'll send it to you in Madrid if you like."

"You can bring it when you come to see me dance in the theatre."

I said: *"¿Quizás?"* and she frowned.

"You're right," she said. "It is a mistake to make plans. They never happen."

"Sometimes they do. We've made it to Málaga."

"Don't be a cynic, it doesn't suit you."

"You get to be that way when you're old."

"Vieja la ropa," she replied. "Remember."

"How could I forget," I said, and glanced over at her. "Your first kind words to me."

233

We arrived at the railroad station. I found a parking place in the street outside the terminal from which I used to ship my car to the north. Carmen insisted on carrying one of the suitcases. Her mother had taken Alicia by the hand and we followed them down the sidewalk. The wind was cold, and she stopped, put down her suitcase and buttoned up her pea jacket. "Is that the only coat you have to wear?" I asked her.

"I have a heavier coat in my suitcase," she said. "For Madrid."

We went inside the main station and she went off to buy tickets for her mother and Alicia. I asked her if she had enough money, she said she did. "Buy a ticket for the quai," I told her, "so that I can take you to the train."

"We can say goodbye here."

"No, I'll come with you and help carry the luggage."

"It isn't necessary."

"Yes, it is. That's what lovers are for. Even short-term ones."

We waited for what seemed like a long time, until Carmen returned with the tickets. Then we walked out onto the platform. There were only half a dozen passengers standing next to the empty track. I looked up at the electric sign that showed the time of departure for the Madrid Express, and the fast train, the Costa del Sol, which was scheduled to leave at ten-forty-five. "We have plenty of time," I said to Carmen.

"Only twenty minutes," she replied. "We are taking the express. It is much less expensive because there are no *literas.*"

"Then you'll have to sit up all night."

"*¿Que más da?*" she said, what difference does it make. "I'll have time to think about you."

There was a small kiosk at the far end of the platform that sold sandwiches. Alicia asked if she could have a hot dog, and Carmen's mother went off with the little girl to buy one. "Children are always hungry," Carmen said. She was making small talk to hide her nervousness.

"Why did you have to leave tonight?" I asked her. "Couldn't you have waited until tomorrow?"

"I am taking the place of a girl who has fallen ill. We rehearse tomorrow and perform the following night." She looked off anxiously in the direction of the kiosk as the train was backing down the track toward us. A few more passengers had appeared.

"Have you reserved your places?" I asked.

"It is not necessary," she said. "Not on the express. You find an empty compartment and hope it will not fill up during the night. It is not a train for tourists."

Alicia and her grandmother were moving slowly toward us, the child munching her sandwich. The old lady was carrying a plastic bottle of water in her free hand.

"Pues, adiós," Carmen said, turning to face me. "I will send Marisa my address."

"I'll write you a note as soon as I know where to send it." We embraced, not like lovers but like friends.

Carmen told her daughter to kiss me goodbye. She left a spot of mustard on my cheek that her grandmother chided her for and that I removed with my handkerchief. I lifted the two suitcases up onto the rear platform of the carriage, then moved along the side of the train to see where my very temporary family had chosen to sit. Carmen tried to pull down the window but it had been locked in place. The side of the carriage was streaked with rain. I waved, and they all waved back. Carmen pantomimed a kiss. An official in a red cap motioned for me to step back. The train started with a jerk, and I stood watching it move slowly out of the station.

It hadn't been much of a farewell but it was probably better that way. We had both known that our affair had been an enactment of Marisa's favorite song—that sentimental ode to the one-night stand, with which she proved, unknowingly, that there was a vast gulf between her troupe and her audience. We were all *estranjeros*, strangers, and would remain just that, even Carmen and I.

I walked back to my car, keeping close to the wall of the railroad station to avoid getting wet. I unlocked the door on my side. As I straightened I noticed that a car had pulled up behind me, a battered green Mercedes. There were four men inside it. I recognized the two in the back, Pedro and his friend, Rafael. The driver of the Mercedes and his companion got out. I turned to face them. The taller of the two leered at me and passed the forefinger of his right hand across his throat. My mouth felt dry. I clenched my fists. Pedro and Rafael had gotten out of the Mercedes. The tall man was only a few feet away. He grunted and said: *"Cabrónazo."* Then he spat at my feet.

I hadn't been in a fistfight since my early days in the Navy, but I remembered what I had been taught in boot camp. The first shot is the one that counts. I feinted, jabbed with my left hand and connected with my assailant's head. It didn't prove to be a very effective blow. His companion had come up behind me. He tripped me with a sweep of his leg and I went down against the wall. Pedro had joined the others. I knew what was coming next—I saw him pull back his right leg and rolled away from the kick. Somehow I managed to reach out and catch him by the heel. He went down on his back on the sidewalk, hard. I heard him groan. The tall thug helped him to his feet. Then the shorter of the two other men kicked hard at my side. He had a round nasty face that was covered with a straggly beard. I heard a woman scream from across the street. He kicked me again, and my head crashed against the wall.

I don't believe I was out for more than an eight-count, but it must have been longer. When I came to, a young Englishman and his blonde wife were standing over me. They took me by both arms and pulled me to my feet. The green Mercedes was nowhere to be seen. "Are you all right?" the young Englishman asked.

"Yes, I think so." The knuckles of my left hand were bleeding.

A short gray-haired woman dressed in black was standing behind the young couple, jabbering excitedly in Spanish. She had seen it all, she said over and over again. A green-and-white Guardia

Civil station wagon pulled up next to my car and two men in uniform got out. The first one saluted and asked what had happened. He was a sergeant. The gray-haired woman who had seen it all gave him a fairly accurate account of the incident. Did I recognize the men who had attacked me? the sergeant asked. Thinking I hadn't understood, he repeated his question.

I took a deep breath. My lungs ached. "Would you be able to identify them?" the other Guardia Civil asked. I could see by his shoulder patches that he was a lieutenant.

"I don't think so," I replied. "It all happened so quickly."

"You poor man," the Englishman's wife said. "Do you have someone you can call to drive you home? We're catching the train in an hour, so there's nothing much we can do . . ."

"I can manage by myself," I said. "But thank you anyway for your kindness."

41

I HAD A HEADACHE but I was pretty sure I wasn't concussed. My mind was clear. I knew that I had to get away from there as quickly as possible. If I told them the truth I knew what would happen. The first thing they would do was call the *cuartel* in Marbella and they would tell them that I had failed to ratify my charges against the same man. Then once they had picked him up again and started questioning him, there was just a chance he would involve Carmen. I didn't want to risk that. Anyway, I was almost even with him. With any luck his back would bother him a lot longer than my arm had bothered me. Nor would there be any more midnight calls, I reckoned, now that he was a free man.

The heater inside my car was beginning to function. The strange thing was that now my clothes were drying, I didn't even feel particularly angry. And as I drove slowly through the wet night, an old Spanish saying crossed my mind. In translation it goes something like this: "You can do anything you want in life, but you have to pay the bill before you're through."

42

MY LEFT HAND HEALED QUICKLY. After three days I was able to put on my golf glove, but given my financial condition I thought it would be wiser to go out onto the practice range and hit some balls before venturing out to play. It was a cloudy day and there were only about six people on the worn strip of grass and mud facing the white markers that show the distance your shots have traveled. I started out with my seven iron, then switched to my five wood. My first few missiles veered crazily to the right, proof that my slice was still with me. I took a shorter backswing and that helped a little, but my shots were anything but straight.

A familiar voice made me turn back to face the bench where I had left my bag of clubs. It was Collins. "Your stance is wrong, Roberto," he said. "When you line up, bring the ball closer to your right foot."

Shirley was with him. She looked sad. "When did you get back?" I asked Collins.

"A while ago," he said. "How have you been?"

"All right. And you?"

"Not too bad, considering everything."

Shirley said nothing, merely stood there with her arms crossed over her chest. Collins was carrying his bag slung over one shoulder. "We might have a game someday," he said, a vague invitation that I knew was meaningless. He glanced at his wristwatch, then turned to Shirley. "Pick me up at five," he told her. "I'll meet you in the bar."

I watched him as he went off in the direction of the first tee. Shirley hesitated, then sat down on the bench behind me.

"Go ahead," she said. "I'm just going to sit here for a few minutes, if that's all right."

I could tell that she had something on her mind. I teed up another ball, altered my stance and hit a surprisingly straight shot well beyond the 150-meter marker.

"That's better," Shirley said, and managed a smile.

I put my five wood back in my bag and sat down beside her. "It's a terrible game," I said. "You're wise never to have taken it up."

She sat there looking down at her hands. I noticed that she wasn't wearing her diamond ring. She sighed, a deep unhappy sigh. "Could I talk to you?" she asked. "Just for a minute."

"Of course."

"I'm sorry . . . you don't know me, but I have to talk to someone." She took a tissue out of her pocket and blew her nose.

"What's the matter?"

"Everything," she said. She lowered her head and ran her fingers through her hair. When she straightened there were tears in her eyes. "I think Cecil has fallen in love with another woman," she began. "He's been back a week and he treats me as if I were a total stranger. Then yesterday I found a letter in one of his tweed jackets. I wasn't spying on him. He'd left the jacket in my car when he went off to change into his golf clothes."

"Did you say anything to him about it?"

She shook her head. "I haven't mentioned it," she said. "I didn't want to provoke him. I was so upset that I just sat there and cried. The letter was signed Elizabeth. Then last night I heard him put in a call to his lawyer's office and ask to speak to this woman. She's a solicitor with the firm he uses in London." She paused. "I don't know what to do. If I confront him there's bound to be a row. He hates people spying on him."

I said: "I know about *that.*"

"After all we've been through," Shirley said. "It's mad, isn't it? I have nothing, you know. No money of my own, no place to go. What do you think I should do?"

"Don't do anything," I said. "It's probably only a momentary infatuation. My guess is that he'll get over it. He's too smart to get romantically involved with a lawyer."

"He's going back to London next week. To see her, I'm sure."

"Go with him."

"He won't take me. He said he'd only be gone for a couple of days."

"Then sweat it out. He'll be back."

"You think so? I wonder. This woman is after his money, I'm certain of that."

"There isn't anything else you can do. Of course, you can leave him and hope he'll come after you."

"And if he doesn't? Then what?"

"You can go back to London and get a job. Make a new life for yourself."

She shook her head. "I'm not that strong," she said. "I don't think I could go on without him."

"Well, you might have to," I said.

She touched her eyes with the crumpled tissue. "Pamela will have a good laugh," she said. "I can just see her . . . gloating and chuckling to herself."

"Yeah . . . well, I wouldn't worry about that."

She got slowly to her feet. "I'm terribly sorry," she said. "I have no right to bother you with my problems. You probably have worries of your own. And you're right. The only thing I can do is wait and hope he'll come to his senses." She held out her hand. "Thank you for listening, anyway."

I said: "My advice, for what it's worth, is pretend you know nothing. No tears, no scenes. That is, if you want to hang on to him. And if that doesn't work, he's not worth hanging on to."

She nodded and released my hand, then turned and trudged off in the direction of the clubhouse. I picked up my seven iron and hit a few more balls. There was a certain advantage to not being rich, I reckoned. No scheming lady solicitor was ever going to set her cap for me.

43

THE BELGIANS LOOKED AT MY *finca* and rented it for three months without arguing about the price. They turned out to be an attractive young couple, and we negotiated in their native language, which pleased them. I told them I didn't want to sell the place, and they both said they understood and were willing to forget about the option-to-buy clause. They deposited two hundred thousand pesetas for possible damages and another hundred thousand for their telephone bill. I couldn't have asked for more, and Cecilia was delighted.

I felt lonely for the first week or two after Carmen's departure. Soon I wasn't sure which it was I missed more, the familiar body or the one that had been brand new. I missed Carmen's tenderness as well as Evelyn's easygoing sarcasms. But if Carmen had stayed on, the hours would probably have gotten to me. I have never been able to sleep late in the morning after a long night. So it was probably just as well that she had left for Madrid when she did. There was a finality about her getting on the train with her mother and daughter that I must admit was less painful than just the two of us saying goodbye would have been.

The weather finally improved. The new Belgians were golfers and they invited me to play, paid my greens fee, as well as for lunch in the sun. Only Kiko grew sourer and sourer. He had received a fax from Susan in which she asked him for a divorce. She admitted she had met someone else, a young American movie producer, and that she wanted to stay on in Santa Barbara.

"Can you imagine sending anybody a fax like that?" Kiko said.

"Why not?" I said. "That way she got it over with in a hurry. Who needs to wait for a letter with bad news?"

"She's just like her goddamned mother, from what you've told me," Kiko said. "A bitch."

I said: "You're not a very good loser, are you?"

"No, are you?"

"I've had more practice."

"Show me a good loser and I'll show you a loser," he replied.

I had heard the wisecrack before and had found it less than charming, a comment on the new mentality in business and in sport. "I don't know," I said. "We're all losers, in the end. Anyway, I've always found it easier to make peace instead of war."

"Cecil Collins feels the same way, but we're not going to let him off the hook."

"Good for you," I replied. "By the way . . . is he still around? What's the word from your gumshoes?"

"He's here," Kiko said. "Moved out of the house and is shacked up with his little typist."

"That's good news."

"Yeah . . . he's fucked himself for real. Cruelty, adultery, desertion. You name it. Lady Pamela has him by the balls."

"I wasn't exactly thinking about her," I said. Kiko looked mystified but I didn't bother to explain that for once my advice had borne fruit. "Love conquers all," I added, without thinking who I was talking to. "Wait and see."

"I don't have to wait," Kiko replied. "I know all about love. It's a four-letter word."

"Did you just think of that one?" I asked him, but he had already turned up the sound of his TV set so that he could pretend that he hadn't heard me.

At the end of the month Evelyn arrived back in town. She looked rested and pretty in her desert clothes, a blonde princess out of the Arabian Nights. We returned to the status quo. My guilt feelings did not interfere with my desire. I told her about the *Penelope* and her passengers, and she seemed not to be in the least bit jealous. All she said was: "I'm happy you weren't tempted to stow away on board."

"I wouldn't have had to," I said. "I could have signed on as a member of the crew."

"Of course. The maiden-in-distress department. But then, why didn't you?"

"Because I thought you just might be coming back to bury the hatchet."

"Well, don't make me sorry I did," she said.

She wasn't altogether reconciled, so it seemed, to our having gotten back together again. Strangely enough, she hadn't inquired whether I had been faithful during her absence, nor had I asked her about her conduct in Marrakech for the obvious reason that I wasn't anxious to open that particular can of beans.

That same Saturday afternoon I came across a brief article in the cultural section of *El País,* the Spanish newspaper I always buy on the weekend. It turned out to be a favorable review of a new flamenco show that had opened in one of the Madrid theatres a few nights earlier. The last paragraph was devoted to praising the performance of one of the featured dancers. "Although no longer as youthful as the other artists appearing with her, Carmen Fernández brings to her interpretation of the classic *buleria* a grace and '*duende*' usually encountered in the renditions of performers half her age. Watching her provided this reviewer with a rare emotional experience."

There was no photograph attached but there was no doubt in my mind that "my Carmen," as I had come to think of her, had inspired these brief words of praise. It was most unlikely that there was another dancer with the same name capable of providing a hardened Madrid critic of the dance with *emoción*. She would be pleased, I felt certain. Then I began to wonder why I hadn't heard from her—no postcard, no early morning telephone call. Then I remembered that she had told me she would send Marisa her address, and that I had promised I would write her as soon as I knew where to send the letter.

Although it was only midafternoon I decided to drive to the nightclub, and if no one was there at least leave my telephone number so Marisa could call me. To my surprise I found the door of the place open, and after parking my car, went inside. Marisa was there, dressed in a tight pair of jeans and a red knitted sweater that clung to the folds above her waistline, as well as to her ample breasts. Around her hair, to hide the curlers, no doubt, she had knotted a yellow silk scarf, the points sticking up toward the ceiling. She put both hands to her face when she saw me and declared that it was a shame I had caught her like this. "*¡Que vergüenza!*" she said over and over again.

"*No te preocupes,*" I told her. "*Estás muy guapa,*" a polite lie she responded to with a frown.

She was directing the efforts of a thin gypsy woman in a faded apron who was waxing the tiled floor in front of the wooden platform used by the dancers. I asked her if Carmen had sent along a Madrid address and she said: "*Que si, que si, que si,*" and hurried off to the bar, where she opened a drawer and rummaged among a disarray of papers. In the end she found what she was looking for, and I copied down the carefully printed street address and telephone number on a paper napkin. Then after promising to return some night soon, I hurried back to my apartment and called Madrid.

Alicia answered the phone and I asked her to let me speak to her mother. Carmen came on the line a minute later.

"*¡Que sorpresa!*" she said, then added in English: "What a nice surprise."

"I read about you in *El País.*"

"So that is why you decided to call."

"I only just now got the number," I said.

"But I wrote Marisa the day after I arrived here."

"I haven't been back to see her. I'm sorry."

"*Que stupido.* I should have called *you,* but I was afraid you would not be alone . . . that your *novia* would be there." She paused. "She's come back, hasn't she?"

"Yes, she has," I said.

"Then you won't be coming to Madrid to see me." It was a statement, not a question.

"No, I don't think so," I said. "I'll wait until you come back in June."

"But I won't be coming back," she replied. "Didn't Marisa tell you? The company is going to London, and then *quizás* to your country, to *Nueva York.*"

"That's wonderful," I said blandly.

"It's very exciting."

"I'll miss seeing you. But anyway, *suerte.*"

"Yes, *suerte,*" she said, and laughed. "*¡Y ojo al toro!*"

It was what friends said to their *matadors* before they went off to the *plaza,* good luck, and keep your eye on the bull. "You don't need luck," I said. "You're the best."

"*Gracias, Roberto. Un beso, querido.*" A kiss, my beloved. It sounded a little too extravagant in English.

"*Un beso para ti,*" I replied. Sending her a last kiss wasn't much, but it was all I had available to offer. I hung up and felt as if a stone had been dropped on my heart.

247

44

A FORTNIGHT LATER I RECEIVED A LETTER from Paul Levin. He was back in California. He wanted me to know that Janet Slater had interceded with her husband on my behalf and that as a result I would be offered a small part in an American movie that was to be shot in Seville not long after Easter. He also suggested I purchase a fax machine. "Someone in the Spanish production office will be contacting you," he wrote, "and since you never seem to be at home it would make it easier for them to reach you."

That should be anytime now. We are in *Semana Santa,* an important occasion in all of Andalucía. Last Thursday night I took my Belgian tenants to Málaga so that they could take in the festivities. We were in a large crowd of locals on the Calle Lario and watched a battalion of the Spanish Foreign Legion parade down the street. Their patron is aptly called *El Cristo de la Buena Muerte,* the Christ of the Good Death, a phrase that has always sounded lugubrious to me up until now. Yet with the passing years it has taken on a more practical significance. A good death often seems desirable. Not too soon, but someday.

In the meantime the letter from the production office has arrived. It advises me that the start of filming has been delayed but that they will contact me again at the end of April. I'm not holding my breath. Even with an influential sponsor I think it's probably too late for my acting career to take off again. As a matter of fact, I seriously doubt that I ever had the potential of becoming a truly top actor or even a minor movie star. My face and figure, I feel fairly certain, were never really meant to light up the silver screen. But then, who knows, with a few good breaks I might even have become the president of the United States.